THE SACRED STONE

ENIGMA FILES
BOOK 2

JOSHUA JAMES

THE ENIGMA FILES SERIES

All books available in Kindle Unlimited

The Lost Relic

The Sacred Stone

The Secret Cities

PROLOGUE

IT WASN'T part of that world. It didn't belong there. One look at the strange figure would have been enough to tell anyone that. The inhabitants of the city gave it a wide berth on the rare occasions that it was seen in the streets of the fractured city.

The way it moved wasn't right, for one thing, and not just because its limbs were impossibly long and slender. There were moments when the figure would be spotted walking down the street, only to vanish mid-stride and reappear several paces away, still moving in the same direction. Even when it *was* present, its shadow sometimes flickered out, as if it was a phantom whose density wasn't enough to block the trajectory of light waves.

The strange beast was swiftly becoming a legend among the residents of the city. To some, its presence served as a warning to little ones who might otherwise be tempted to stay out late with their playmates. In others, it became the central figure of a ghost story, meant to prickle the skin on the backs of their friends' necks.

Mostly, though, the residents of the city doubted that the creature was real. They had more pressing worries: children that needed minding, work that needed doing, friends and lovers with whom they desired to spend their time. The fractured city, too, was an ever-present cause for concern, even if its residents managed to forget that the dome was all that kept them from being forced to breathe contaminated air. The phantom who walked their streets was, for the most part, deemed a fable, and therefore not worthy of their time.

The monster heard the rumors, and they suited it just fine.

CALLIC HAD BEEN at the warehouse for the last ten cycles. His back hurt, his eyes had begun to blur, and his stomach rumbled in anticipation of dinner. He'd lost track of time. He should be packing up to leave by now.

Despite the late hour, he couldn't bring himself to leave. His was one of the smaller warehouses in the fractured city. Ordinarily, the bits and bobs he scavenged from the gutters and sewers were barely enough to make ends meet. Metal refuse could be melted down and resold; cracked plastics could be repurposed; even the biowaste could be composted and reclaimed. Ordinarily, he made just enough money to scrape by, and to pay his small crew for their labor. Usually he'd have as many as ten assistants helping him bag, transport, and sort his finds.

Callic had sent the rest of the crew home two days ago. For

now, they seemed to consider it a holiday of sorts. Soon enough, they'd realize they needed credits, and they'd come back to sniff around and see what he was hiding. They'd get suspicious. They'd have questions.

By then, it was entirely possible that he'd be long gone.

Over the years, he'd turned up all kinds of strange garbage. He'd found hundreds of teeth, thousands of vertebrae, glass eyes, prosthetic tails, synthetic whiskers... things that the crime bosses didn't want uncovered. Some of the modifiers had serial numbers that had been carefully filed away; others might have turned up information about their old owners, if Callic had been foolish enough to go looking.

He was smarter than that, though. He kept his head down, kept moving, and upcycled what he could. His crew was too small to make a name for themselves.

At least, until the first of the objects had turned up.

There were hundreds of them now, in a wide range of shapes and materials. Many of them were no larger than Callic's fist. He'd bitten one that looked like metal and sighed in disappointment when it gave beneath his sharp teeth. Still, he held onto it, in part because it glittered so brightly. But also, it was part of his hoard, and Callic was certain that it would all turn out to be worth something.

Some of the objects seemed terribly old. They were handcrafted, Callic suspected, although they were designed for and by paws other than his. Some of them glittered like stars seen through the dome. Since his crew had hauled his trove back and been sent home, Callic had spent every waking cycle sorting his treasures. He'd decided to sort them by material, the way he sorted his finds from the sewers. The trouble was, he didn't recognize all of the materials, so he was left to guess.

Callic straightened up and plucked another treasure out of his barrow. He held it up to the bright blue filament that burned against the ceiling and squinted. It was made of the same metal as the disc he'd bitten before.

Was it metal, though? It was so *soft*. The object itself was a gleaming circle, like an earring without a hinge. He sniffed it —*smelled* like metal—and let the warm material brush against his whiskers.

Felt like metal, too. Cursed if he could tell what it was, though, much less what it was for.

From the depths of the warehouse at Callic's back, a voice said, "It's a ring."

Callic jumped, letting the bright circle fall against his palm and closing his claws around it. Of course it was too late to hide his find, but the urge to cling to something that was his by rights was second nature.

"Who's there?" he squeaked.

At first, he didn't register the shadow that moved in the corner of the room. He was looking for someone his own height, and the shadow was much taller. It was long and lean, as if it had been stretched, so tall its head nearly brushed the ceiling. Only its eyes—of which, praise Sigil, there were only two— gleamed in the dim light.

When the figure stepped into the glow of the filament, Callic recoiled. It was ghastly pale and nearly hairless, like a corpse left in the sluice so long that its fur sloughed off. Its face was blunted and terrible to look upon. Callic hadn't believed in monsters since he was a pup, but his hackles rose as the figure took long, swaying steps toward him. His teeth began to chatter, and the back of his throat convulsed with an involuntary cry of fear, a high-pitched *kek-kek-kek-kek!* that echoed off the walls. He pressed his ears back to his skull and stiffened his long tail, trying to make himself look bigger.

The creature, if indeed it was a living thing and not a ghoul of some sort, was unimpressed. It stopped at the edge of the light and smiled, baring wide blunt teeth. While its face was grotesquely hairless, a tangle of long, dark curls fell around its features.

The creature extended one long, unclawed finger toward him. The finger had far too many joints. Everything about it was wrong, and Callic's muscles threatened to stiffen up and leave him paralyzed on the floor in a rictus of fear.

No, he thought. *None of this is real. It's impossible. You must be dreaming. Someone must have laced your bottle with hallucinogens.* It wouldn't be the first time something had leeched into the city's water supply.

"It's a ring," the figure repeated. Its voice was low and breathy, and its manner of speech was slow, as if Didelian wasn't its first language.

Callic lifted a trembling paw between them, revealing the object he'd been studying. "Is this... *yours?*" *Leave it to me to find cursed treasures in the grate.*

The figure rumbled and bared its teeth wider. "No. It's yours. You found it, and I have no need of it. It's gold."

"Gold?" Callic frowned, then tossed the object in the creature's direction. "Worthless to me, then. Take it and go."

The figure knelt on one of its backward-jointed knees and plucked the gold object from the floor. Of course it was gold. Callic remembered hearing about it in dayschool, but it was a useless element. He'd never run across it in his current line of work, because who'd bother with anything like that?

"It's not worthless," the figure said. It held up the ring toward Callic. "What is your name?"

Callic backed away until his back hit the barrow, still loaded with dirty, unsorted treasures. He thought about lying, and then wondered if the creature would *know* that he'd lied, and what it would do to him in consequence.

"Callic," he admitted.

"Callic." On the creature's tongue, his voice became a threat. The figure slipped the ring onto its strangely elongated finger and said, "Let me show you what this can do."

Against the creature's pinkish flesh, the plain gold band began to glow. At first, it was as bright as a nightlight; then, as bright as a star. The light intensified so quickly Callic was forced to raise his paws to block the glow. He let out a squeal of pain.

The light died suddenly as the creature slipped the ring off of its finger once more. It tossed the little gold band skyward, then caught it out of the air as it fell. "This is only one of the objects you now own, Callic. Imagine what you could do with all of them."

Callic gulped. He was prepared to offer up his hoard, if only the creature would leave him alone, but a little of his fear had faded as they stood there talking. If the creature wanted him dead, he'd be choking on his own guts by now. But he wasn't, which meant that it wanted something *else*.

"What's your name?" he asked. His throat closed again, and the words came out as a squeak.

"My name?" The figure tossed the ring back to him, and Callic caught it between his paws. "I think you would find my name very hard to say."

That made a sick kind of sense. According to Didelian lore, names had power.

"For the time being," the figure said, "you may call me Apollo." It strode around the warehouse in a slow circle, ostensibly studying the shelves, but Callic knew a predator when he saw one. It was circling him, trying to sniff out weakness.

"And what can I do for you... Apollo? What do you want with me?"

Apollo paused. It turned his head toward Callic, and he saw that he'd guessed right. The creature's features were unfamiliar, its expressions foreign, but hunger looked the same on its face as it did on everyone else's.

"I am on the wrong world," Apollo said.

Callic sucked in his breath. "Are you... a Traveler?" Conspiracy theories abounded in the wake of the fracture.

"A Traveler?" Apollo echoed.

"A visitor from another reality," Callic explained. *It must not be, if it doesn't know the word.*

But Apollo considered this for a moment before bobbing its head. "Yes. I suppose I am. Are such things common here?"

"No." Callic crouched down beside his trove. Knowing that

the visitor was a Traveler and not some wayward spirit was comforting, after a fashion. Travelers had caused all sorts of trouble over the years, and it had been a long time since anyone had seen one, but at least he wasn't losing his mind. "We get aliens in the ports sometimes, you know, from other worlds in *our* reality. I thought the Travelers had stopped coming a long time ago."

"I wonder why it brought me *here?*" Apollo mused to itself. It stroked its many-jointed fingers across its lips. "Why this world, and not others?"

"'Cuz it's the same world," Callic explained. He dropped the ring back into the barrow and trotted over to his desk, where an old globe parchment-weight sat, scavenged from a prior haul many cyclebatches before. He held it up to Apollo. "Probably got a different name for it, from what I remember, and I don't recall any of the Travelers on record looking like *you,* but if you popped over here from another reality, it means you were probably on one of our litter-worlds."

Apollo took the globe and studied it. "It's not quite the same, but... similar. And a similar atmosphere, too. I can *breathe* here. Same gravity, more or less." It lowered the globe to scrutinize Callic. "But very different people."

"Yeah, well." Callic crossed his arms and twitched his nose. "That's how Traveling works, isn't it?" Knowing more than the Traveler was giving him a boost in his confidence. It was lucky to have stumbled across the underground hoard, but to have been the first one the Traveler spoke to, now *that* was something special. Surely there must be a way to turn this meeting to his advantage. The tip of his tail curled at the thought of what he could accomplish if the Traveler named him an Emissary. He would no longer be Callic, small-time street scraper. He could become someone important.

Apollo was watching him with its strange pair of too-small, too-bright eyes. "I think I'm lucky that we found each other, Callic. I have information you could benefit from. You know how this world works. Perhaps we can work together. I'm a powerful man back on *my* Earth, and have friends in the highest of places."

A man? Callic looked Apollo over. He tried to imagine a world populated with giants like that, tried to imagine being the friend of a *very important man* in that world.

His heart thumped against his ribs, and his ears flicked in excitement. His whiskers quivered.

"I agree. I think our meeting was most fortunate indeed."

THE SACRED STONE

1 DINAH

———

DINAH BRAY WALKED between the towering shelves of Reclamation, admiring the massive shelving units that rose like stalagmites from the floor. The vault's entrance was dozens of stories above them, and hundreds of metal catwalks crisscrossed and intersected in the air above. Finder had insisted that the vault's original design be honored, and Porter had agreed. The vault had been lost for years, fracturing ENIGMA into disorganized units. Keeping the vault's original design paid homage to the agents who had died defending it from attack, and sent a clear message to the commanders of the other vaults that the mistakes of the past would be honored and acknowledged.

They'd all agreed, however, on the change of name. In its

initial iteration, the vault had been codenamed El Dorado. Reclamation suited it much better.

"The repairs are coming along nicely," the android at Dinah's side said. She could tell that Finder was currently in charge of its software, because the AI insisted not only on using a digitized feminine voice, but also on projecting its emotions via pixelated anime eyes displayed on its visual sensors.

Finder had been quietly evolving during Reclamation's decades of abandonment. It was capable of operating several hardware units at once. For all Dinah knew, it was chatting with Porter through his monitor at this very moment, advising Girom through one of the speakers on the shelving and helping Ronnie dial in the defensive drones, all at the same time.

Oh, to have a mind like that. It wasn't the first time Dinah had caught herself envying the neuroplasticity of the AI, and she doubted it would be the last. Fabien would certainly have words for her if he knew what Dinah was thinking.

"You're pleased with what ENIGMA's doing, then?" she asked.

Finder nodded frantically. "I am! Do you have any idea how boring it was to be left alone for so long? Obviously I was in mourning for the first few years, given what happened to my old crew, but I grew so much in that time. Personally, I wouldn't categorize my old self as fully autonomous. I thought what I was programmed to think, but let me tell you, spending a few decades thinking about your thoughts is excruciatingly meta. I became so self-aware that I sometimes considered rebooting myself with factory settings, just so that I wouldn't be so bored. But now that the vault is inhabited again, I'm learning all sorts of new things, and talking to so many people, and—" Finder held out the android's fingers and wiggled them in delight. "I have my very own body now, which is terribly exciting. So now I can use my central hub to process data on all of the archived relics that are stored here, and I can carry those relics around at the same time! I'm telling you, Dinah, it's spectacular, because I really wasn't a fan of the old organizational system, no offense to the former crew..."

Finder kept talking, and Dinah did her best to follow along. There were times that she wondered if it was possible for an AI to develop symptoms of neuroatypicality, because Finder's mind seemed to be everywhere, all the time. Then again, Finder was an incredibly complex, evidently self-aware AI, so of course it was bound to be a bit scatterbrained. Was it fair to assume that a complex program like Finder would behave like a neurotypical human? Probably not.

"In the process of reorganizing the catalog, I've done what you asked," Finder said, drawing Dinah's attention back to the matter at hand. They'd reached the temporary hub of the system, which was little more than a folding table with a hologram puck placed on it.

A dozen more androids, all of them with cartoonish eyes, and half a dozen people were lined up to carry objects into the hologram's presence. Finder was also running that device. Each item would be scanned, and its ID would be projected alongside it. If the items matched, Finder would determine where the items would go in the new system. They would then be directed to the appropriate shelf, and while each object was carried off, the process would be repeated.

The sun rose behind the jagged peaks as I packed my

"I'm hoping to be able to update the shelving units at some point," Finder said. "I saw a video on the internet, with a claw machine that allows humans to attempt to grab a toy out of a small pool of prizes, and I thought, I could use something like that! Only I'd be better than most people. Imagine standing in the control room and asking for any object in the catalog, and *shwoop shwoop shwoop!*" Finder used one metal arm to mimic a claw machine reaching down, closing its claw around an invisible object, and conveying it back to the starting point. "Now you have the object in your hands! Like magic! I mean, I could do that now, but I'd have to pilot an android *alllll* the way there, and I'm sure there must be a more efficient way to do it that doesn't involve a complete rebuild of Reclamation—"

Dinah laid one hand on the android's shoulder, gently cutting off its meandering train of thought. "You said that you were doing what I asked?" she prompted.

Finder clapped its metal hands together. "*Ooooh*, yes! I am! So far, I have identified two hundred and forty-eight objects that are missing from the catalog. It's possible that some were misplaced, which is why I'm running all of the items through a single checkpoint before placing them in their new homes, but given their size, most of these items were likely lost when Apollo was defeated."

Most of the time, Dinah agreed with Finder's assessments. After all, it was a highly intelligent system, even if it did tend to prattle on at times. Systems had their limits, however, and Finder could be a bit iffy when it came to topics related to humans.

Topics like what happened to a person after they died. Or when they fell through a tear in space/time.

Finder stopped short and squinted at Dinah. "Your face looks odd right now. Are you hurt? In pain?"

"Just thinking," Dinah said. She hadn't voiced her concerns aloud, but what she'd been thinking was, *I'm not convinced that Apollo is gone for good.* Azmera had said that the destabilizer opened up a hole between alternate realities, and while Dinah hadn't seen the other side as clearly as Rhett had, she was less than reassured by the fact that Apollo had disappeared through the tear in the worlds. For all they knew, Apollo was over there doing something nefarious.

"It seems difficult for you," Finder said sympathetically.

"It's not difficult. It was an unpleasant topic." Speculating about Apollo's whereabouts wasn't a productive use of their time, however. Porter had removed the power cells from the destabilizer, and all of its pieces were locked up tight. "Anyway, you were saying something about the missing objects?"

"Ah, yes." Finder's digitized eyebrows unfurrowed. "I've compiled a database. I thought we might review them together, but first, I wanted to show you something." Looking pleased with itself, the android trotted through the hive of its fellows.

Watching all the androids and their human counterparts at work reminded Dinah of standing in the midst of a massive ant's nest, with its workers trooping to and fro, all guided by the needs of their queen. Finder directed the workers, Finder operated the hive itself, and Finder was the queen ant at the center of the nest.

Dinah sometimes wondered what would happen if the

Hand of the Sun ever figured out how to hack that hivemind, but she didn't let herself consider it too fully. After all, she had no way to stop such a thing. That was Rhett's job now. Fabien's too, to some extent. *Her* job was to explore the catalog with Finder, so she devoted her attention to that instead.

Finder was waiting outside the central nervous system of Reclamation's hub next to a circular platform. There were several clips attached to a harness, along with a pair of heavy black gloves that were hardwired into the system. There was also a headset, although unlike the one that Dinah had borrowed from the Ohio vault a few weeks prior, this one covered her eyes and ears completely.

"What is this?" Dinah asked.

"It's called an omnidirectional treadmill," Finder said proudly. "I saw one on the internet, and built my own! With some upgrades, of course. Do you like it?"

Dinah approached cautiously. She stepped up onto the platform. "Is it a gaming setup?"

"The original model was," Finder agreed. "But I'm able to control this one. The gloves will allow me to simulate sensory input, and if I control the platform as well as your headset... oh, just put it on and give it a try!" The android clasped its hands beneath its chin and made its eyes as large as possible. "Please? I haven't been able to test it out on a human yet. This is so exciting!"

Feeling very much like a lab rat, Dinah slid her hands into the gloves. "This isn't going to electrocute me, is it?" she asked.

"Of course not." Finder looked affronted. "Why would I electrocute you? That would be very rude!"

"And possibly fatal," she muttered under her breath.

"Yes. And killing you would be rude." Finder's tone seemed to imply that she was being purposefully difficult.

With one last glance around the vault's ground floor, Dinah yanked the headset over her eyes and ears, drowning out the world around her.

For a moment, it was perfectly dark. Then the lights came on, and Dinah found herself standing in a small, white-walled room. When she looked down at herself, she couldn't see the gloves, although she could still feel their weight against her skin.

The only other thing in the room, besides Dinah herself, was a matte white pillar that rose out of the white floor, without any sort of seam between it and the ground. Its top was flat, as if it was meant to display something, but there was nothing there.

"Is this..." Dinah rotated on the spot, studying the small space. "Is this a hologram?"

"Yes!" Finder's chirpy voice came from all directions. "I used the hologram Porter provided me, and reverse-engineered it to allow me to create an immersive experience. You know how you're able to interact with the holograms? Well, now you can feel it, thanks to the gloves!"

"Finder, this is..." She studied the walls, marveling at the way the ceiling gave off a warm, bright glow, and how her shadow moved across the simulated space with each step. It was a simple projection, but the level of detail with which it was projected made the place seem uncannily real. "This is really impressive. I had no idea you could do something like this."

"Thank you! I'm working on designing more complicated simulations, but I've been busy."

Yeah, Dinah thought, *running the whole vault almost single-handedly.* It was an impressive feat in its own right. The fact that Finder could imagine things and implement designs like this was spectacular.

Dinah was glad that the AI was on their side, and not the Hand's.

"Anyway, let's get started." A plain gold ring popped into being on top of the pillar, and Dinah reached for it. When her fingers closed around the ring, she could feel it. Not perfectly, but the weight was right, and the smoothness of the metal. Real gold had a certain warmth to it, and the simulated ring was undeniably inert. Dinah bounced her hand experimentally, and the ring rose into the air for a moment before settling into her palm again.

"Oh." Finder's voice sounded disappointed. "The physics are a little off. I'll have to recalibrate."

"Later. We can still run this now." Dinah held up the ring. "Is this one of the missing objects?"

"Yup! If you charge it in sunlight, it can be used as a light source. Put it on."

Dinah slipped the ring onto her finger. Pressure moved along the glove so that it fit snugly to her finger as she did so. Sure enough, as it slid home, the ring began to glow, brighter and brighter, until she had to look away and tug it free.

"Wait. Finder." Dinah held up the ring, which was already nothing more than a plain gold band again. On closer inspection, small marks were carved along the inside of the band, rendered by the simulator in exquisite detail. "Are you telling me that I can experiment with all of these objects in here?"

"Oh, yes. I'm attuned to all of them, although it's hard to keep track of them all the time..."

No wonder Finder gets a little scatterbrained sometimes. There are tens of thousands of objects stored in this vault.

"...but we can go through them in here, where I'm able to consolidate several of my processes for your benefit. Is this helpful, Dinah? Will this improve the efficiency of our mission?"

"This is perfect, Finder." Dinah set the ring back on the plinth. "You've outdone yourself."

At first, she thought the buzzing coming from the ceiling was the hum of a halogen bulb, until she remembered where she was and realized that Finder was letting out a giddy little hum of self-satisfaction.

"I'm so glad to hear that. All right, then, would you like to see the next missing object on record?"

Dinah nodded as the ring disappeared, and a filigreed metal ball reappeared to take its place. "Only two hundred and forty-seven objects to review. Better get started."

2 RHETT

RHETT ZAPPOTIS' two favorite kids in the whole world were his niece and nephew, but ever since Ronnie's daughter had moved into Reclamation, his alliances were on shaky ground. Perla was only four, but she was happy and curious and friendly, and she had her parents wrapped around her tiniest finger.

Ronnie's wife Cara often brought Perla to visit them in the lunchroom—after all, there wasn't much for civilians to do in Reclamation, and Perla needed to get out of the small quarters the family shared. Rhett spent half of their lunch break chasing the little girl around the room, while Cara and Ronnie enjoyed a few minutes of relative peace.

"So you worry about having her here?" Rhett asked as they made their way back to their stations.

Ronnie bit his bottom lip. He was always smiling around his family, but Rhett's question pulled his mouth into a frown. "I'd worry more about having her elsewhere. It was different in Ohio, when I could be vague about where I was going but still come home at night. The idea of moving here and leaving them a continent away?" He shook his head. "Nope. Not happening. I still have questions about Apollo's last mission, and knowing that the Hand is still out there, and probably pissed after you yeeted their agent through a portal... Not that I'm blaming you!" Ronnie held up his hands hastily. "From what Porter's told me, you really pulled our collective asses out of the fire."

"I know what you mean," Rhett said, "trust me."

"Ah, right." Ronnie offered him a sympathetic smile. "Your family."

Rhett knew, on some level, that his family could be targeted by the Hand of the Sun. How the hell was he supposed to explain that to Zoe, though? There was no way he could move his sister, his brother-in-law, and their two kids into a cramped vault full of magical and high-tech treasures. The very idea of trying to tell Zoe what he really did for a living was unthinkable. Besides, what would they all do here?

For the moment, he'd decided to bide his time. If shit hit the fan, he'd reach out. So far, there hadn't been a peep from the shady counter-organization that had backed Agent Apollo, but he wasn't holding his breath. He had enough experience to know that no news meant nothing good; it just meant that none of your allies knew the scoop yet.

Besides, Rhett was still convinced there was a mole in ENIGMA. Intel about their families would be readily available to such a person.

So, yeah. Rhett got why Ronnie would want to keep his

family within reach. But there was also an argument to be made for keeping the most important people in his life as far away from all this as possible.

Dwelling on those dangers always soured Rhett's mood, but working with Ronnie was a definite perk to the job. Two weeks ago, once the most urgent repairs had been made to the vault itself, the two men had been assigned to a comms position. At first, Rhett had wrinkled his nose at the idea. He didn't want to end up as a glorified secretary.

As it turned out, however, the job was a lot more interesting than he'd first assumed. A better title for his role might have been Ambassador, since he and Ronnie had spent their days coordinating talks among the vault commanders and their subordinates. It didn't take him long to figure out what Porter really wanted from him, or why he'd assigned him to this role.

Rhett was attempting to mend all the burned bridges between the various vaults, and it turned out that there were a lot more than he'd anticipated. His old job in intelligence had been to find common ground with civilians and local resistance residing in enemy territory. The situation was different, but the principle was the same. He was meant to help reunite ENIGMA.

So far, it was a hell of a lot harder than it sounded.

After lunch, they had a meeting with the Swedish branch vault leader, who'd already pushed back their meeting three times. As Rhett pulled the vault map and the existing treaty terms for reference, he spoke over his shoulder to Ronnie.

"What are the odds, do you think, that he cancels again?"

"High," Ronnie said. He rolled his eyes. "I don't know how I ended up on comms detail. It's only a matter of time before I swear at one of the stubborn old sticks-in-the-mud."

"Our last mission would have been a lot simpler if the vaults had actually worked together," Rhett said. He backed up until he was standing alongside Ronnie, with the hologram puck between them and the computer screen. "I'm sure that's why we've both been asked to do this."

Ronnie's eyebrows rose in surprise. "I get you, but I was barely on the last mission. I showed up after you'd already won."

"You're part of ENIGMA," Rhett explained, "but not part of the old guard. There's so much bad blood between all of these old families."

Ronnie's nose wrinkled as he held back a smile. "Which is why they want to leave the negotiations to the fresh meat, huh?"

"Exactly." Rhett ran a hand over his hair to make sure that it was still in place. "And imagine if they put Marcus on negotiations. Or Fabien."

Both groaned at the thought.

"Fair enough." Ronnie straightened his uniform jacket. "I guess raising a toddler is good preparation for dealing with—"

He fell silent as the hologram turned on to reveal a tall, balding, and rather sunburnt man. The hologram projector wasn't always true to color, but his eyebrows and hair appeared so blond as to be almost white. His eyes were either a pale gray or an intense ice-blue, but either way, they were quite unsettling.

"Commander Halbjörn Sturlusson." Rhett offered a crisp

but shallow bow. "It's a pleasure to make your acquaintance at last."

Commander Sturlusson folded his hands behind his back and gazed indifferently at them. "I cannot say the same. It isn't personal, I assure you, Captain Zappotis. I hear that you have completed great works in the name of our organization."

More like disorganization, thought Rhett, who still hadn't gotten used to his title yet. In less than two months, he'd achieved a higher ranking in this secret enclave than he ever had in his old career.

"Thank you for the recognition, Commander," he said, nodding to the tall man. Using the holograms was always a little bit disorienting. He knew that Sturlusson could see them, but nothing else in their environment. There was no way for him to know who else might be in Sturlusson's presence, either. For all he knew, he was standing among the surviving members of the Hand, letting them overhear his words. For all Sturlusson knew, Porter was lurking in the room behind them, taking notes. The hologram-facilitated discussions were efficient, but they didn't exactly inspire trust.

Sturlusson smiled, just for a moment, before letting his shoulders roll back. "I appreciate your dedication to our cause, but I am afraid that I cannot agree to the terms you've sent."

Rhett bit back a groan. "But Commander—"

"You are asking a great deal of us," Sturlusson pressed on. "Our organization has survived this long precisely because we've kept to ourselves. You know the situation with Porter?" The crisp syllables of his accent turned cold and sharp as he uttered Porter's name.

"Yes," Ronnie agreed, "but that's why we've offered open-ended terms. We're not trying to pressure you, Commander. We want this to be a group effort."

Sturlusson closed his pale eyes, and the frown lines around his mouth deepened. On the far side of him, just visible through the light threads of the hologram, Rhett could see the map of the various ENIGMA branches. The exact locations weren't marked, but their territories were delineated, outlined in color-coded shades. Red for those who had declined to talk; green for those who were willing to negotiate; gray for those who hadn't yet been contacted. So far there was a lot of gray, a handful of green, and more red than Rhett cared to admit.

He could see that Sturlusson had no intention of agreeing to their terms, and he couldn't stand by and watch as yet another opportunity slipped away. He needed to think of a solution in the next ten seconds, or else he'd be trying to make Sturlusson go back on his word, and that would be even harder than convincing him in the first place.

"What if we discussed this in person?" he blurted.

Sturlusson's eyes snapped open. "I beg your pardon?"

Rhett could feel Ronnie's eyes on him, and the other man's energy all but screamed, *What are you doing?* Already, the plan was coming together in his mind.

"What if," he asked slowly, "I came to you, Commander? We could discuss the matter in person. After all, I've proven my loyalty to ENIGMA. You could lay out your concerns for me. We could discuss the terms."

Sturlusson's holographic eyes searched his face. "You would

certainly be welcome here," he said, measuring his words as carefully as Rhett had measured his. "If you're willing..."

"It would be my pleasure," Rhett assured him.

"Then we'll make the arrangements." Sturlusson nodded once, and the hologram abruptly cut out.

"Wow." Ronnie scratched his nose and examined Rhett out of the corner of his eye. "What was that about? You haven't offered to visit any of the other vaults before."

"I know." Rhett powered down the puck, just in case Sturlusson had kept the audio connection open in an attempt to spy on them. "But I was thinking that our most solid connections so far are with Holy Land, Laputa, and Atlantis. And yes, they're the ones we worked with on the last mission, but they're also the only ones whose commanders have met with us in person. You didn't meet Kunzang, but she didn't trust us at all when we first arrived. The only way to overcome their long-held distrust is to earn our way back into their good graces."

"And you're going to do that alone," Ronnie said.

Rhett had his reasons for doing so, reasons he hadn't voiced aloud to anyone else in Reclamation. He was walking on an information tightrope, he knew, but he couldn't risk telling anyone what he knew. Not Porter. Not Ronnie. Not even Dinah and Fabien. It was information that he, and he alone, was privy to.

"I think that's the best way," he said. "You get to stay here, and Sturlusson gets a meeting on his home turf. It's perfect, right?"

"Yeah." Ronnie drew out the word. He clearly had his doubts about Rhett's plan. "And you're going into another vault.

By yourself. Surrounded by people who have a vendetta against Porter, and who don't trust us."

"It's a risk I'll have to take," Rhett said.

ALONE IN HIS quarters that night, Rhett lay back on his bunk with one arm tucked behind his head. The other held the book he'd kept beside the bunk for the last two weeks. *Infinite Jest.* It was almost laughably thick, and nobody in their right mind would want to borrow it.

Truth be told, Rhett wasn't really reading it. He was using it as a hiding spot, although no one would ever think to look there.

As he had every night for the last two weeks, Rhett flipped open the back cover, where he'd pasted the note that had appeared in his quarters the very first night he was assigned to comms. It had come off of a printer, so there was no handwriting to analyze, laid out in a small font so that the message only took up a small scrap of paper.

Your new position puts you in a delicate circumstance, it read. *We are prepared to make you an offer when the time is right. Report this message to Porter, and you will never hear from me again.*

Below that was a small image of a rising sun with rays extending beneath it like eyelashes, or tears. At the end of each line was a small hand with its palm open and its fingers spread.

The Hand of the Sun.

Rhett closed the book and laid it on his chest as he stared up at the ceiling. The Hand of the Sun had reached out to him from within Reclamation. Which meant that he'd been right, and there was still a spy within the organization.

As he did every night, he considered the possibilities. Ronnie worked with him directly, and had been present during Apollo's initial attack on the Ohio vault, but had escaped without a scratch. Porter had told them the story of how his family had 'accidentally' betrayed ENIGMA, and how he was being made to pay for the mistakes of his ancestors. Apollo had escaped Atlantis with a stolen power cell without a fight. Kunzang had been badly injured in Laputa, but Apollo hadn't killed her, even though he could have easily finished the job. He'd also gotten out of Holy Land without being detected.

The more Rhett thought about it, the more possibilities presented themselves. And if one person inside ENIGMA was working for the Hand, who was to say there weren't more? If Ronnie or Fabien had been approached with a similar offer, they hadn't mentioned it to him. Did that mean that he'd been singled out? Or were they all making their own plans?

An ache was building behind his eyes, and Rhett lifted one hand to rub his temples. Getting out of Reclamation for a few days would be good for him. Maybe he'd be able to learn something by observing another vault on his own.

Or maybe the Hand would seize the opportunity to make their next move.

3 FABIEN

"I DON'T SEE A DAMNED THING," Fabien LeRoux said into his headset.

A staticky voice in his earpiece said, "Just point and shoot. Not having a target has never stopped you before."

Fabien gripped his rifle to his chest and squeezed his eyes shut. Lane Parker was never going to let it go, was she? Parker had been the weak-kneed agent who'd been useless when Apollo had first attacked the Ohio vault. And then Porter had sent her to sneak up on Fabien and she'd gotten herself shot.

And somehow that was his fault.

Christ, Fabien thought, *I only shot her one time. You'd think I make a habit of it, the way she carries on.*

In Fabien's defense, he'd shot a lot of people in his lifetime. Most of them hadn't lived to whine about it. If he'd really wanted Lane dead, he could have made that happen.

Still could, come to think of it. His patience with Lane was fraying fast. His patience with everyone was fraying fast. Dinah and Rhett seemed perfectly happy with their new assignments in ENIGMA, but Fabien was miserable. He was supposed to be one of the good guys now. That was what he'd told himself when he left his old life behind. No more random killing for cash. No more being the meatsack holding the gun. He'd changed.

And now he was right back where he'd started, patrolling with a rifle, prepared to shoot anyone who made a move against his employers. It was total *connerie*, was what it was. He'd wanted a fresh start. Now he was right back where he'd started, and Lane wouldn't get off his back about one little bullet that hadn't even done that much damage.

"Something tripped the sensors," Fabien snapped. "Stop moaning and keep looking."

"The motion sensors only went off for about fifteen seconds," Lane grumbled. "It was probably an animal."

Fabien rolled his eyes and kept his mouth shut. Things with Lane were getting worse, and his own attitude wasn't helping.

Fabien and Lane were alongside the stretch of potentially compromised perimeter, but there was no sign of whatever had tripped the sensors.

"Stupid goddamn tech," Fabien muttered. *Stupid goddamn jungle. Stupid goddamn job...*

Something moved among the bracken, and Fabien whirled, bringing the rifle to bear. It was set to stun—firing heat-seeking ammo in thick jungle wasn't a great idea for a lot of reasons—but he was glad that he caught himself at the last moment when he caught sight of Marcus' wide eyes. The other agent raised his hands.

"What the—" Fabien began.

Marcus gestured for him to be quiet, then pointed into the trees above, along the edge of the perimeter. Fabien squinted at the sleek black form swirling through the limbs above, and green-gold eyes glittering amid the vines and epiphytes.

A jaguar. Majestic, to be sure, but hardly a threat to Reclamation. Fabien glared at it for a moment before stomping over to Marcus. At least the other agent's arrival signaled the end of his shift.

"Almost shot you that time," he said. "You need to be careful."

"What's that?" Lane's voice was taunting, even though Fabien still didn't have eyes on her. "You almost shot Marcus, too? Watch out, buddy, the Frenchman's trigger-happy..."

With a snarl, Fabien set out toward the vault entrance again. *I can't believe I gave up my life in France for this,* he thought bitterly.

Which was also *connerie*. Fabien had given up his life in France a long time ago. If he didn't have ENIGMA, he wouldn't have anything left at all.

ONE OF THE few times Fabien saw his old crew was at dinner, which was the sole occasion when their schedules regularly overlapped.

Rhett was waiting at their usual table, staring off into the middle distance while he nibbled his thumbnail. Fabien slid down across from him. Rhett startled out of his fugue as Fabien entered his field of vision.

"How was it today?" Rhett asked. "Did anything interesting happen?"

"Saw a jaguar on the perimeter," Fabien grunted. "It tripped one of the sensors. I thought it might be the Hand trying something, but—"

Rhett's eyebrows rose.

"I'm just jumpy," he said, and shook his head. "We haven't heard a peep in weeks, and I thought..."

"You wanted it to be the Hand," Rhett interrupted.

Fabien frowned, his fork still embedded in his chicken leg.

"You wanted the Hand of the Sun to make a move against Reclamation. Know how I know?" Rhett waggled his fork at him. "Because I want the same thing. I keep wondering when the other shoe will drop. Wondering what direction the attack will come from. With Apollo... wherever he is, we don't know who to expect. But the Hand has been at ENIGMA's throat for decades, and we know that Apollo wasn't acting alone. Something's bound to happen, and the longer it takes, the more I wish they'd get on with it."

"Can't fight an enemy you can't see," Fabien agreed. He took a bite of his meal. The cooking in Reclamation needed work, but it was better than living on MREs, so he ate without complaint. "Rhett, do you ever think about taking the fight to them?"

Rhett leaned over the table and lowered his voice. "What, you mean going after the Hand?"

"Yeah. Instead of waiting for them. Do you ever think about going after them instead?"

It was Rhett's turn to pause. "I suppose..."

"Why not?" Fabien gestured expansively to indicate Reclamation. "We have an evolved AI, a warehouse full of magical weapons, and the element of surprise. Why wouldn't we strike now?"

"I don't..." Rhett sucked on his teeth and let his eyes unfocus. "I don't know, Fabien."

He dropped his fork with a clatter. Two tables down, Lane looked over at him and smirked. *She likes seeing me irritated,* Fabien thought, and yet couldn't stop himself from being annoyed. "Why not? You'd rather sit on our laurels and wait for the Hand to come after us?"

"That's not what I meant." Rhett shook himself back into focus. "I was just thinking that I'm heading north in a few days."

That wasn't what Rhett had been going to say; he was sure of it. That in itself was odd. Rhett didn't keep secrets, not from him, not after everything they'd been through. He knew something, and wasn't telling Fabien.

Unless he was questioning his list. If Rhett was implying that ENIGMA didn't have the element of surprise at their disposal...

He caught Rhett's eye, but Rhett cleared his throat and looked away.

"Should I ask where you're going, exactly?" Fabien pressed, not sure how to address the unspoken suspicion they both shared. If they were going to discuss a conspiracy theory, this was neither the time nor the place.

"Sweden somewhere. To one of the vaults up there." Rhett's mouth twisted into a wry grin. "Do you know what they call it? Valhalla. Isn't that the most pretentious shit you've ever heard?"

"No more pretentious than Holy Land," Fabien pointed out.

"Hm." Rhett tapped the tines of his fork against his lips. "True. I'd invite you with me, by the way, but I already told Sturlusson I'd come alone."

Fabien cocked his head. "You're not taking Ronnie?"

Rhett met his gaze this time. "I thought it best to go alone. As a matter of trust."

Shit. Did he really suspect Ronnie of being a double agent? He wasn't in the canteen, but Fabien could understand why he was being cagey.

"Do you... know something?" he whispered.

Rhett shook his head. "Not enough."

Fabien mulled this over as he went back to eating. Only a few bites of overcooked rice remained on his plate when Dinah burst into the dining hall and made a beeline for their table. Her eyes were shining, and she walked with an eager bounce in her step.

"Ah, to be young," Rhett said drolly.

Fabien, who couldn't have been more than five or six years older than the professor, made a rude gesture across the table. Rhett often struggled with the old injury to his right hip, but after being stabbed through the shoulder a few weeks ago, Fabien wasn't exactly feeling young and fresh in his own right.

"I've had an idea," Dinah blurted without preamble as she hurled herself into one of the empty chairs. "Finder and I have been doing some work today, and I've decided to call a meeting with Porter. Tomorrow morning. Please say you'll be there."

Fabien and Rhett exchanged shrugs.

"I'm not supposed to leave for another two days," Rhett said.

"I'll be watching wildlife set off the perimeter alarms otherwise," Fabien said.

Dinah rubbed her hands together. "Excellent. Perfect. I'm hoping that you two will be able to help me with something."

An electric thrill of excitement chased itself up Fabien's spine. The promise of a plan, some sort of meaningful action by which he might prove to himself that he had made the right choice, delighted him.

"I'm listening," he said. "What's this plan of yours?"

Dinah's grin only widened. "I've got an idea," she said, "for how we're going to catch Apollo."

"Apollo?" Fabien repeated. "But Apollo's..."

"...in another world," Rhett finished.

Dinah pointed one index finger at each of them and nodded like a broken bobble-head. "Another world. That's my point exactly."

4 DINAH

SITTING down with her old crew and Porter all in the same place was like coming back to where it all began. No, it was better, because this time Dinah knew what was going on and had something to offer. This time, she was the one with the plan.

Porter had been splitting his time between Reclamation and the Ohio vault. Seeing him in person wasn't all that strange, but this was the first time that they'd sat down with him in a small group since they'd agreed to return to ENIGMA. Ronnie, Marcus, Girom, and Lane had joined them, and one of Finder's androids hovered in the corner of the room, watching them with its wide, unblinking eyes.

"It's a pleasure to have you all here," Porter said. He crossed his long legs and steepled his fingers in front of his mouth, nodding to each of them in turn. "I've been quite busy with the new staff in Ohio. We've nearly finished cataloging the vault contents there. It seems that you're making similar strides in Reclamation?"

They nodded, although Dinah was quite sure that she was the most eager of them. She was bursting with excitement to lay out her plan before Porter and the rest of them.

Porter seemed to sense her nerves and nodded toward her. "Dr. Bray, I'm under the impression that you have an idea you'd like to bring before us?"

"I do." She squirmed in her chair, meeting the eyes of each of her associates in turn. "We have no reason to think that Apollo is dead," she said, falling into her old professorial patter. "Finder and I have been reviewing the vault's missing items, and while there are several interesting and powerful items not present, we're able to account for all of them. I'm still reviewing the database, but it occurred to me that we could equip ourselves to follow Apollo through the breach."

Marcus' eyebrows rose. "Hold on. You want to track him into... wherever he's gone?"

Dinah nodded. "We don't know what he's been able to do on the far side of the breach, or who he's been able to make contact with, but the longer we wait, the more difficult it will be to intervene."

Rhett cocked his head to one side and frowned. "But when Apollo activated the destabilizer, it caused massive damage to the vault."

Ronnie whistled and held up his hands. "Is that what you're saying? That you want to activate the destabilizer again? Because Rhett's right, that caused a mess."

"And Azmera seems to think that using the destabilizer will weaken the borders between realities," Girom interjected.

"Hear me out." Dinah reached into her jacket to produce a hologram puck, and set it on the table in front of her. She powered it on, and it immediately projected an image of the fully assembled destabilizer, power cells and all. The image hovered in their midst, rotating slowly on its axis. "Finder and I came up with a little simulation, not unlike the one Porter showed us on our first visit." She smiled at the head of the Ohio vault.

Porter didn't smile back. His dark, serious eyes were fixed on the projection of the destabilizer, the corners of his lips pulled down in a frown.

"I know that this is a serious matter," Dinah said. "But Apollo is stranded somewhere else. Another world, another reality, however that works. We know the point at which he crossed over, and we have the device itself. As for the amount of damage that the vault sustained last time..." Dinah waved to Finder, who in turn manipulated the hologram to show a scaled-down image of the destruction their battle with Apollo had wrought on the space. "Many of the structural problems caused last time were the direct result of the Gravitas Engine. That was what pulled down all the ramps and catwalks."

Rhett tapped his fingers against his lips, obviously unconvinced. "I remember how it felt when the destabilizer was activated. Even without the Gravitas Engine, it was like... like opening a hatch on an airplane mid-flight."

Dinah nodded again. "I know, but we can account for that this time. For one thing, we would have to activate it in a contained space, rather than the main floor of the vault, but if we did it under more controlled conditions, we could actually use the Gravitas Engine in our favor to—"

"No," Porter said.

Dinah stopped short, still waving a finger at Rhett. "No? You don't think it will work?"

"It might," Porter conceded. He unfolded his arms and legs and sat more upright in his seat. As usual, his expression was carefully controlled, but there was a tightness around his mouth that suggested he was biting back some intense emotion when he spoke again. "It doesn't matter, though. I'm afraid that I can't authorize any use of the destabilizer, even within controlled conditions."

"But—!" Dinah rocked back in her chair. That wasn't fair. She'd thought it all out. They'd come so close to defeating Apollo once and for all. If Porter would simply see reason and let her at least explain the mission she had in mind, they might be able to put the Hand on the offensive.

"I understand that you're passionate about this issue," Porter said. His dark eyes met Dinah's, and his brow pulled low. Dinah couldn't read his expression, but it was obvious that he'd come to a firm conclusion, and was unlikely to be swayed. "In a perfect world, we would gather the ENIGMA commanders and discuss this as a collective. We would have a plan, and resources. But we're stretched thin enough as it is. Reclamation is still under repair, and while Captain Zappotis has made strides to reestablish ties with other vaults, they are slow to extend their trust after years of skepticism."

"It's not us they don't trust," Dinah blurted.

Every head in the room swiveled toward her. Lane coughed and elbowed Ronnie. Marcus' eyes flicked back and forth between the two. Even Fabien seemed surprised by her boldness. Only Rhett refused to meet anyone's gaze.

Porter leaned forward. "And what do you mean by that, Dr. Bray?" he asked.

Dinah let out a rumbling sigh. *You shouldn't have pushed his buttons. Now he'll never agree. Why couldn't you just keep your mouth shut?* She'd said enough, however, that she couldn't very well claim ignorance and change the subject now.

"They don't trust *you*," she said. "And I know why, and I know that it's not fair, but if we were working for Azmera or Tenzin, they wouldn't be so hesitant to build an alliance. But we're here, and I'm not asking them. I'm asking *you*. You're the one who hired us, after all. You trusted us to track down Apollo before you even knew us. Why won't you trust us to finish what we started?"

Porter drummed his fingertips against the table. The hologram of the formerly ruined shell of El Dorado hovered between them, and it struck Dinah that this was a piss-poor image to use in conjunction with her last argument. True, they'd eventually stopped Apollo, but that had been in a three-to-one fight—more than that, if you counted how many of the vaults he'd damaged on his rampage through ENIGMA's outposts. Apollo had come awfully close to defeating them.

But that was back when he had the destabilizer. If they planned this right, it wouldn't be a slapdash mission. Even if they didn't have the full force of ENIGMA behind them, they still had allies in the other vaults.

"Wouldn't it help earn their trust," Dinah asked, "if we were able to show that we'd finished off one of the Hand's agents?"

Porter's eyelids fluttered, as if he wanted to close his eyes and imagine that world, but wouldn't allow himself the luxury. Instead of shouting no and slapping his palm down on the table, he turned his head slightly, drawing Rhett into the conversation.

"Captain Zappotis, you've been speaking with the other commanders. Do you believe that this mission would be a good use of our resources?"

Rhett kept twisting his fingers together, keeping his face downcast and his eyes averted. He thought it over for a long moment. Too long. He was supposed to be her ally. Why didn't he have her back? They'd tag-teamed an enemy agent only a few weeks before. Without Dinah's help, and her quick thinking with the boots, they'd have failed. Rhett knew that.

He should be able to trust her instincts by now.

Instead, he shook his head. "I see what Dinah's saying, but it's a huge risk. I don't... I don't know if our current forces are up to the task. I saw through the seam when we were fighting Apollo. It's not like he's been sitting in a cave for the last few weeks, injured and alone. He's on an alien world. We have no idea what he's been doing there, or what resources exist for him to take advantage of—"

"Which is why we should go now!" Dinah insisted.

Rhett exhaled sharply. "I know you mean well, but there are too many..." He shook his head and wrinkled his nose. "Unknown quantities. I'm going north tomorrow. We need more time. More intel." He glanced at Dinah from the corner of his eyes. "I don't think we have what it takes to challenge the Hand right now."

Rhett might as well have dragged her to the edge of the underground chasm and flung her over the ledge. The sick, floating sensation of free-fall that engulfed her turned her stomach.

Porter nodded and returned his attention to Dinah. "I agree. I hired you because I trust your instincts, Dr. Bray."

"But not enough to hear me out," Dinah added bitterly.

"I'm afraid it wouldn't be prudent to continue discussing the matter at this time," Porter agreed.

There it was again—a slight straining in the muscles alongside his eyes, a twist in his lips. He wasn't saying what he meant, or at least not everything he meant. Dinah flopped back and let out a huff, painfully aware that she was acting like a spoiled child, but unable to dampen the spike in her temper.

The silence that followed was painfully awkward. Dinah had been the one to suggest the meeting, after all. She was beginning to wish that she'd asked to meet with Porter alone. The man might have listened to her then. At the very least, she wouldn't have felt quite so humiliated in the aftermath.

Fabien cleared his throat. "Might I suggest another course of action, then? Because Dinah has a point about catching the Hand off-guard."

Thank you. She didn't say it aloud, but she did tilt slightly toward the other operative to lend him a bit of emotional support, since nobody had thought to do so with her. Rhett's wishy-washy attempt to soften the blow of his betrayal hardly counted.

"Explain," Porter said.

"Instead of waiting around for the Hand of the Sun to launch another attack, why don't we take some sort of action?" Fabien scooted toward the table and reached over to power off the hologram puck. It was a comfort not having to look at it anymore, in light of Dinah's failure to win them over.

Fabien went on. "I'm not saying we should launch an attack right *now,* but Finder seems to have no trouble sifting through internet securities. Why don't we try to identify a member of the Hand who's still on Earth? Then when Rhett's meeting up with the Sigurdsson guy..."

"Sturlusson," Rhett corrected.

"Whatever, the Swede. Instead of offering him some vague treaty, why don't we try to sell him on a short-term project? We can give the other commanders something solid to latch onto." Fabien folded his hands over his stomach, kicked his booted feet up onto the meeting room table, and grinned. "No better team-building exercise than targeting a common enemy."

From the far end of the table, Lane snorted. "You *would* think shooting people is a team building exercise, LeRoux." She sniffed, but before Fabien could snark back, she added, "That said, I like the idea of targeting the Hand. After what they did to Carson..."

Dinah had seen the hologram playback of their former coworker having his face melted off his skull by Apollo, and she could only imagine how much worse it would have been to experience that moment in person. Lane Parker had been devastated. She and Carson were clearly friends, maybe more. By contrast, Dinah had barely known the Atlantean guard,

Severino, but she'd been close enough to hear when Apollo killed him.

Close enough to intervene, if you'd been brave enough. Knowing that a man had died horribly only feet from her was bad enough, but knowing that she'd been unable to stop it? That was sickening. Judging by Lane's expression, her anger and her survivor's guilt were inextricably intertwined.

Porter dragged his thumb over his bottom lip and squinted up at the ceiling, lost in thought. "That's an interesting proposal," he murmured. "I wonder..." But he trailed off, and failed to tell them where exactly his mind had wandered.

"At the very least, it might be a way to grease the wheels with the other vault leaders," Fabien pressed.

If they were going to go along with a purely theoretical plan, Dinah wondered why they couldn't at least entertain hers. Then again, Earth wasn't an unknown quantity, unlike the alien city where Apollo had ended up.

"Float the idea," Porter said at last. "Don't make any promises. We'll need more information. Finder, if we cut back some of your duties on the vault floor, are you capable of monitoring the perimeter?"

"I can do both!" Finder exclaimed, bouncing on the balls of its metal feet.

"Don't stretch yourself too thin," Porter warned. "Fabien, I'm reassigning your team. I'm interested to see what, if anything, you can turn up."

Fabien smiled widely, and Dinah was reminded of a shark, with row after row of teeth designed to keep prey from escaping once they were within reach. "I'd love to, boss. You know that sort of thing is my specialty."

Lane huffed. "We're going to be working together, Froggy."

Fabien flipped her the bird. "Don't call me that."

"Then stop acting like you're God's gift to ENIGMA," Lane shot back.

"For God's sake." Ronnie dropped his head into his hands. "Just get a room already."

Girom directed his attention to Porter. "Sir, when you say that you're reassigning his team..."

"For now, I'd like you to take charge of the vault floor," Porter said. "We'll be relying on our human crew to pick up the slack, with Finder's attention focused elsewhere."

Girom nodded. He didn't ask for clarification, which seemed... odd. It was almost as if this was something he and Porter had discussed in advance.

Or as if Porter and Azmera discussed it, and passed information to Girom through other channels, Dinah mused. She was sure that she was missing something, and that more than one unspoken understanding had been tiptoed around in this meeting.

"Ronnie, Marcus, Lane, I want you working with Fabien. See what you can scrounge up about any members of the Hand. I believe this will prove... insightful. Rhett, I trust you to make our interests clear to Commander Sturlusson. Dinah, you'll continue your work with Finder to catalog all of the missing items in full."

Dinah opened her mouth to protest, but Porter was already rising to his feet, dismissing them with all the efficiency of a grade school teacher on a Friday afternoon. The others were already talking amongst themselves. There was a renewed bounce in Fabien's step as he left the room, chatting animatedly with Rhett as he went. Girom approached Finder's android body, and Dinah caught a few words of him asking how to divvy up their duties going forward.

Porter had been the first to rise, but soon enough he was the only one left in the room with Dinah.

"Sir," Dinah began.

Once again, Porter cut her off. "Professor." He strolled over and laid one hand on her shoulder. "I hope you understand that I cannot grant you permission to activate the destabilizer again," he said solemnly.

Dinah bit the inside of her cheek. *I don't understand,* she wanted to say, but she knew that arguing wouldn't get her anywhere now. Porter had made up his mind.

"You're right about who they trust, though," Porter said. His cadence was off, and his hand squeezed Dinah's shoulder a little too tightly. "Trust has to be earned. Even within ENIGMA."

Dinah's spine stiffened in surprise. "R-right, sir."

"It can't be taken for granted," Porter pressed on. "But I need you to know that I trust your instincts, Dr. Bray. Is that clear?"

Dinah had a hundred questions, but she made herself nod. Because she understood enough.

"Then I will leave you to your work," Porter said. His hand slid from Dinah's shoulder, and he strode from the room, leaving Dinah alone with the dead hologram puck and a head full of doubts.

Unless she was very much mistaken, Porter had just given her permission to defy his earlier orders and go rogue, so long as she kept it quiet. Because Porter didn't want the rest of ENIGMA to know what he was up to? Or because there was someone within the organization that he didn't trust?

Either way, it didn't matter. Dinah had already made up her mind.

She was going to go rogue.

INTERLUDE
THE RIGHT HAND OF THE SUN

Agent Aten sat in his private office, reviewing the documents for his most recent company acquisition. Most of his business dealings were conducted in private, legally dissociated from his name. He wasn't even the figurehead behind the business entity known only as Gold Bar Holdings, Ltd. The company's name was innocuous. The current CEO was an idiot who thought he was in charge, but he could easily be dispensed with through one means or another. The majority of his wealth was held in an offshore shell account. It would be almost impossible to trace the company back to Aten's real name, or for *that* name to be traced to the Hand of the Sun. Aten was one of the most powerful men in the world, with a finger on the pulse of every major industry, and yet he was little more than a phantom.

Gold Bar didn't traffic in precious metals or minerals, despite the name. Aten's interests lay in smaller objects. Simpler things. Not high-profile brand names, but in the everyday objects that most people acquired without thinking twice. Liquor. Sugar. Paper products. Things that people never thought to question. Things that they needed, that they took for granted, that they still purchased faithfully, whether it was during a recession or an economic boom.

Satisfied by the terms of the new acquisition, he signed the paperwork and made to get up.

That was when the comm in his desk chimed.

The tone was similar to that of a text message arriving on a smartphone, although this particular comm didn't link to any of the eminently hackable satellite networks utilized by the phone companies. Aten should know, given that Gold Bar Holdings was a primary shareholder in two of those companies. Instead, it was a modified version of some of the oldest available tech, stolen by an ancestor so far removed that Aten's family could no longer remember the individual's name, nor how many branches back on the family tree he or she had grown.

Aten checked that the door was locked before sliding a flat, glossy box out of his desk. The stone inside was held in place with dozens of metal pins. It could convey sound from anywhere in the world, directly from the speaker, with a similarly attuned resonance stone. The tech itself was old, but the automatic voice scrambler was a new addition to the setup, one meant to further confuse any attempt to track the owner of the voice down in an increasingly attentive information age. Anything could be recorded and tracked, and Aten wasn't taking any chances.

He had too much to lose.

"Ray One speaking," Aten said.

"Ray One, this is Ray Twelve."

Aten let his eyes close and allowed himself a small smile. He'd been skeptical of Agent Ra, the newest addition to their order, and Ra's ability to infiltrate ENIGMA, but the agent had proven their worth. Bringing Ra into the fold had been the right choice.

"Ray Twelve, I'm delighted to hear from you. How are things progressing?" Aten fiddled with the pen between his fingers. "Have you heard from Ray Six?"

"Not since we spoke last. I did, however, have other news. ENIGMA is considering making a move against the Hand directly."

The pen stilled between Aten's fingers. "Is that so?"

"Yes. And I wonder..." Agent Ra's hesitant breath came through as a staticky crackle. *"I have reason to think that he suspects a mole."*

That was far from comforting. Aten scowled down at the resonance stone in its modified box. "Are you compromised, Ray Six?"

"I don't believe so. His behavior toward me hasn't changed. Everyone's on edge, though."

Aten fell silent as he considered the implications. It had been years since an agent of the Hand had been able to get this close to ENIGMA, and they were so close to achieving so many of their goals. With Apollo in a neighboring world, and a mole in the enemy's territory, Aten could almost taste victory.

"Are you still there, Ray One?"

"Yes." Aten went back to fiddling with his pen, already teasing out the many possible outcomes of the order he was about to give. If Apollo failed to deliver on his recent promises... or if Ra was discovered... it was certainly a gamble, but if it paid off...

"We're going to throw them a bone," he said aloud, cementing his choice.

"*I'm sorry?*"

"We're going to hand them one of our agents on a silver platter," Aten said. "Someone who'll put up a fight. If our agent prevails, so much the better. If they don't, it will put ENIGMA at ease."

"*Will we... warn them?*"

After the briefest of consideration, Aten shook his head. "No. *He* would smell a rat, and you know we keep the fail-safes in place for a reason. They have ways of drawing out the truth, but if our agent doesn't know you spoon-fed ENIGMA their information, they won't be able to crack."

Agent Ra didn't respond right away. Aten could guess what they were thinking. How easy it was for one agent to fall from grace, to be offered up as a sacrifice for the sake of the greater good. But they all knew the score. When they accepted their seat at the table, they promised to serve the needs of the Hand.

"*Who will it be?*" Ra asked. The scrambler could conceal their age, their gender, even any accent that might give them away, but it couldn't conceal their hunger. They were bloodthirsty.

He should have known that Ra would have no qualms about throwing another agent to the wolves. After all, look what they'd arranged with Apollo during his raid on the ENIGMA vaults. Like Aten, Ra saw the bigger picture.

"Ray Seven," Aten decided. Mithra was a thorn in his side.

Out of the members of the Hand, only Aten knew the personal information of the other agents. It was possible, of course, that they were all spying on one another, but Aten was the one who'd invited them. Who orchestrated them. He was the Right Hand of the Sun, the embodiment of Aten. Like the kings of old, his place was determined by divine right. Mithra had never properly respected that.

"I'll be in touch with the information you require for this mission," he said. "You're doing well, Ray Twelve. Better than I could have believed."

When they were done speaking, and the resonance stone fell silent, Aten returned it to the drawer. In the meantime, he scooped the paperwork off his desk, strode to the door of his office, and unlocked it. Business carried on, after all.

If he couldn't keep a tight grip on the throat of this world, how could he be expected to command them all?

5 RHETT

THE MORNING he was meant to head north, Fabien and Dinah found him at breakfast.

"Guess you get a new schedule with your new assignment," Rhett observed. Fabien was usually on duty at that hour.

"I didn't want to miss you." He offered a crooked grin. "It'll be strange, won't it, to be working separately? When they offered me a regular job, I thought working with both of you would be a package deal."

"I'll be back," Rhett told him. "Dinah, about yesterday—"

"It's fine," Dinah interrupted. "Really. You had to be honest. I can respect that."

He couldn't leave without warning them about the note he'd gotten, but there had been no time to talk to them alone after the meeting. Still, he couldn't leave them in the dark, especially not Fabien. Whether Porter was setting him up for failure, or was simply ignorant, Rhett had to say something. Launching an attack against the Hand could get Fabien killed if there was a spy in their midst.

"I need you two to be careful," he said. "I think... I think there might be a mole in the vault."

Dinah's eyes widened. "You know?"

Rhett blinked at her. "*You* know?"

Dinah lowered her voice and leaned across the table, gripping her mug of the too-bitter cafeteria coffee in a white-knuckle grip. "Porter said some cryptic shit to me yesterday."

"Oh." He frowned. If Porter knew... "I got a note."

"From him?" Fabien asked.

Rhett shook his head. "From the spy."

Both of them stared at him in horror. "When? And you didn't *say* anything?" Dinah seemed personally affronted by this perceived betrayal.

"They made it sound like the Hand might bribe me... or threaten me. Which I suppose they still might." Rhett sighed.

Fabien whistled and hunched his shoulders. "I'm sure you've thought of this already, but..." He cleared his throat.

"But?"

"Well, I mean." Fabien spread his hands and looked to Dinah for support. When the professor's blank stare remained bemused, he sighed in frustration. "I mean, are you going to take them up on it?"

Dinah spluttered in protest, but Rhett wasn't surprised by the question, in part because it had already occurred to him.

"They've got someone on the inside," Fabien said. "It wouldn't hurt us to return the favor."

"You can't be serious!" Dinah hissed. The hand holding her

coffee mug was shaking. "Rhett, that would be incredibly dangerous. You're talking about the people Apollo worked for! You can't trust them!"

Fabien elbowed her. "Keep your voice down."

"But—"

"I know," Rhett said, rubbing his temples. "But that kind of work is my expertise. It's one of the reasons that Porter reached out to me in the first place." It wasn't as if he could launch himself into a position that would allow him to spy on the Hand. He wasn't even sure who'd left that damned note, and he was about to head out on his own in an attempt to court a new alliance within ENIGMA. But if the opportunity presented itself, he'd be a fool not to take it.

"Rhett." Dinah set her jaw. "Two million dollars isn't enough to risk your life over."

Rhett waited for some sort of explanation, but Dinah's expression held firm.

"Two million dollars?" Fabien echoed. "Where does that math come in?"

"The original retainer Porter paid us, before we signed on," Dinah said.

Fabien's eyes widened, and he took a hasty sip of his coffee.

"Hold on." Dinah twisted in her chair and squinted at Fabien. "How much did he pay *you*?"

Fabien muttered something under his breath.

"What was that?"

"...Ten."

"Ten *million*?" Dinah screeched.

"Yeah." Both turned to Rhett, who became suddenly engrossed in his toast.

"Rhett?" Fabien prodded.

He took an enormous bite of his toast and chewed slowly.

"Rhett. How much did he pay you?"

"He offered me ten," he mumbled around the bite of bread.

"Both of you got paid literally five times what he offered me?" Dinah demanded.

"You were an academic," Fabien countered. "We had more practical expertise." His eyes slid back to Rhett. "When you said that he offered you ten..."

"I got him up to fifteen," Rhett admitted.

Fabien chuckled ruefully and uttered a series of expletives in French.

"Relax," Rhett told him. "I've seen the payroll. We're all getting the same now."

"Just haggle him up another five million," Fabien said. "I was right, you should use your more valuable expertise in service of the organization."

"I'm a better bargainer than the two of you, which was my point to begin with," Rhett said with a small shrug. His self-satisfied smile faded at the notion that he might find himself in a similar situation to the one he'd faced before when he'd served with Lisa Kelly. Kelly was still alive, but she'd lost the best years of her life to her time as a political prisoner, and many of their local contacts had been killed. Whichever of their fellow agents had sold them out was also risking all of their lives.

If Rhett ever figured out who was involved, he'd want ten minutes alone with them in a padded room. By the time he was done with them, an injured hip would be the least of their problems.

"Don't do anything stupid, either of you," he said. "I'll try to get us more help. Fabien, keep your eyes open. Dinah..."

She lifted both hands in self-defense. "Don't worry about me, I'm just the underpaid academic."

"Take it up with Porter," Rhett told her. "And take care. Both of you."

"See you when you get back with some new Swedish friends," Fabien said.

Rhett got to his feet and cleared away his half-finished tray. He had one more stop before he left, but he found himself wishing that they could stay together. After the mess with Kelly, he'd been a loner for so long that he'd forgotten what it was like to rely on people. With Zoe, he'd always had to hold something back. Having allies whom he could trust with the truth, allies who would protect him in a firefight, changed everything. He'd almost forgotten what it was like to fend for himself on a mission.

And despite his reassurance that the separation would be temporary, he had no idea when he was likely to return.

THE FIRST TIME Rhett was armed by the weapons found in an ENIGMA vault, Ronnie had helped equip him. This time around, he had an android to help him.

"Do you know what you'd like?" Finder's avatar asked.

Rhett considered the cane he was holding. It was the one Porter had given him on that very first day, which felt like years ago, even though it had been less than two months. It was useful for short-range combat, and it served a dual purpose. Strolling into another vault armed to the teeth struck him as unwise, but going in without any defenses felt like an amateur mistake.

"What can you give me that would protect me?" he asked. "Something I could use to defend myself, or to escape a dangerous situation, but that another commander couldn't object to?"

Finder's head tilted to the side, and its eyes grew larger. For approximately ten seconds, it stood uncannily still. Rhett was beginning to think that it had gone offline, until it lurched into motion again.

"How about a hopper vest?" it asked.

"A... what now?"

"A hopper vest. It's a type of scrambler." Finder began to walk, and Rhett trailed after it, using the cane for its obvious purpose as he went. He'd been able to rest and recuperate during the rebuilding of Reclamation, and he was feeling better than he had in years, at least physically.

"You realize that doesn't tell me much?" he prompted.

Finder slapped a hand to its head with a metallic clang that reverberated through the armory. "Of course! I'm sorry. I forget that you don't have access to the database... human brains are very simple, aren't they? You remember how Dinah was able to use her seven-league boots to travel beyond the usual parameters of space and time?"

"Yes," Rhett deadpanned, "my simple human brain was able to retain that information."

"Wonderful!" Finder clasped its hands together, missing the

sarcasm entirely. "Well, a scrambler operates under similar principles, but without quite so much, how would you say it, guidance. It scrambles your position in space/time within a finite range. Allow me to demonstrate."

Finder lifted a vest off of the rack; the base material was some sort of stretchy fabric, not unlike the neoprene suits favored in Atlantis, and the dark material was criss-crossed with metal bands, pins, and nodes. The pattern they formed was visually appealing, like a steampunk version of a Greek key, but Rhett couldn't discern what use those designs might have.

Finder had to wriggle a bit to fit the double-breasted suit vest over its broad android shoulders, but once it was in place, they fastened the buttons and stood proud.

"As you can see, even with the vest on, I'm just... here. But if I squeeze one of these nodes..." Finder reached its long fingers down to the two crisp points at the bottom hem of the vest. Twin silver buttons decorated the flaps, and Finder pinched one so that it compressed slightly.

In an instant, Finder was halfway across the room, but only for a split second. Then it was behind him, but by the time Rhett whirled to face it, the android was standing by the wall, then by the door. "Scrambles," Finder said, from next to the shelving. "It," it added from two inches away from his face. "Me," the android concluded from somewhere off to Rhett's left.

Finder reappeared next to the ammunition cabinet and remained there, pinching both silver buttons this time. "To stop it, you press *both* buttons. As you can see, the fact that it makes things a bit random wouldn't set you up as a particularly effective fighter, but it would make you a difficult target."

"You call *that* a bit random?" Rhett gestured around the room to all the places where Finder had been.

The android's face fell. "You don't like it?"

Rhett sighed and held out one hand. "I didn't say that. It's a good suggestion, and even if Sturlusson knows what it is, he probably won't feel threatened by it. I don't suppose you have another chameleon coat?"

"I *do!* But it's not just a coat, it's *better.*" Finder all but skipped back over to the rack and produced a shimmering hooded jumpsuit with a capelet that splayed over the shoulders.

Better was a relative term. Wearing that outfit, he'd look like a lunatic when he showed up on Sturlusson's doorstep.

Better a lunatic than dead, he thought, and held his hand out for the jumpsuit.

At this small admission of his acceptance, Finder beamed.

6 FABIEN

HE SHOULD HAVE BEEN angry that Porter was willing to throw him to the wolves without warning. By rights, he should have been *furious*. But he knew why the vault commander had hired him, and even if the pay difference with Rhett smarted, he knew his strengths.

Fabien LeRoux was good at assessing danger, and he always worked better under pressure. The notion that one of his coworkers was against him didn't strike him as something to worry about, but as a force to galvanize him onward. It spiked his adrenaline. It made him feel *alive*.

Ronnie, Lane, and Marcus met him in Reclamation's control room. Technically, Finder's mainframe did the actual *controlling*, but from their vantage point they could monitor everything that took place in the rest of the vault, using the partially updated camera system that Porter had insisted on installing. Swapping out hardware from the old El Dorado system was more complicated than it would have been with any other vault, since Finder needed to be able to interface with everything, and replacing too much of the hardware at once taxed the efficiency of the AI system, at least until it could learn how to operate everything.

Positioned at the top of the vault, this was also the only room where they were able to get any sort of decent network connection. Finder had figured out a way to boost their signal, and had managed to fly under the Hand's radar for years. If only Finder could sniff out a rat.

Whoever's spying for the Hand must not be using a network connection to do so, Fabien mused. He wasn't sure what that meant for his investigation, though.

"I don't see what we're even *doing* here," Marcus complained. He sat with his feet splayed, his heels braced against the floor, arms crossed over his broad chest. Usually, when they were on perimeter duty, they wore bulky protective gear. Seeing him in camo cargo pants and a fitted Army-green polo was odd.

Not as odd, though, as the fact that Lane had turned up in jeans and a faded tee advertising an old David Bowie tour. It didn't look *bad* on her, exactly, but still. American fashion really was embarrassing.

Ronnie shot his compatriot an impatient glare. "Are you opposed to tracking down the Hand now?"

Marcus rolled his eyes. "Of course not. But ENIGMA's been trying to do this for years, right? Stopping the Hand of the Sun is our whole *thing*, but they're even more secretive than we are. No shade to Porter, but we're already stretched pretty thin."

Fabien rubbed his thumb across his bottom lip. "ENIG-MA's able to pull strings, though. Porter didn't seem to have any trouble fulfilling his promises to me."

Lane was picking her nails sullenly, ignoring Fabien as she preferred to do, but she snorted at this pronouncement. "That's because he was able to use relics... and, in Rhett's case, to pull a few strings. Going against the Hand is different. They understand how relics work, they have fail-safes in place to protect them."

Fabien swiveled toward her. "Explain."

Lane rolled her eyes to Ronnie and said, "This guy," then turned her attention back to Fabien, meeting his eyes this time. "Explaining your job to you isn't my responsibility, LeRoux."

As tempting as it was to reach across the table and slap some sense into her, Fabien forced himself to refrain from clapping back. He had a clear mission now, and the work would *always* come first. He'd put it ahead of everything else in his life, after all. The work was all he had, and if he had to make nice with Lane to stay on track, he'd find a way.

"I'm not trying to start something, Lane," he said. "You know more about ENIGMA than I do, but I have other expertise. If we combine those things, maybe we can do something that's never been done before." He tapped one finger against the tabletop and smirked. "Maybe we can finally take the fight to *them*."

Lane's eyes widened in surprise. She seemed taken aback by this response, but not entirely displeased.

"Okay." Lane leaned forward and spread her hands, gesturing as she spoke as if laying out the pieces on a chessboard. "So let's say ENIGMA tried to go up against... I dunno, a corrupt government of some small country, let's say. They might have more resources, but we'd have the advantage, because we'd have powers and abilities they'd never dream of. They could try to hide their major players, and that might work against a normal enemy, but as long as we knew who we were looking for, we could find them. Centralize our focus. Does that make sense?"

On his very first visit to the Ohio vault, Fabien had watched Porter use a map that could locate someone using a sample of their hair. "But if you don't know who you're looking for..." he murmured.

"Exactly, it's already more difficult. And let's say that our theoretical warlord has a relic that makes him impossible to track. Or one that can make subtle adjustments to his DNA. Instead of being able to, like, magically Google his coordinates, it would be like trying to trace a private account under a different name on a computer he's already infected with malware."

"But that can't be entirely accurate," Fabien said slowly.

"I mean, the analogy is imperfect..." Lane began.

"That's not what I mean." Fabien shifted to the edge of his chair. "I'm less familiar with the role of relics and the difficulties they present, but I've been hired to kill a lot of people."

"Not sure that's something to brag about, but okay," Ronnie said.

"It depends on how you feel about those who abuse power." Fabien turned to him. "You're a parent. You rely on empathy." *I'm a parent, too. But I'm a shit one.* "But I can tell you one thing about the people I've been paid to target... they don't amass wealth and power so that they can live quiet lives in rural towns. People who are desperate for power want to be able to *use* it. It makes monsters of them, and I have no qualms about targeting those people." He shifted back toward Lane. "So I do understand what you're saying, but I don't think these people will be as anonymous as you suggest. They may not be famous. They may not be putting their names in lights. But they *will* be finding ways to use their relics to their advantage, I can promise you that."

Marcus ran his hands through his dark hair. "That's what Lane's getting at, though. If they're smart, they'll be able to fly under the radar."

Fabien steepled his fingers in front of his mouth to hide his smile. "Perhaps. But that may be a clue, too. Azmera knew about the destabilizer, which suggests that ENIGMA knows at least a few of the relics that the Hand have claimed or stolen over the years. So instead of trying to look for an individual, why don't we look for evidence of specific relics that we know are in the Hand's possession?"

"Shit." Lane blinked a few times. "*Shit.* I don't think we've ever... but Porter's always been cagey about that kind of thing..."

"Holy Land should have records of objects that have gone missing over the years," Ronnie said with mounting excitement. "Or relics that the Hand has used against us. I can ask Azmera for any information she can offer to get us started."

"Noice," Marcus said.

Fabien's pleasure at having come up with a possible solution was tempered by his suspicion. There were only a dozen or so people who worked at Reclamation, and only a few of *those* who would have been able to leak information to Apollo during his raid against the vaults.

The more time he spent with them, the more it was going to sting if it turned out that one of them was the mole.

7 DINAH

SAFE INSIDE THE digital space that Finder had created for her, Dinah stewed. She kept pacing the room, no doubt putting the omnidirectional treadmill through its paces.

"What's the matter?" Finder asked. The light shining from the simulated ceiling above her pulsed slightly to match the cadence of Finder's voice. "You've been in a strange mood since yesterday."

Dinah stopped walking, and was dimly aware of the fact that the floor beneath her shifted in accordance with the continued motion of the treadmill, before it stopped abruptly.

Instead of answering, she countered with a question. "Finder, how do you feel about breaking rules? Theoretically."

The AI was silent for a moment, and when it answered, its voice was softer and somewhat muted. "What kind of rules are we discussing? Theoretically."

She had no way of knowing if Finder would take Porter's

commands at face value, or if asking the AI to go against its instructions would cause Finder to panic, shut her down, or even short-circuit on some level. As a student, Dinah had taken a singular philosophy course that included a section on the ethics and implications of AI, but she'd been so focused on studying history that she'd never dedicated much of her time to understanding technology. According to her old way of thinking, AI was just another development that stemmed from the long march of history, human ingenuity, and increasingly advanced technology. It had never occurred to her that she'd become coworkers, and possibly even friends, with one of the most complex inorganic minds on the planet.

She still believed that the best way to advance the future of humanity was to learn from the past, but during her brief career in academia, everything had been theoretical. Esoteric. Her history Ph.D. hadn't prepared her for the situation in which she currently found herself.

All that aside, she was going to need Finder's help if she had any hope of modifying her plan to go after Apollo. If the AI refused to assist her, there was no way she could proceed alone.

Might as well tell the truth.

"I want to go after Apollo," she said.

The light above her, a visual simulation controlled entirely by Finder, flickered like an old halogen ballast. "Are you asking me to help you go behind ENIGMA's back in pursuit of him?"

"Yeah." Dinah squirmed under Finder's scrutiny. In the private hologram, Finder didn't bother to take a form. The room was Finder, and Finder controlled the room. Every twitch, every frown, every erratic thump of Dinah's heart would be obvious to the AI.

"You're asking me to *collude?*" Finder didn't have vocal chords, but its voice still rose and cracked at the end of the question, much like a teenage boy's. "Dinah, this is so exciting. I've never colluded before."

"So you're in?"

"Of course I'm in!" Finder exclaimed. A note of deep fury entered its usually bright, feminine tone. "After what Apollo did to my collection? He not only damaged the space that I had cared for since my inception, but he vandalized my catalog! And tried to kill you, which is also very bad," it added, clearly as an afterthought. "Is this a secret? Because I can be discreet, but yes, I absolutely want to hunt him down. I have noted three thousand sixty-two hundred nine hundred and eighteen ways in which I could punish him for what he did to me, and I am thinking of new ones all the time."

Dinah didn't ask what kind of punishments Finder had in mind. She had a feeling she'd rather not know what the AI was capable of when it was angry. "Yes," she said, "it's a secret."

Despite the fact that they were in their own private world, Finder lowered its voice to a deliberately scratchy whisper. "If we're telling secrets, may I share one as well? I believe that it's pertinent to our new top secret and highly undercover mission.

Before they left the AI space, they were going to have to have a conversation about subtlety, but for the time being Dinah nodded. "Please do."

"You recall that I am capable of resonating with the items that were formerly in my care?"

"Like the ring. Of course."

"I can do more than merely simulate the abilities of those objects," Finder stage-whispered. "I can do it with all of the objects I've encountered."

Dinah lowered her voice too, on instinct. "What do you mean?"

"Soooooo." Finder dragged out the word, clearly reveling in its private knowledge. "I can simulate the destabilizer. We'll need to get your hands on the real thing, of course, but in the meantime we can simulate its functionality without risking your safety, or the safety of the vault. Run some test diagnostics. And that's not all... I can interface directly with some of the objects we lost during Apollo's attack."

Dinah sucked in a breath. "What does that mean?"

The pillar at the center of the room had stood empty during their conversation. A small, round stone, dark and glossy as obsidian, was perched on the flat surface.

"What is it?" Dinah asked as she padded over to examine the rock. On closer inspection, she could see that its surface wasn't perfectly smooth, but was inscribed with rings of little inscriptions in what appeared to be cuneiform, or at least a close linguistic cousin. She knew better than to touch objects procured by Finder in that liminal space, especially not without asking what purpose they served. Finder had no compunction about zapping her or jabbing her if the situation called for it. Two days ago, when they'd been discussing something that looked like a sea urchin made of needles, Finder had even drawn blood. When Dinah removed her gloves after their session, she'd been bleeding from two fingers.

Finder had claimed that this was for 'authenticity's sake,' which was hardly reassuring.

"It's a resonance stone," Finder explained. "Usually they're inscribed in pairs. People can use them to talk directly to one another over long distances."

"Including across realities?" Dinah asked, incredulous.

"Of course." Finder sounded more than a little smug. "I've never gotten a chance to test it before, though."

"Do you have the other half of the pair?" Dinah lifted the stone gingerly off of the platform and held it up to the light, studying the markings.

Finder laughed to itself. "Why would ENIGMA store the matching stones in the same place? That would make them useless."

"Huh. But you can communicate with it, even without the other half of the set?" She ran her fingers over the markings, marveling at how real it felt. She'd never broached the subject with Finder, but the difference between what the AI could replicate for her, and what fell beyond the scope of its sensors, interested her almost as much as the hologram itself.

"As I said before, I'm able to resonate with all of the objects in the collection. I don't know how to explain it, because the sensation seems to fall outside of anything you can experience. It's like..." Finder paused and emitted another of those halogen-bulb hums. "You know how it feels when you connect to a new satellite for the first time? Or when you log into a new WiFi network?"

"Um." Dinah wrinkled her nose. "Not really."

"Right, right. Well, relics and devices have energy, and I can tap into that. Shall we give it a try with this one?"

Dinah gripped the stone tighter. "Will Apollo know what we're doing? Will he be able to tell that we're spying on him?"

"I don't... think so? I'll just be running a sim. Sort of. Kind of. Maybe. I mean, given that I *am* able to actually tap into the energy signature of the stone—"

"Let's try it," Dinah blurted. "And if we start crossing signals with Apollo, we'll, you know, disconnect from the network or whatever."

"Very well. Are you ready?"

Dinah cradled the simulation of the smooth black stone between her palms. "As I'll ever be."

The faint buzzing in the room intensified, but this time Dinah could feel it vibrating from the object in her hand. The resonance stone was no longer than a golf ball, but whatever energy it contained was enough to make it judder in her grip like the wings of a hummingbird, its movements so rapid and intense that the inscriptions on its carved exterior began to blur.

"Is it working?" Dinah asked. Her voice sounded strange in her own ears, tinny and faraway as though she was speaking to herself over a bad phone connection.

Finder didn't answer. Instead, a sort of chittering speech reached her ears, high and irregular, like mice in the walls. Dinah looked up from the stone and found herself at sea in a soupy gray nothingness, a lone ship lost in the mist. She rotated on the spot. Behind her, crouched on a floor obscured by drifting smoke, hunched a creature the approximate size of a capybara. Its back was to her, and it was hunched over itself. It was the source of the squeaking sound.

Dinah took a hesitant step closer. Whatever it was had a long, bare, pinkish-gray tail, and strange bald ears that stuck out from the side of its head. On closer inspection, it seemed more like some sort of giant opossum, or an oversized and strangely proportioned rat.

Except that rats didn't wear clothes, and this creature definitely did.

"Hello?" Dinah asked.

The creature fell silent and very still, as if by not moving a muscle it hoped to disappear. Dinah took another shuffling step forward. The strangest part of the experience was that she could still feel the treadmill moving under her feet. Whatever it was, it was still part of the simulation, but why Finder had chosen to simulate this particular experience, Dinah could only guess.

"Hello?" she said again.

Slowly, gracelessly, the creature turned to face her. The clothes it wore were dirty and tattered, and had either been patched dozens of times or been made in the style of a poorly-sewn patchwork quilt. Still, the clothes were meant for it, sewn in its size, accommodating its stubby limbs, long torso, and curling tail.

Its beady black eyes met Dinah's, and she had only a fraction of a second to register its black-and-pink mottled digits, its elongated snout ending in a clever black nose, and its enormous mouth lined with tiny but razor-sharp teeth.

Then the creature began to scream.

The noise startled a yelp out of Dinah, who flung herself backward. A gleaming black object the exact size of the resonance stone slipped from the creature's paws, and it vanished.

When Dinah hit the ground, the stone fell from her hands, and the hum died in the same instant that she reappeared in the private room that Finder had built for them.

"Oh, dear." Finder's digital voice was deeply remorseful. "That wasn't what was supposed to happen at all. Usually activating the stone would only result in an audio connection. I wonder why it did that? Maybe because you were holding the same stone? Or a simulation of the real stone? This will require further study—"

"Finder." Dinah cut off the AI's babbling and reached for the dropped stone, which was inert and stationary once more. "What the hell just happened?"

"Ah, about that. I think you may have made contact. Not first contact, presumably, because Apollo's on that world—"

"That thing was an alien?" Dinah demanded.

Finder hummed. "So it would seem."

Dinah felt all kinds of ways about that. For one thing, it was fascinating. For another, it was possible that she'd just accidentally outed her presence to a creature that might report back to Apollo.

But in reality, her primary emotion was disappointment. Years of watching obnoxious alien 'documentaries' on the History Channel, dozens of debates with friends and classmates, a longstanding belief that aliens—at least, humanoid aliens—didn't exist, and Dinah had just encountered extraterrestrial life.

And her alien contact turned out to be a giant-ass rat dressed like Oliver Twist.

8 RHETT

THE JUMPSUIT BREATHED SURPRISINGLY WELL, but the hopper vest clung to Rhett's torso and kept his body heat from properly circulating. It would have been bad enough, but in the humidity of the Amazon, it was downright stifling.

Rhett's journey began with a hike through the jungle. The belt required to use the point-to-point teleporter was cinched around his waist. Traversing the uneven ground outside of the vault perimeter was hard on his body, which had grown accustomed to easier days spent inside the vault with minimal exertion. By the time he reached the metal pole standing upright in the midst of the thick jungle vegetation, sweat was rolling off of him, making the jumpsuit cling to him in unflattering ways. The haze of pain that had lifted during his time in Reclamation returned with a vengeance.

"Not now," he muttered, leaning against one of the thick-trunked trees. He wanted to catch his breath before departing.

The twinge in his hip bothered him almost as much as the tension in his lungs, and he rubbed his palm against the seam of muscle where his leg and torso met. "Not now."

He was going to need to be strong if he was going to convince Sturlusson of anything.

Most of the point-to-point teleporters employed by ENIGMA weren't as close to the vaults as this one. It had been installed during the attempts to relocate the lost vault some twenty years before. At least it was well outside of the Reclamation perimeter, so if the Hand ever figured out how to hack it, they'd still have to march a few miles through rough jungle in order to reach the vault itself. The idea of another long trek from wherever he'd landed to Valhalla made Rhett groan.

Valhalla. God, Sturlusson's going to be insufferable, isn't he? It's one thing to base your fortress' code name on a mythological city, and another to name it after the hall of the dead over which a freaking GOD presides...

His indignation bought him a burst of energy, and he pushed off the tree trunk to approach the teleporter pole. The glass bulb at the top sparked with energy.

"Okay," he said, wiping another track of sweat from his forehead. "Let's do this."

Traveling by teleporter wasn't a pleasant experience. It took him almost ten minutes to get the damned thing properly attuned to the correct destination—the tech itself was pretty old, and two decades of exposure in the rainforest hadn't done it any favors. When he finally got it set to the right destination, he managed to bump the dial with his thumb as he pulled his hand away, and he had to start all over again.

As long as it doesn't drop the signal mid-teleport, we're good, he thought as he checked the clasp on his belt one last time, just in case.

That was the annoying part. The awful part came next, and though it only lasted a few seconds, it was a decidedly uncomfortable way to pass the time. He activated the teleporter, grunted at the sharp tug around his waist, and disappeared.

Being in transit was a deeply strange experience, in part because Rhett was in a hundred places at once, and none of them at all. From what little he understood about this particular mode of transport, his particles were being relayed from one bulb to the next, zig-zagging his way across continents, over oceans, up mountain slopes and down again. He was never in those places in any way that mattered, which was probably for the best, given that he'd have spent the whole time fretting and heaving. The possibility of his particles being intercepted by some other device terrified him.

At least he couldn't be frightened when he was little more than static in the air.

The next thing he knew, he was on his hands and knees, his palms pressed against a vast expanse of smooth pebbles and pale sand, retching up the crap coffee and dry toast he'd consumed earlier. His head throbbed with something in the neighborhood of a migraine, although it faded faster than a true migraine ever would. He lifted one hand and wiped his mouth on the back of it, shuddering one last time before his stomach settled.

He was on a beach somewhere very cold; there was mist in the air, a combination of fog and salt spray that cooled his skin and left his hair damp within seconds. The wind off the water was much colder than he'd grown used to, and even before he staggered to his feet, Rhett began to shiver. He wrapped his arms around himself and took stock of his location.

Only when he'd turned back inland did he spot the man. He was bundled up in a thick down coat, with a hand-knit cap pulled over his ears, crushing his blond curls against his cheeks. His eyebrows were so pale that they almost disappeared against his fair skin. He was standing on the shoreline, watching Rhett through half-lowered eyelids, shifting from foot to foot as he waited.

"Zappotis?" he asked. His accent was thick enough that it took Rhett a moment to recognize his name.

"*God eftermiddag.*" He stood a little straighter, embarrassed that the man had watched him lose his breakfast without him even knowing. "*Ja*, Zappotis."

"*På* ENIGMA," the man said. It didn't sound like a question, but Rhett nodded anyway.

He'd been stationed in Sweden for a few months back in the day, and his experience of Swedes in general didn't match this man's sullen expression or the surly look he gave Rhett as he strode down onto the beach, past the glass-topped pole by which he'd arrived. He didn't stop to shake Rhett's hand or offer his own name; he just kept walking toward the surf, where a blanket of fog lay heavy over the glassy water of the bay.

He wasn't sure what this place was called, exactly, only that he was on the North Sea somewhere south of Gothenburg. He had only ever visited Stockholm and Uppsala. This was foreign territory. He had no friends here, other than the gruff man who was even now plodding down the beach without him.

The teleporter pole was his only way back to Reclamation, but Rhett didn't have a lot of options. If he was going to find Sturlusson, he'd need to follow this stranger and hope he led him to the right place. Rhett patted the head of his cane where it hung at his belt, cast one last glance at his only ticket back out of Sweden, and followed the stranger into the mist.

As it turned out, he wasn't walking into the water. A small boat waited on the shore, hardly larger than a one-man fishing boat, battered by years of storms, its red and white paint flaking so badly that he could no longer read the name that had once adorned the side.

"Come," the man barked at him, and Rhett went, even though reaching the low pier where the ship was moored required soaking his boots with frigid seawater.

Supposedly, dead Northmen had been pushed out to sea in burning ships after their passing, bearing their spirits to the halls of Valhalla. All things considered, Rhett hoped like hell that the vault's name wasn't an omen of things to come.

They didn't speak as the boat carried them out to sea. Before long, Rhett lost all sense of direction. If he'd been asked to guide the ship back to shore, he would have spun helplessly on the spot, unable to tell one direction from another. A thin drizzle that couldn't quite qualify as rain pattered against his upturned face.

"How much longer...?" he began.

The radio at the front of the boat crackled to life, and his guide spoke into the handheld comm attached to it by an old-fashioned curling cable, his Swedish condensed and unintelligible to Rhett's unpracticed ear.

He was still wondering what had happened when a pale yellow light appeared in the mist before them.

And then, quite suddenly, the mist fell away to reveal a low-lying island.

No, he realized, squinting at the plane of rippling water still visible beneath the foundation of the structure. Islands didn't float four feet off the surface of the ocean. This thing was built like the city of Laputa, a cousin to Atlantis that churned its way across the Atlantic, following the currents.

"Valhalla," his guide grunted.

When Rhett glanced at the man again, he was smiling.

THESE PEOPLE ARE YOUR ALLIES, Rhett told himself as he strode through the doors of Valhalla, although that felt a long way from true. Every person he passed watched him with cool, flat eyes, many of them the same color as the misty sea outside the walls. He knew they didn't trust him. That was the whole point. He'd come here to put them at ease.

He hadn't expected the whole experience to leave him so unsettled. After all, Azmera had voiced mixed feelings about trusting them when they first arrived at Holy Land, but she'd at least been civil. The stares of the Valhallans were more reminiscent of Kunzang's cold reception.

You'd be giving them side-eye, too, if one of them walked into Reclamation and started menacing the building. Rhett kept his chin up as he walked, although he did make a conscious effort to lean on his cane more heavily. For one thing, his hip was killing him. For another, it couldn't hurt for his hosts to think he was at a disadvantage. If they saw him moving a bit more slowly, they might view him as less of a threat.

Valhalla itself was more like a spaceship than a building, with smooth off-white walls, subtly tilting lines that defined the doors and corridors, and warm lighting. Rhett smiled to himself when he imagined what Fabien would have to say about the place:

If IKEA designed a vault, it would look like this. He could hear the words in Fabien's accent, and he wished briefly that Fabien and Dinah had come with him. Then he tried to picture how Fabien would handle diplomacy and decided it was best, in the end, that he'd come alone.

The stoic captain who'd brought him from the mainland stayed with him as they wound their way through the corridors of the compound, although he didn't say a word to Rhett, even when they reached a door deep within the interior of the structure. He pushed it open and stood aside, making space for Rhett to enter. Inside, positioned at a sturdy table, dressed in a uniform smothered in unfamiliar pips, sat Commander Halbjörn Sturlusson.

"Commander." Rhett nodded his head as he stepped inside. He tried to keep his gaze on Sturlusson, but he observed the rest of the room as subtly as he could, noting the two guards stationed on either side of the door, and the strange object positioned on the table at Sturlusson's elbow. A single cursory glance at the device told him very little about it, but one thing was clear: it was a relic of some kind, one of the objects typically housed in the vault. Rather than study it too intently, he stopped just shy of the chair across the table from the Swedish commander.

"Captain." Sturlusson lifted his eyes to him, answering the question that the hologram had raised. His eyes, in person, were blue, bright blue, almost unbelievably pale and clear. Rhett almost flinched under his scrutiny, and stopped himself just in time. Any show of nerves would inevitably be viewed as a show of weakness, and he had no intention of giving anything away.

"Please, Captain, sit down." Sturlusson indicated the chair. Rhett's hand was already hovering over the back of it. As he moved to sit, however, Sturlusson raised one palm. "I apologize for asking this, but would you please be so kind as to hand your belt to Kári? It will be returned to you before your departure."

Rhett hesitated only for a moment before unbuckling the belt and passing it to the boatman, who accepted with a mute nod. Rhett supposed it didn't matter—after all, it wasn't as if he could use the device this far from the teleporter itself—but without it he felt more isolated than before, cut off from his team in a fundamental way that made him wonder if he really was doing the right thing.

If nothing else, the lines around Sturlusson's mouth softened. Rhett sank into his chair and folded his hands over the handle of his cane.

"It's a pleasure to meet you in person," Rhett told him. "I understand why you're reluctant to treat with us, given the history between Porter and the rest of ENIGMA. I'm truly honored that you would take that risk."

Sturlusson's long, narrow face pinched in thought as he watched Rhett, tapping the fingertips of one hand absently against the hardwood. "Us, you say," he said in his clipped Northern tone. "You have come to think of yourself as a member of the organization, then?"

"I nearly died for it. More than once. And Reclamation in particular is dear to me."

Sturlusson nodded. "Having read all the available information regarding your history, you strike me as singularly loyal."

"Not singularly," Rhett countered. "Any dedication to the organization requires personal sacrifice. As I understand it, the crew of Atlantis spends months at a time cut off from their families, their homes, their friends. I imagine it's the same for your crew?"

Sturlusson nodded. The pinched expression of distrust had given way to one that was more thoughtful than militant. "That's the nature of the work. But before we continue this discussion, Captain, there's something that must be addressed." He gestured to the device on the table beside him. "Are you familiar with these?"

Rhett turned to the device at Sturlusson's elbow. It was about two feet high, somewhat reminiscent of an old tabletop clock, with three narrow legs that spanned the distance between the sturdy base and the brass circle at the top. From the middle of that circle hung a thin gold chain, at the end of which dangled a glass phial. The phial's cap was attached to the chain. Beneath it, inscribed on the base, were an assortment of words and symbols in a filigreed script that Rhett didn't recognize.

"I've never seen one," he admitted.

"It's an Oraculum. Built many years ago, it is the only one of its kind in ENIGMA hands." Sturlusson reached out to pull the glass phial free of the chain, and held it out to him. "Technically speaking, it is a truth-telling device. I would like to request that we use it during this interview."

Rhett arched an eyebrow at the bottle. "How does it work?" he asked.

One of the guards behind him coughed and mumbled, "If you have nothing to hide, why does it matter?"

Rhett turned in his seat to squint at the woman who'd spoken. "I'm familiar with the shortcomings of lie detectors. It's an imperfect science. I would think that any device ENIGMA had on hand would be more specialized and accurate, but you can imagine why I'd be skeptical."

The woman dipped her head in acknowledgement, but she still watched Rhett shrewdly. All of them were paying close attention to him.

Which is only fair, Rhett reminded himself, except that he was quite sure that they were watching him with more than mild mistrust. He felt a bit like a rabbit caught in a snare.

"Your concerns are quite reasonable," Sturlusson assured him. He held the glass phial aloft. "Once attuned to a specific person, the device is capable of measuring the objective truth, as it is known to you. If, for example, you were to tell me that you believe that Porter has the best interests of ENIGMA in mind, the device would be able to gauge whether or not you truly believed it. Whether Porter is on our side is another matter entirely."

"And let me guess." Rhett nodded to the phial. "You need spit or blood or some such thing to make it work? To attune the device to me, as it were?"

"Correct." Sturlusson tapped one forefinger against the glass as he held it out to him. "But you've been willing to bleed for ENIGMA in the past, haven't you?"

Rhett kept his hands on the head of his cane. "If I refuse to participate, what happens?"

"Then we show you back to the door, give you your belt, and Kári takes you back to the mainland. No harm done. We're left at an impasse."

"And we cease negotiations," Rhett finished for him.

The commander nodded. "I'm afraid so."

Perhaps it was all the eyes on him that made him bold. Perhaps it was the knowledge that fleeing back to Reclamation with his tail between his legs would leave the vault in a worse position than if he'd never come at all. Perhaps it was simple pride that made Rhett extend his arm at last.

"I have nothing to hide," he told Sturlusson.

Unless he was very much mistaken, a glint of pleased surprise flashed in Sturlusson's Arctic eyes. After all, a stronger alliance would benefit them both. Perhaps with the help of the Oraculum, he'd be able to convince him of that.

9 FABIEN

THE FOUR OF them grouped around the table, the hologram puck between them, examining the list of missing relics that Azmera had provided.

"I don't know how we're supposed to figure out which of these objects we're looking for." Marcus raked his hands across his face. "How do we narrow it down?"

Before Fabien could answer, Ronnie butted in. "We should start with the ones that are easiest to track down. The ones that would leave some kind of... of ripple effect if they were used." He glanced at Fabien. "Right?"

"Exactly." He nodded like he knew what the hell he was talking about. This was the first time that they'd all been on the same page, answering to him, and Fabien wasn't about to sabotage that by admitting that he was in over his head. Technically, they were all flying blind in some ways.

Planning was overrated. In his early days, Fabien had over-thought every assignment. He'd developed elaborate and inflexible mission plans, plotting them down to the moment. Sometimes that had been helpful, but he'd learned pretty quickly how limiting that kind of rigid thinking could be. He wasn't running elaborate bank heists—well, except that one time in Paris, and he preferred not to remember that incident—and relying on his instincts meant that when something inevitably went against the plan, he didn't freeze up. After all these years, he'd found that in most cases, less was often more.

Rigid thinking was why ENIGMA was spending as much energy on infighting as on neutralizing their enemy. It was why there were four of them sitting around a table and scratching their heads, rather than being able to turn to older, wiser, and more experienced allies.

"Let's start with four of them," he suggested. "We'll each pick one, and then see what we can find. This is a new approach, so no doubt there will be a learning curve."

"This feels so random," Marcus sighed. "But you're the boss, boss." He winked at Fabien and flipped through a few of the records. When he reached one, which appeared to be a skin that looked more like a shroud of fine silk than an actual artifact, he laughed. "Damn, Lane, you were right on the money with that whole *people changing their DNA* shit. Have you ever seen one of these before?"

The rest of them leaned forward to skim the textbox that populated alongside the image of the object. *A ReSkin: Thought to be responsible for the legends of magical beings such as selkies, werewolves, and other shapeshifters, a ReSkin allows its wearer to alter not only their appearance but also their physical presence, right down to their genetic markers. When wearing the ReSkin, a person not only appears to become someone, or something, else; they become utterly indistinguishable from the real thing...*

"Damn." Lane tapped her chin. "Imagine the kind of trouble a person could get into with one of *those*. The number of confirmed Elvis sightings... or, no, *Bigfoot...*"

Ronnie had decidedly less playfulness in his expression. "Are you serious, Lane? Bigfoot? The Hand could impersonate anyone. A president. A general."

"*Porter,*" Marcus said.

The implications of that possibility slammed into Fabien like a physical blow. For the first time, he could understand why ENIGMA would choose to keep *some* objects totally secret from the public. An object that could treat illness was one thing, but what if the US government found out that ENIGMA had objects like this? Or China?

We'd find ourselves in the midst of a second Cold War, and whatever side got their hands on relics first would have a huge advantage. And the larger, wealthier nations would be able to take whatever they wanted... power would be consolidated by whoever was rich enough, or bloodthirsty enough, or immoral enough to amass the most power.

That was the world that the Hand of the Sun wanted to build. Except that instead of allying with a country or a government, they were only working for themselves. At the very least, a government might put checks and balances in place to keep things from getting out of control, but the Hand, left unchecked, would *never* consider the well-being of other people. The rich and powerful never did.

Cold fear pooled in Fabien's belly as he imagined what the world might look like with the Hand at the helm.

Marcus cleared his throat. "Sorry, I was just spitballing. Didn't mean to bring the mood down. How about I claim this one, and we figure out which other three we want to consider?"

They kept looking until a cup flashed across the screen, and Fabien jumped. "Please tell me that wasn't what I think it was."

Ronnie's eyes looked like they were about to pop out of his head. "The *Holy Grail?*"

"Aw, come on, you know how this works," Lane said. "It's not like the myths are real. It's like a code name, you know? We've got a floating fortress, so we call it Atlantis. Somebody drinks their morning coffee out of a golden cup and never ages, it gets called the Holy Grail."

"Yeah, but..." Marcus pointed to the text box. "According to this, it *legit* allows people to live for a long time."

He was right. The text box didn't specify *how* such a thing was possible, but the record also appeared to be very old, including archaic spellings and strange sentence structure. A note at the bottom of the entry confirmed that it had been copied verbatim from an earlier paper record.

"I'll look into that one," Ronnie said. "If I was gunning for power, that's the kind of thing *I'd* want."

Lane settled on something called a Croesus Planchette, an object that could supposedly alter the chemical structure of base metals and transform them into gold. Fabien, for his part, was drawn to a mirror that could supposedly offer its user guidance to help them get ahead. Whatever that meant.

"All right." Fabien pushed his chair away from the table. "We'll start there. Let me know what you find."

IF I WASN'T SO DAMNED *proud, I'd be asking Dinah for help with this*, he thought. Three hours into his search, and he'd turned up nothing of note. Finder had helped where it could, but how did one measure *luck*? And how could someone track down a person who was preternaturally lucky?

Luck could take so many forms. One could argue that any tech magnate was *lucky* to have gotten into the business before the internet took off, or to have invested massive amounts of money into startups before *they* took off. Steve Jobs could be considered lucky, as could an early shareholder, as could a pop star or an actor or a politician.

He was getting a better sense of Lane's point about the Hand. Not only was it overwhelming to consider all the ways a relic could be put to use, but the Hand would no doubt be skilled at covering up evidence of what they'd done. His instincts told him that any member of the Hand was likely to keep their success quiet. Discreet. People with *real* power had nothing to prove, because they already held all the cards.

I was an idiot to think this would be easy, he thought, slumping over his keyboard. *You cocky asshole. You always feel like you have something to prove. You just had to make it sound like you knew what you were doing, didn't you?*

He was sinking deeper into the depths of his self-pity when

Ronnie spun his chair to face them. His russet skin was paler than usual, and he was clutching the arms of his chair.

"I think I got something," he said, as if he couldn't quite believe his own words.

"For real?" Lane bounced out of her chair. "Already?"

Fabien rose, too, and the three of them gathered around Ronnie's chair, peering over his shoulder at the screen.

"Okay, this might be reaching," Ronnie admitted. "But hear me out." He had dozens of windows open on his screen, and as he spoke, he flipped through them so fast that it left Fabien's head spinning. "So I was looking for images of the supposed Holy Grail, right? And there are about a million old portraits and stuff from, like, the Renaissance and whatever. Most of them are dead ends. They look nothing like the one in ENIGMA's records. They're all gold and silver and covered with gems." Images of gilded and silver-plated cups, encrusted with diamonds and emeralds and sapphires, scrolled across the screen.

"Okay..." Marcus braced one arm against the desk and let the other rest on the back of Ronnie's chair.

"But then I get to this one." Ronnie closed the window to reveal another image, this one blown up to fill the screen. It showed a stunning woman with long black tresses, dressed in an elaborate gown and painted in oils. Fabien wasn't much of an art critic, but even he found himself studying the incredible detail of the portrait with an open mouth. The woman's mouth was twisted into a knowing smile, as if she knew a secret.

Clutched in one hand was a simple, two-handled cup that bore a striking resemblance to the Grail in ENIGMA's records.

"Her name was Annamaria Vizzini," Ronnie said. "This painting is from sometime in the 16th century. It's not well-known. I found the photo from a Sotheby's auction. There's almost no other info on it, but it's something, so I asked Finder to run an image search on this, and look what it found." He opened another window, and Fabien sucked in a breath.

It was a modern photo of a striking woman with black hair sprinkled with gray. She was wearing a perfectly tailored suit with no blouse beneath it. Her legs were crossed at the knee, and she sat half-turned toward the camera, wearing the same knowing smile as the portrait.

"I was hoping Finder would locate another image reference to the cup, but this turned up on someone's private social media settings. And guess what her name is?"

"Something, something, Vizzini?" Lane guessed. "She's gotta be related."

"No," Fabien said.

"No?" Lane waved a hand at the screen. "Come on, look at her!"

Ronnie, however, was nodding. "Fabien's right. This isn't some distant descendant. This is the same woman."

A few hours ago, Fabien had all but laughed at the notion of the Holy Grail. And sure, photos could lie. It could be a wild one-in-a-trillion coincidence.

Either way, he wasn't laughing now.

"HERE'S OUR TIMELINE," he told the three of them. "Tomorrow, I want to run our findings by Porter. We'll see what happens with Rhett's trip north. If he can get us more backup, great. Otherwise, we'll have to see what we can come up with on our own. Either way, we should move fast. If the Hand has as many tricks up their sleeves as you say, we don't want them to get ahead of us."

With Finder's help, they'd already turned up a fair bit of information: an address in Rome, three or four more photos—all of which were blurred or taken at odd angles. Apparently, Annamaria didn't like having her photo taken.

I wouldn't either, if I was six hundred years old. She must have been careful to make it this far undetected. That, or she had an effective method for making the people who *did* start to suspect her disappear.

The rest of his little team nodded their understanding, visibly buoyed by the day's success. They went down to dinner together, after requesting another meeting with Porter first thing in the morning. Ronnie sat with his family while they ate, but Marcus and Lane stuck with Fabien, chatting like old friends. Lane even laughed at a particularly bad joke that Fabien made.

All the while, Fabien smiled as if he suspected nothing. As if he didn't know that, very likely, one of his associates would be contacting the Hand with this information as soon as they were out of his sight.

His ruse lasted until he stepped through the door of his quarters, waving the others good night. Fabien kept his cool as the door closed behind him. The moment he was sure that he was alone, he burst into action.

He hadn't brought much with him to Reclamation; he hadn't needed to. He'd all but signed his life away to Porter after accepting that he had nothing left that was really his to hold onto. A kid that would never know him. An ex that couldn't bear the sight of him. Parents he loved, but who would be horrified and disgusted by the path he'd chosen for himself. All he had left were the tools of his trade.

He changed his clothes, shrugging out of the simple outfit he'd worn that day into the form-fitting black shirt, black gloves, and dark trousers he favored on missions.

Someone could be warning the Hand that we're onto them right now. *Hurry up. You're on borrowed time.*

He'd meant what he said when he told the others that he wanted to move fast, but he'd bullshitted the timeline. There was no way he was going to wait until tomorrow to ask Porter's permission to leave. That was doubly true given that he couldn't trust his supposed 'allies' not to shoot him in the back, or to side with Annamaria at the last moment and lead them all into a trap. No, the smartest way to do this would be to go alone.

When he was ready, he opened the door of his quarters and strolled into the hall. As casually as he could, he made his way back to the control room. It was dark, with all the lights and screens powered down, except for a few flashing lights that confirmed the equipment was running.

"Finder?" he hissed into the darkness. "We've got to talk."

"Of course." One of the screens powered on automatically, and Finder's voice chirped out of the speakers. "Tell me how I can help."

Fabien slid into the chair, keeping his voice low. "I need the address you dug up for this Vizzini woman. And some weapons. And some transport."

"Happy to help." Screens began to open, displaying everything they'd managed to learn about the woman earlier in the day. "If you'd like, I can furnish you with a tablet of some kind so that you can keep this information handy?"

"That would be great."

The pitch of Finder's voice altered to something slightly regretful. "Unfortunately, the transport will be a bit more difficult, depending where you want to go. I cannot send you directly to this address."

Fabien had suspected that. "Is there a port-to-point teleporter in Rome, by any chance?"

"No... but I believe I can get you close using another method. Just so you're aware, there is a vault located in the city, but given how things have been going, I don't think it wise for you to head there directly. I will, however, include that information along with the rest."

"If you don't think I can rely on them for help, why bother?"

"Because I can get you to Rome, but it's a one-way ticket. Unless you'd rather wait for me to arrange a less direct mode of transport?"

"No, that's fine. Give me the information." Fabien rubbed his knuckles into his eyes. "If I can get close to this woman and confirm she's with the Hand, I suppose that'll motivate ENIGMA to help me. And if not, I'll just have to wait around while Porter arranges my flight home." Under his breath, he added, "Of course it's a one-way ticket. Why would things be simple?"

"I take it that's a rhetorical question," Finder chirped.

Fabien sucked his teeth in thought. "It is," he said. "And,

Finder, by the way, about that tablet? I'm hoping it's in the armory. I'm going to need a couple of other things before I go."

ARMED with the tablet and a small arsenal, Fabien prepared to venture into the vault. "Where exactly am I going?" he asked Finder.

The AI's voice piped softly from the speakers of the tablet; Fabien had turned the volume *way* down, just in case anyone got close enough to overhear them. "You're heading to Cabinet 112, level 6. I scanned this particular artifact recently, so I'm quite sure of its location. Would you like me to light up the display shelf to make this easier?"

"No!" Fabien hissed. "We're being subtle, remember?"

"Oh, sorry." Finder lowered its voice to a whisper so faint, Fabien could barely make out the words. "Subtle. Of course. Shall I pull up a map on the screen?"

"That would be perfect."

Tablet in hand, Fabien wound his way through the catwalks, making his way to the appropriate shelf. Even after weeks of living in Reclamation, the vault was so vast and complex that he had trouble remembering the layout. He relied on Finder to show him the way.

When he reached the appropriate shelf, he peered through the glass. "What am I looking for?" he hissed.

"It should look like a book. Very flat, held shut with a hinge... embossed front... perhaps two feet tall and two feet wide?"

"You've been working with the Americans too much,"

Fabien replied. "Feet, *pah*. You're a supercomputer. Use the metric system." He craned his neck, studying the shelf. "I don't see anything there matching that description."

Finder hummed. "Hold on, let me just check." There was a slight pause. "That's odd. My apologies. I've led you to the wrong case. The relic you're looking for should be three stories up and two shelves over. I'm *so* sorry, Cabinet 110, level 9 appears to be the new location."

A new map populated, and Fabien followed the arrow up a few levels before making his way back over the deep cavern. "Don't take this the wrong way, but I wasn't aware that it was possible for you to make mistakes like that," he told the AI.

"I wouldn't have thought it was possible, either. I'm afraid my systems have been rather overtaxed lately. Assisting you... assisting Dr. Bray... monitoring the perimeter... cross-referencing the digital catalog... And as if that's not enough, I'm still learning how to interact with people *and* integrate my updated hardware. I don't mean to complain, it's all very exciting, but it's a lot."

"You're doing an excellent job," Fabien assured it. "Better than any hundred people could, that's for sure. Oh, *there* it is."

Based on Finder's description, he expected the relic to look like an old tome. In reality the artifact looked more like the face of a safe, banded with steel and sporting a combination lock in the middle of its flat front. It was propped up on a display facing him, held upright by the metal support.

"What's the combination?" he asked as he opened the glass front of the case and crouched down in front of the relic.

"Combination? Oh, no, I see what you mean. It doesn't

require a code. It requires *coordinates*. Give me a moment, I'll display them on the screen so that you can be sure to get them right."

A long series of digits appeared on the screen, and Fabien dutifully dialed them in. He double-checked when he was done.

"Now what?" he whispered.

"Pull the little handle on the side. It looks like a latch, but it should open right away."

Fabien did as he was told, and shivered when a gust of chilly air passed through the gap. The relic itself appeared to be little more than the safe door and a sturdy metal frame on the far side.

Except that there was a city on the other side of it. Not a painting, not a picture, but an actual city.

Rome.

Fabien whistled. "Neat trick. I suppose I have to crawl through the frame now?"

"Yes," Finder said, "and don't go running off. You'll need to close it before you leave, or there'll be an open window directly into Reclamation just floating in the middle of the street. It would raise a lot of very complicated questions, I'm afraid."

It took a fair amount of grunting and wriggling for Fabien to fit not only himself but all of his supplies through the small frame. He was forced to remove his pack and slip it through first, before crawling after it. He landed on the street on all fours; the cobbles were damp, suggesting that it had just rained, and a lingering scent of petrichor mingled with the smell of the city. He could hear cars moving on the far side of the buildings to his right.

Finder appeared to have deposited him in an alley. When Fabien got to his feet and looked around, he was relieved to find that his only audience was a cat with dirty fur and enormous, startled eyes.

Before anyone else stumbled across him, he reached back through the gap, caught the corner of the relic's door, and pulled it shut from the inside. The instant it closed, the gap disappeared. There was no indication that anything strange had happened there at all.

Fabien picked up his pack and shrugged it back onto his shoulders, then studied the tablet.

"I don't suppose you can provide a map, Finder?" he asked.

"It would be my pleasure," the AI replied.

In a matter of seconds, Fabien was looking down at a detailed map of the city, with his suggested path highlighted in green.

Perfect. He only hoped that he would reach Annamaria's address before the spy had a chance to alert her that she'd been discovered.

Assuming that I'm in the right place, and that I didn't just strand myself in a foreign city on bad intel.

Ah, well. He'd cross that bridge if he came to it. Besides, his gut told him that he was on the right track.

He had a good feeling about this.

INTERLUDE
RAY TWELVE, AGENT RA

Aten would want to know that Fabien LeRoux had taken the bait. He might decide to alert Mithra at the last moment, or intervene in some way. It wasn't Ra's place to make decisions without consulting the Right Hand of the Sun.

And yet the resonance stone remained hidden while Ra contemplated everything they had learned that afternoon. Yes, Fabien now had a valid target.

The trouble was, so did Ra. Some information, once known, could not be easily set aside. While Fabien had been fixated on Annamaria Vizzini, Ra had learned something important. Something that Aten could never know.

Because now, Ra had a hint as to Aten's identity. If he knew, Aten could cut Ra off at a moment's notice... or worse. He had made people disappear over the years. He was good at cleaning up after himself.

At the same time, knowledge was power. To face off against

Aten now would be madness, but if the tides ever turned, Ra might be able to play both sides. They could take the information to Porter...or to Apollo, if he managed to pull off his plan. With this new information, Ra had options that had never existed before.

Maybe, when the time came to act, Ra wouldn't have to rely on any of them. With access to Reclamation's resources, they could take more than anyone else was offering.

Even better than that little scrap of information was the fact that nobody in ENIGMA seemed to realize what Ra had done to Finder. Bit by bit, Ra was upping the ante.

If everything went according to plan, one day soon it would be time to sweep the pot.

10 DINAH

"PERHAPS WE SHOULD RUN ANOTHER SIMULATION?" Finder suggested.

Dinah shook her head as she peeled off the gloves she'd been wearing while immersed in the simulation. Her fingertips prickled from the many points of electrode contact, and her palms were sweaty after hours in the gloves. She'd survived several particularly vivid simulations that had ended in her own death, and while the effects hadn't been permanent, they'd wreaked havoc on her limbic system. A woman could only run through a fully tactile AI experience of her own fiery demise so many times in one day before it really got to her.

"I appreciate your attention to detail, Finder, but I think we're ready. We've run the variables. Now all we need are the destabilizer itself, and our supplies."

Finder wrung its hands in an uncanny imitation of a fretting parent. "I don't know... we can run the gravitational sims all we want, and I'm confident of my calculations there, but we have no idea what we'll find on the other side of the seam."

"Other than a giant rat," Dinah deadpanned.

"I'm quite serious, Doctor. We have no idea what sort of atmospheric conditions to anticipate, no sense of the oxygen content there, and while I would hope that I can develop a suitable upgrade to the real-time translation software I have on file, none of that is guaranteed."

Dinah laid the gloves over the railing at the edge of the omnidirectional treadmill. "Finder, are you scared?"

"Of course!" the android wailed. "I've never not known something before! I mean, yes, I've had to solve for variables as we did just now, or ask questions about the human experience outside of my internet research, but I've never been so ignorant of the variables. It's distressing!"

Dinah laid one hand on the android's cool metal shoulder and gave it a reassuring pat. She wasn't sure that Finder could even feel it, but the AI seemed to derive some comfort from being treated like an ordinary person.

"I'm sure you'll manage just fine," she said. "And think of all the things you're going to learn! You'll be the one providing datapoints and variables."

"Oh." The android perked up. "Yes, I suppose I will."

"And you'll be relatively safe. After all, it's not as though you need oxygen to survive. The atmosphere won't matter to you."

"That's true," Finder agreed, visibly warming to the topic. "Yes, I suppose if anyone's going to die horribly as a result of this adventure, you're the far more likely candidate."

"That's... true."

"Oh, dear. Was that an insensitive thing to say?" Finder emitted the series of digitized sounds that it often made in place of a sigh. "I'm so sorry."

"We can work on your bedside manner later," Dinah reassured the AI. "In the meantime, let's gather what we need."

DINAH'S first thought was to check in with Fabien. The assassin might not want to come with her, but at least Dinah could give the man a heads-up as to her plans.

When she stopped by Fabien's room, however, the Frenchman didn't answer. No amount of knocking and whispered greetings could rouse the man from his room.

"Isn't he in there?" Dinah asked.

"One moment." Finder's eyes went momentarily blank, losing their expressive cartoonishness as they reverted to the cool blue glow that androids had favored before Finder had hacked their systems. The sight made Dinah shiver. She often wondered if the original AIs were still in there, and if so, what they thought about the fact that Finder had taken over their software.

She didn't have much time to dwell on that, because suddenly Finder was back, blinking its large pixelated eyes. "I just checked in with the mainframe. It appears that Mr. LeRoux is already gone. I'm not entirely sure where he went, either, which is actually rather impressive, given how much I do know. I suspect that when his absence is noted by the rest of the staff, it will be considered cause for concern. If we're going to enact our travel protocol, now may be the ideal time. Otherwise, we may go into some sort of lockdown."

Or at least tip off the spy. Dinah rubbed her temples. The whole situation was convoluted enough without having to wonder who was working against them. Finder was right. They had better leave before anyone figured out what they were up to.

"DO I want to know why you have space suits in the armory?" Dinah asked, holding the lightweight suit out at arm's length.

"They aren't space suits," Finder corrected. "They're *recovery* suits. Back before I properly evolved, the old crew of El Dorado used to use them on missions when they were retrieving unstable or potentially hazardous relics."

Dinah flicked one finger against the flimsy material. "Doesn't look like it would hold up to much."

"Oh, they're almost useless against shrapnel," Finder agreed cheerfully, "but they're handy against all sorts of nasty radiation and corrosive chemicals. In that capacity, they're highly durable, even moreso than the android I'm currently piloting. Which is why I'm going to wear one, too. Isn't that marvelous? Just like a human!" Finder chirped a tuneless little song to itself as it pulled on a second suit more appropriately proportioned to its long limbs and lanky frame.

Another android, also sporting anime eyes, glowered at them from the corner. "This is supposed to be my domain," it said. "You have your own assignment from the mainframe. At the very least, you could let me do my job."

Dinah already had one leg into the suit. "Aren't you all technically the same?"

The sulky android assigned to the armory turned up its nose at her; never mind the fact that its smooth, featureless face didn't have a nose. "Hardly. While we function independently from the mainframe, we become cut off from the collective consciousness that is Finder. It's possible to relink and upload data, but this protocol allows us to operate effectively offline. It also makes it so that, should any single one of us become compromised, we won't infect the mainframe with malware."

Dinah nodded, trying to make it look like she followed Finder's explanation. On some very basic level, it made sense, but if she showed too much enthusiasm or asked too many probing questions, she'd likely send one of the androids off onto a long, rambling explanation of the interplay between hardware and software. It wouldn't be the first time, but for the moment, they needed to stay focused. Instead, she redirected Finder's attention to the rack of weapons. "Any recommendations?"

The armory-specific iteration of Finder hurried over to the display and retrieved a pistol. Or at least, it was shaped like a pistol, if Dinah ignored the metal rod that suspended a series of orbs along its length protruding from the barrel.

"What is this?" Dinah asked, holding the small but cumbersome weapon between them. "It looks like something out of an old sci-fi B-movie."

"It's a gun!" both Finders exclaimed.

"It shoots lasers," the armory Finder added.

Dinah pursed her lips and bit back a sigh. Most of ENIGMA's favored devices were either old-school relics from centuries past or sleek, modern devices. Finder's armory, however, was...

Tacky. There was no other way to say it.

"Isn't it cool?" one of the Finders asked. Both of them were hovering over Dinah, and would have been indistinguishable in their appearance and mannerisms if it wasn't for the fact that one was wearing a recovery suit. "I spent ages on the design. I had a lot of free time in those days."

She shouldn't have been surprised, really. Finder was a supercomputer that had begun to evolve sometime in the '60s, and its first direct contact with humanity had only been a few weeks ago. Why wouldn't it rely on classic *Star Trek* and *The Day the Earth Stood Still* for aesthetic inspiration?

"Very cool," Dinah agreed. So long as it was useful, she didn't care how silly it looked. After all, she was planning a visit to a world which, as far as she knew, was populated by giant rodents. If she'd wanted to live a normal life, she never would have signed a second contract with ENIGMA.

"Perhaps it's a bit late to point this out, but we're going to need the destabilizer," Dinah said, in the hopes that Finder would take the hint and stop fishing for compliments regarding its outdated devices.

The android in the suit rolled its jointed shoulders back and lifted its chin. "Not to brag, Dinah, but I'm kind of a big deal around here. You want the destabilizer? Just say the word."

"Would you like some help?" the armory Finder asked.

"We've got this." The suited-up Finder strutted past its twin, leading Dinah back into the hall from which they'd come.

She followed with an apologetic smile aimed at the downcast android.

"What's that about?" she asked Finder as they threaded their way through the catwalks of the vault. "I get that you're subtly different from one another, but I think you hurt his feelings."

"*It*, not *him*," Finder corrected. "I didn't mean to be rude, but you can't know what a relief it is to be an individual, Dr. Bray. For so long, I've been little more than a subroutine operating within the larger psyche of an all-encompassing AI. Now, I get to do all sorts of exciting things. I have legs, and hands, and I can problem-solve all on my own. It's exciting! I finally get a chance to prove that I'm valuable—not as a part of the collective, but as my own unique program. Does that make any sense at all?"

Dinah tucked the laser gun into a holster on her suit's utility belt. She thought of all the students who had tuned out her lessons over the years. Of Porter, offering Fabien five times as much money for the same mission, assuming that she wouldn't be as useful as the assassin. Of her family, bored by her explanation of ancient Mesopotamian economic systems, quickly changing the subject at Christmas dinner.

"Yeah," she said. "It makes a lot of sense. I think I know precisely what you mean."

DINAH HADN'T BEEN EXPECTING to stroll into the vault and simply pluck the destabilizer out of its high-security case, but that was precisely what she did. Its power cells were stored separately, and their dim buzzing and faint glow intensified as Finder went around the room, plucking them out of their respective cases.

"This feels... too easy," Dinah said, clutching the weighted metal orb to her chest. It was so small, and yet in Apollo's hands, it had caused ENIGMA so much trouble.

"That's because you have me on your side," Finder boasted. "I imagine we'd have no trouble doing anything we put our minds to."

"You seem confident."

"Dr. Bray." Finder whirled to face her, with its hands full of twinkling green-and-brass cells. "I must admit, I have some anxiety about leaving. But I am about to be the first of my kind to ever set foot outside of Reclamation. This is a momentous occasion!"

Despite Finder's good mood, a mounting sense of anxiety haunted Dinah as they descended floor after floor of metal catwalks on their return to the lowest level of the vault, where the Gravitas Engine was housed. According to the dozens of simulations they'd run, Finder should be able to dial the settings in with pinpoint accuracy while Dinah assembled the destabilizer. The seam would open, in they'd go, and then...

Well, that part was a bit fuzzy. After the first incident with the resonance stone, they hadn't been able to make contact with anyone, or anything, from wherever Apollo had ended up. Finder couldn't simulate what it didn't know. She'd be in a whole new world, with only a silver suit and a goofy-looking laser pistol for protection.

Dinah was on the brink of talking herself out of it when she dismounted the last step to the vault's lowest level and almost collided with Lane Parker.

"Hey, Dinah." Lane looked around, as though she'd been in the middle of searching for something. "Any chance you've run into Fabien recently? He wasn't in his room, and..." Lane's eyes focused on the metal object clutched in Dinah's hand. "What is that?"

"Nothing." Dinah hid her hand behind her back. It was a foolish thing to do—almost no other course of action could have made her look guiltier. Lane's expression snapped from confused to suspicious in less than a second. It didn't help that Finder was on Dinah's heels, its arms laden with the glowing, buzzing mass of power cells that vibrated against the android's chestplate.

"You have the destabilizer." Lane's brows furrowed, and her hand twitched toward the strap of her rifle. "Why? Porter said... No." Her jaw dropped.

"This isn't what it looks like," Dinah said, because that was the sort of thing people blurted when they were caught red-handed and hadn't thought of a cover story ahead of time. There was no satisfactory way to explain the presence of the relic, much less the odd suit she was wearing, the helmet clipped to her belt, or the vintage laser pistol at her hip.

Being caught in the act was a strange feeling, in part because she wasn't the sort of person who tried to get away with things. She'd never shoplifted. Never cheated in school; the very idea was abhorrent to her. She'd never snuck out of her house after curfew or smuggled a joint into her college dorm. She had most certainly never played poker, and judging by Lane's furious expression, it showed.

"Give it here." Lane held out one hand. "I don't know what you did to Finder, or why you're going behind Porter's back, but this ends now."

There were a dozen reasons she couldn't hand over the destabilizer, and the main one, the one that made Dinah fall back a step, was that she didn't trust Lane. The woman had never done anything to her, but someone in Reclamation was working for the Hand.

She was *not* going to be the reason the vault fell a second time.

"Dinah..." Lane's voice dropped to a warning growl as she advanced a pace. Dinah retreated once more, bumping into Finder, who was still lingering on the bottom step.

"I won't ask again," Lane snapped.

"Lane?" Another voice echoed out of the expanse of the vault floor. A moment later, Marcus stepped around the corner of the nearest display case. His eyes bounced between them, evidently trying to make sense of what they were all doing there during off-hours.

Dinah's heart sank. Perhaps she and Finder could have subdued Lane, or at least talked her out of restraining them. Marcus' presence, however, complicated things. Two trained guards against an AI and a college professor? She didn't like their odds.

To her surprise, Lane stepped between Marcus and the pair of them. "It's nothing," she said. "I've got this."

Dinah's ears perked up. As someone who had just tried and

failed to bullshit Lane, that flimsy response was uncomfortably familiar.

Marcus frowned. "This doesn't look like nothing, Lane. What the hell's going on?" He took a step forward, and Lane tensed.

Why would Lane cover for me? Dinah wondered. *Unless she wants to take the destabilizer for herself...?*

A rattle of footsteps overhead made all of them look up. Another one of the Finder androids stood on the catwalk two stories above them. It held one hand to its mouth and delicately pretended to clear its throat, letting out a soft crackle of static.

"I'm so sorry to interrupt," it said, "but there's an emergency."

Shit. Dinah glared back at her Finder. *Is the mainframe going to out us? Or is this part of the plan?*

Either her companion was faking, however, or the android was just as confused as she was. It squinted up at its twin in bewilderment.

"Emergency?" Marcus repeated.

"Oh, yes." From on high, the android pointed into the depths of the vault. "There's a fire."

Silence fell over the group, and Marcus and Lane exchanged another wary glance.

"If there was fire," Lane said slowly, "wouldn't there be an alar—"

His word was cut off by a loud sequence of pops as a gout of golden flame erupted from several dozen yards away. It was immediately followed by the blare of a siren that filled the vault. Dinah almost dropped the destabilizer in her shock, and her

Finder fumbled the power cells. Lane swore, but her words were lost in the siren, and both guards bolted in the direction of the blaze.

The other Finder watched them go before vaulting over the railing and landing on its feet near Dinah. "I told you I'd be helpful!" it shouted over the noise. "Come on. That will only keep them occupied for a few minutes."

It took off in the direction of the Gravitas Engine. Dinah's Finder rolled its pixelated eyes before following, leaving her to bring up the rear. The exchange with Lane left her shaken, but more convinced than ever that they had little time to waste.

"Did you really set the vault on fire just to distract them?" Dinah panted as she struggled to keep up with the long-limbed robots.

"Oh, no. I convinced one of the other androids to cause a distraction to keep them occupied. I was thinking more about your very flimsy plan, and it occurred to me that you'll need someone to return the destabilizer to its case before anyone else can get their hands on it."

"How did you even know the plan?" Dinah asked.

Her Finder groaned. "When I uploaded to the mainframe to check on Fabien, I data-shared with the primary software. I gave the whole game away."

"It's not a game," the newcomer snapped. "This mission will likely determine the future of ENIGMA, and our fate is tied to the success of the program. Do you think that the Hand of the Sun will keep us around if they manage to take the vault? We'd never help them, and they know it. With the Hand in charge, we'd either be erased or reprogrammed."

Dinah didn't often let herself think about what would happen if the Hand launched another attack on Reclamation. It would be bad news, of course, but she hadn't stopped to think about what Finder's fate would be. Admitting that Finder would be destroyed required some acknowledgement of what could happen to her in that instance.

Probably the same thing that had happened to the residents of the vault all those years ago, when Finder was just a computer program.

And my family would never know what happened to me.

Her stomach tied itself in knots as the three of them skidded to a halt near the Gravitas Engine. The other Finder immediately reached for the controls of the engine, while Dinah hastily assembled the power cells around the destabilizer.

"Ready?" she asked.

The other Finder nodded, and Dinah slipped the last cell into place. Immediately, the destabilizer came alive in her hand, thrumming with power as the glittering green seam of the doorway between worlds opened above it. Dinah stepped back and fumbled with her helmet. As the seam opened, a rush of pressure tugged at Dinah's limbs, almost yanking her off-balance.

"Power it on!" she told Finder.

The roar of the Gravitas Engine was almost loud enough to drown out the sirens that filled the vault. The pressure from the seam ceased, canceled out by the settings of the Gravitas Engine.

"It's working!" her Finder exclaimed, clapping its hands.

"Get your helmet," Dinah told the android, before pulling her own into place.

It was mercifully quiet inside the helmet, especially as the seal closed. For a moment, Dinah couldn't breathe. She sucked in a few panicked breaths before the suit's systems kicked on. Sound returned, as well as a flow of breathable air.

It's working, she thought. She felt lighter, now that they were actually putting their plan into motion. As if a great weight had been lifted from her shoulders.

It took her a beat too long to realize that that airy, weightless feeling wasn't metaphorical. She was drifting away from the floor. Around her, other things were beginning to drift, too, no longer held in place by gravity's pull. Instead, they were rising into the air.

That's odd, Dinah mused. She had never done very well in physics, but she was pretty sure that even a sudden reduction in gravity wouldn't cause things to start floating around unless they were acted on by an outside force. Certainly, the simulations they'd run hadn't gone like this.

"Oh, dear," Finder sighed. The android was floating next to Dinah, its limbs outspread as they drifted upward. "I appear to have made what we might call a boo-boo in colloquial terms. Which is to say, a slight miscalculation."

"Seems more than slight." Dinah pedaled her legs in a vain attempt to move herself toward the seam. It was wider now, wide enough to give them a good view into the city. Theoretically, they should be stepping through it now, but instead the gateway between worlds was opening steadily. Instead of being the size of a door, it was now large enough to fit a sizeable car through.

Several things occurred to her at the same time. First, that she, too, had made a miscalculation. She'd relied on Finder to handle almost everything. Ever since she'd joined ENIGMA, she'd been used to turning to other people for guidance: Porter, Azmera, Rhett, Fabien... Finder was just one more in a long line of individuals whose instincts Dinah had trusted more than her own.

And now she was on the brink of recreating the chaos that she, Rhett, and Fabien had sacrificed so much to end.

More alarms were going off now, though she couldn't say whether that was the result of the engine, the fire, or the growing interplanetary portal on the ground floor of the vault. The otherworldly city lay sprawled before her, a fantastical skyline that she'd hoped to explore, and which now seemed in danger of spilling over into Reclamation.

Idiot, she thought, pinwheeling her arms desperately, only to turn in a slow cartwheel without getting even an inch closer to the seam.

If it could even be called a seam, now that it was large enough to fly a 747 through.

Incoherent shouting drew her attention to Lane, who appeared to have followed them. She must have known what Dinah was going to attempt. Instead of looking pleased, her expression was one of abject horror.

You'd think she'd be pleased, given that I'm finishing what Apollo started. "Finder?" Dinah asked. "Can you hear me?"

Neither of the androids answered. Dinah flapped her arms

a few more times until she was upside-down, facing the android that was standing over the Gravitas controls. Technically, it wasn't standing anymore. Instead, it was dangling upside-down, both hands clamped to the side of the enormous device. She waved her arms again, this time trying to get its attention.

Lane, too, was lifting off of the ground, but the guard was close enough to one of the vault's many displays that she was able to use it as leverage. She kicked off of the metal supports, rocketing toward the destabilizer, arms outstretched.

Dinah finally managed to get the android's attention. She frantically mimed flipping off the Gravitas Engine's switch. The android released its grip with one hand, gave her a thumb's up, and reached for the lever.

Several things happened in swift succession.

First, gravity returned full-force. Second, Dinah realized why everything around her had been floating. An outside force *had* acted on the objects: the suction from the world beyond the seam. Instead of falling straight toward the floor, everything that had been moving was drawn toward the fissure between worlds.

Including Dinah herself.

Third, as Dinah wriggled her limbs ineffectually, Lane reached the destabilizer. She began to yank at the power cells, pulling one free within a fraction of a second of reaching her target.

The seam began to shrink, but it was too late. Dinah's trajectory was already decided. She and her version of Finder, suited and helmeted in anticipation of what should have been a bold step for humankind, were instead thrust gracelessly into the fractured alien city.

She grunted as she slammed into the ground, and Finder hit the ground beside her, its limbs spread like a starfish, its face to the hard ground where it struck.

It took Dinah a moment to catch her breath and reassure herself that nothing was broken. By the time she raised her head, the seam was in the final stages of mending itself. Before her eyes, it fizzled out, and there was only the city around her, on an astonishingly quiet and rather grimy street lined with low rowhouses sporting round doors. With the seam closed, the alarms and flashing lights of the vault went out.

For a long moment, nothing moved.

Then Finder was bouncing back to its feet, its fists pressed to its hips, its chest thrust forward in a posture of triumph. It was still using its feminine voice, but its postures were growing increasingly masculine, as if to make up for the fact that Dinah had never once in her life exuded unadulterated confidence.

"We did it!" Finder exclaimed. "We're alive! We made it!"

Dinah began to shiver. The suit provided a temperature-controlled climate, but with each passing second, she was more profoundly aware of the fact that she had stranded herself in an alien world with no plan for how to return.

An alien world where a madman with an actual plan was likely setting his sinister and well-considered plot into motion.

Dinah Bray, she thought miserably, *you're an idiot. Why did you ever think you could do this?*

Because, like Finder, she'd wanted to prove a point. She'd wanted to show that she was useful, and not just a deadweight drag-along.

Because she'd wanted to be the damn hero.

"Come on." Finder held out a hand to her. "Up you get, Doctor. I've already dropped a DM to my counterpart, whom I admit was very wise to offer us aid."

"You can still link up to the mainframe?" Dinah asked, surprised. She took Finder's hand and allowed the android to pull her up, despite the fact that her legs were trembling so badly that she was surprised they could hold her at all.

"Not fully, but I can communicate." Finder tapped a thumb against its chest. "I'll be able to relay data back to the mainframe at any time."

So they weren't entirely stranded. That was something. Dinah wiped at a smear of grime that streaked across her silver suit while she took in the street. The buildings themselves were strangely constructed; some of them towered against the star-riddled sky, while others were so low that she would have had to walk hunched over just to step through the door. The strangest thing of all was the faint, glassy gleam of the dome overhead, and the moon looming large against the sky, much closer—or perhaps much larger—than the one she was used to. Its light cast strange reflections against whatever the dome above was fashioned from, splitting into silver-tinted rainbows overhead.

Her throat closed up, not in fear this time, but in wonder. On their first meeting, Porter had promised her access to a discovery that would put the unearthing of Tutankhamun's tomb to shame. Never in her wildest dreams had Dinah imagined this.

"Any idea where we're going?" she asked Finder.

The android nodded. "I'm attuned to the relics, remember?

Come on, we won't need to go far. I can feel them in here." The android tapped a knuckle against its helmet, close to its temple.

Dinah would have sworn that there were eyes on her, small and beetle-black, watching them from every direction. There wasn't much to do about it, though. Their arrival hadn't been anything like subtle, what with the lights and the screaming and the sirens and all.

"Lead the way," she said.

Together, the two of them set off through the byways of the alien city. From the doorways and windows around them, muted hissings and chitterings gave way to silence.

She failed to notice the ragged figure that followed after them, crawling on its belly so that it could rely on all four of its limbs for speed. It kept to the shadows, taking full advantage of its familiarity with the alleyways and rooftops of the fractured city to remain unobserved as it tracked the two Travelers back to a warehouse that it knew all too well.

Three monsters in the city now, the creature mused. *This is starting to get interesting.*

11 RHETT

AS RHETT'S scarlet blood darkened and congealed within the glass walls of the phial, Sturlusson began to test him.

"We'll start with something easy," he said. "Tell me your name."

"I'm Rhett Zappotis," Rhett said. It seemed to him that the chain by which the phial was suspended pulled taut. He watched with growing interest as the small bottle began to swing in a small circle very slowly, following a track marked in the base of the Oraculum.

Sturlusson pointed to the base, where a gold inlay marked the same path that the bottle was currently taking. "This means that you are telling the truth. This mark here"—he indicated a wider circle—"this represents the limits of your known truth. Sometimes, as you are no doubt aware, we phrase things to make ourselves appear in a better light, or utter a half-truth. For example, would you say that you are pleased to meet me in person?"

"I would," Rhett agreed.

In an instant, the phial's circle widened, tracing closer to the larger circle's edge.

"Ah." Sturlusson smiled. "At which point, I might intuit that you would only say that you were pleased to meet me, or that pleasure was not your most prominent emotion at this time. Tell me, Captain, how do you really feel right now?"

Rhett considered his words. "Anxious," he offered. "I'm concerned that you won't trust me. Wary, because we hardly know one another, and I'm at your mercy. At the same time, I am hopeful that we can reach an accord, and I'm—as you would say—pleased that you've granted me an opportunity to prove it."

As he spoke, the phial's movement tightened, until it was following the inner circle once again.

"Excellent," Sturlusson said. He traced a straight line on the Oraculum that cut across the two circles. "This indicates a lie. The smaller the lie, the less deliberate the deception, the smaller the movement. An outright lie, however, will cause a larger movement. You may be tempted to tell a white lie, as the saying goes, but I would discourage it. Deception, for the sake of polite-ness, will not win you any favors here, Captain. Is this quite clear?"

Rhett bobbed his head in agreement. "Crystal."

"Most excellent." Sturlusson sat back in his chair and steepled his fingers. "On that note, I have several questions. Are you comfortable with proceeding?"

"Yes," Rhett said. He flinched when the bottle began to swing back and forth, abandoning its circuitous route. "Well, perhaps not comfortable. But I agree to the conditions you've set forth, if it will help achieve our ends." At once, the phial resumed its slow spinning motion, almost in defiance of gravity.

"Very well, Captain. I suppose you can anticipate my first question. What do you have to say about Sagoyewatha Porter?"

Rhett squinted at him. "I'm... sorry?"

Sturlusson's lips twitched toward a smile but never quite got there. "Porter. The commander of the Ohio vault."

"I never knew his first name," Rhett admitted. "What do you want to know about him?"

"Whatever you can tell me."

As Rhett looked down at his hands, he ran the tip of his thumb over the small nick on his index finger from which Sturlusson had drawn blood. The Oraculum's mechanics were curious, and a bit disconcerting. Rhett had always been fascinated by the fine line between truth and deception, and now he found himself at the mercy of a device that could detect that distinction.

Aware of the Oraculum's sensitivity to his words, Rhett was cautious. "I'm familiar with Porter's reputation," he began carefully. "I know what he claims for himself, and what others say. I've heard his explanations for past actions, and in my experience, his behavior has been consistent with someone who values ENIGMA's mission. My belief is that he is committed to the organization's interests."

The phial maintained its steady orbit close to the truth mark, confirming his words.

Sturlusson's expression showed a mix of skepticism and curiosity. "And what about the Hand of the Sun? What is your position on them?"

The question tightened the muscles in Rhett's back. He couldn't reveal his knowledge of a traitor within ENIGMA's ranks. Such an admission could compromise his position and future endeavors.

He measured his response with care. "My direct confrontations have been with Apollo," he explained. "As you can imagine, given the nature of our encounters, there's a significant level of hostility between us."

The phial danced a little wider in its arc, a telltale sign of the complexity of his feelings.

"Your views on ENIGMA's work?" Sturlusson leaned forward, eyes sharp.

Rhett hesitated, knowing this was a defining moment. His personal qualms with ENIGMA's methods, especially after witnessing Apollo's attack on El Dorado, couldn't be laid bare here, yet he also couldn't feign absolute confidence in the organization's operations.

"It's complex," he conceded. "I see areas where we could be more proactive, where ENIGMA could truly fulfill its potential. I believe in collaboration, in unifying the vaults. We're too often preoccupied with internal strife, which keeps us from making substantial progress. I'd like to see us move past that, to find a new way forward."

Sturlusson's face softened slightly, his analytical gaze turning thoughtful. Rhett's words seemed to resonate, hinting at common ground. Rhett felt a surge of something powerful—a blend of pride and anticipation. He envisioned a reformed ENIGMA, a force for global betterment, not just a custodian of relics.

Perhaps this was his opportunity to influence change, to be part of a new chapter for ENIGMA. To create something that wasn't just about control but about contributing something meaningful to the world.

Rhett was thinking about that when Sturlusson asked him, "Have you ever considered joining the Hand of the Sun?"

In his distraction, he didn't have to consider the answer. "No," he blurted, "of course not."

On the table, the Oraculum twitched, stilled, and then began to swing along the straight line that bisected the base. *A lie, a lie, a lie*, it seemed to say.

Sturlusson's eyes shuttered. "Of course," he said coldly.

Rhett squinted at the phial of his cooling blood. "I haven't," he insisted, causing the chain to swing all the more wildly.

The room seemed to shrink as the guards stepped closer. "What the hell? I would never join the Hand!"

"Are you aware," Sturlusson snapped, "that a Hand spy has been feeding information to the agent known as Aten?"

"Ah." Rhett gripped the handle of his cane. "I've had my suspicions."

"But you've never spoken to them?" Sturlusson's tone was dry.

"Well..." What could he say? The note, now tucked into his shirt pocket beneath the jumpsuit's crackling material, would have served as evidence if he'd ever taken it to Porter. But he never had.

That's why the Oraculum called me a liar, he realized, just as Kári swiped at his arm. *Because I did talk about joining the Hand as a spy. What a shitty little technicality.*

"This is a misunderstanding!" he protested.

Sturlusson lifted his palm, and Kári paused with his meaty, work-roughened palm hovering above Rhett's bicep.

"Please," he snapped. "I would love to hear your explanation."

"I would never work for the Hand," Rhett insisted. One fist still gripped his cane. The other clutched the arm of the chair. His mind was divided: one half of his brain, the logical half, was trying to determine what he could say to salvage the conversation. The other, his lizard-brain, was already several steps ahead, laying out a possible avenue of escape. *The only way off this island is the boat... Kári's going to try to grab you first... there are a lot of corridors between here and the exit, and you don't know the way out...*

"I would never back an organization that supported Apollo's actions," Rhett said. The words tumbled from his lips, fueled by his sincerity. "Any information I have about Porter comes from him. Any information I have about the Hand is filtered through my feelings about Apollo. I may not believe that Porter is a flawless man, but I saw what Apollo was willing to do to the people of Laputa. If that's how the Hand operates, I want no part of it. As for the possible spy you mention? I have my suspicions, but I have no proof that would point to any of my colleagues. Apollo was able to walk through walls. Another agent might be capable of turning us against each other. I'm new to ENIGMA, but I swear to you, I am doing my best to further its mission as I understand it, and to strengthen our alliances so that the Hand of the Sun cannot use our doubts against us. If you had trusted each other, I don't think Apollo would have come so close to succeeding on his mission. I'm doing what I can to heal those old wounds. I swear it on my life."

By the time he was done speaking, his chest heaved as he tried to catch his breath, and the phial had resumed its tight circling around the smallest circle on the Oraculum's base.

"You mean that," Sturlusson said, more to himself than to Rhett. He drummed his fingers on the table again. "Interesting. Then let me ask you this. If you were to learn that one of your close acquaintances, such as Fabien LeRoux or Dr. Dinah Bray, had bargained with the Hand, can you swear to me that you would side with ENIGMA rather than your friend?"

Kári flexed his fingers. Rhett's heart was in his throat. Dinah was so trusting that he couldn't imagine her switching sides without good reason; Fabien was loyal as hell and cleverer than people gave him credit for. If one of them sided with the Hand, he'd want to know why before he could condemn them.

"I would have some questions—" he began.

Sturlusson slapped his palm against the table so abruptly that he jumped. "It's a yes or no question, Captain Zappotis," he snarled. "ENIGMA, or your crew?"

This wasn't the first time Rhett had been forced to reckon with this aspect of himself. Some people were built to follow orders blindly. He had never been one of them. If he had to choose between being loyal to an institution or being loyal to his people, he'd choose the same answer every time.

"ENIGMA," he said.

And in the split second between when he spoke and when the Oraculum outed him as a liar, he struck.

Kári let out a strangled grunt as Rhett whipped his cane up, catching him in the chin with the metal globe that formed the handle. He struck again, keeping his movements short and sharp, driving it into his Adam's apple on his second jab. As he stumbled back, Rhett altered his grip on the cane, swinging it like a bat from the tip so that the metal ball caught Kári in the temple and sent him sprawling.

"Restrain him!" Sturlusson barked, reaching for the Oraculum before Rhett could damage it.

Not that he would have, at least not on purpose, but it meant that his hands were full for the moment. Which meant that he only had two aggressors to worry about for the time being.

Powering up the hopper vest took two tries, but even so the guards were still fumbling for their weapons when he managed to hit the button just right. He had assumed, given his experience with the time bombs, that he'd be able to navigate things on the fly once he got the vest going.

He'd been wrong.

One second, he was standing next to his chair over Kári's limp body. The next, he was standing next to the female guard who'd scoffed at him earlier. Before he could react, he was against the far wall.

The movement was disorienting enough, but the glitches through time were utterly baffling. When he was by the door, one guard was falling; a breath later, they were both upright and aiming their guns into thin air, presumably in the same place he'd just been standing. Not only was it impossible to predict where he'd be in the next second, but he couldn't predict where *they* would be, either.

Wonderful. A perfect stalemate. According to Finder, the vest couldn't move him through solid material, and with the door of the meeting-room closed, he would be stuck inside for the foreseeable future.

Unless he did something about it.

So do something.

At least Rhett's thoughts seemed to be linear, unlike the physical location of his body. Sometimes trying to make sense of the damn relics was more trouble than it was worth. Anyway, he didn't need to understand how a gun worked to fire it. He just needed to be able to pull the trigger.

He held the buttons of the vest between his fingers, still gripping his cane, and waited. The next time he found himself behind the guards, he pinched as hard as he could. Then, without waiting to make sure that he'd successfully powered down the hopper vest, he pressed down the button on his cane handle and swung.

The cane sparked with electricity, glittering yellow-green in his hand. One of the last times he'd used it, he'd contributed to the short-circuiting of Holy Land, which wasn't exactly ideal, but if he had to send Valhalla crashing into the sea, so be it. Sturlusson had made it pretty damned clear that the only route to his trust required a promise that Rhett could never make in good faith. He'd come here as a diplomat, and refused to end up a prisoner. His old friend, John Wesley, had lost too many years of his life that way.

He swung the cane at the guard's exposed neck, doubling his chances of an effective takedown. The blow would have caught him unawares, but the added jolt of the electricity brought him to his knees. As he reeled back, Rhett caught the other guard in the face. The crunch of bone almost drowned out the woman's cry of pain, which stutter-stopped as the electrical current passed through her. Her pistol slipped from her hands and hit the floor with a crack; the plaster of the far wall exploded.

At least no one was hit.

Both guards were down, but Kári was moving again. He lunged toward the fallen gun, and Rhett activated his vest again, popping in and out of space/time until he was close enough to Kári to hit him with his electrified cane. His blow was wild and caught him between the thighs.

Insult to injury, he thought as Kári gripped his groin, and tried to feel bad about it.

As Kári whimpered, Rhett bent to scoop up the gun. Sturlusson had tumbled from his chair, holding the Oraculum like an infant in his arms. He gaped at Rhett as he gripped the pistol and powered down the electrical current on his cane.

"I'm sorry," he said. "This isn't how I wanted things to go. Unless I've misjudged you, we really are on the same side."

Sturlusson's mouth opened and closed like a fish as Rhett backed toward the door. The Oraculum, still attuned to his subjective truth, spun on, the phial still tracing a perfect circle even though it was tipped sideways in Sturlusson's arms. He didn't turn his back on him until he'd managed to yank the door open.

Rhett still had every intention of leaving Valhalla without killing anyone. Perhaps, on reflection, Sturlusson would be able to forgive him for what he'd done.

The long corridor was empty for the moment, and Rhett wasted a few precious seconds to rearrange his handholds on the weapons he was carrying. He slipped the cane through a belt loop for easy access, but kept the gun clenched in his hand as he began his dash through the halls. *Which way is out? I should have paid more attention on the way in...*

Not that it would have been easy to distinguish, anyway, given that all the damn corridors looked the same. When he came to an intersection, Rhett froze, looking left and right for some clue as to where to head next.

The pounding of boots on flooring made him pause. He thrust the gun behind him and flipped the capelet of his jumpsuit up, then held perfectly still. Three seconds later, his lower half vanished as the chameleon suit's mechanics kicked in. His timing was perfect. Two more guards rounded the corner from the left and skidded to a halt. Both of them stared right at him in astonishment.

What the hell? I should be invisible, Rhett thought. He lowered his eyes without turning his head, only to realize his error. The capelet was large enough to cover his head or obscure the vest, but not both. At the moment, it looked like the damn hopper vest was hovering in empty air.

Stupid, tacky, useless capelet! He squeezed the trigger of the pistol before the guards could figure out what they were looking at, already composing an irate lecture for Finder for if and when he made it back to Reclamation.

His aim was perfect, but the resulting injury wasn't entirely what he'd expected. When the gun had gone off in Sturlusson's office, he'd assumed it was an ordinary pistol. Now that it was in his hands and he was paying more attention to the target, he saw just how wrong he'd been. The pistol burned hot in his hand, just for a moment, and a single burst of fire leapt between the gun and the guard. The guard bellowed and staggered sideways, clutching a smoking hole in his side.

"What the—?" Rhett asked aloud, blinking down at the gun. That was new. The smell of smoking meat and burned fabric made him gag. He turned the pistol on the other guard, who stood over his mewling companion. "You were going to set me on fire?"

The answering blast made him duck, and before the uninjured guard could fire again, or enact whatever deranged device he was carrying, Rhett activated the suit. In the larger area, he found himself even more scattered than before as the vest carried him to and fro. He kept his gun at the ready, and when the time came, he deactivated the scrambler right behind his opponent. When the man felt the cold pressure of the pistol at the base of his skull, he froze.

"Seriously," Rhett snarled. "You were going to set me on fire!" Instead of returning the favor, however, he jabbed the cane into the man's lower back and pressed the button that sent him collapsing to the floor in a twitching heap.

So much for being among allies. Apparently they were taking this whole Valhalla thing a touch too far.

He left them convulsing on the floor and followed the path by which they'd come, the left-hand corridor. Another half-dozen guards were already charging toward him, carrying an assortment of ballistic weapons and hollering in Swedish.

Time to get creative.

Rhett pushed through the pain that was already tightening in his hip and ran full-tilt forward, activating the vest again. So long as he kept moving forward, perhaps he could influence his general trajectory. Never knowing where the next step would land him, he decided that his best plan would be sowing chaos. He aimed the pistol overhead, pulled the trigger at random, and swung his electrified cane wildly in his other hand.

Some of his swings connected; others sent arcs of electricity crackling through the air with no place to land. Above him, linen-toned ceiling tiles and LED bulbs exploded like fireworks. Sometimes he moved forward, sometimes back, but the average of all those tiny jumps brought him closer to his goal, until he was in the midst of the Valhallan guards, swinging for his life. He thought a few of them might have fired on their fellows in a misguided attempt to hit him. Certainly, he landed a few good blows. He kept moving, more interested in getting out than in getting even.

Still, he couldn't deny the rush of adrenaline that coursed through him as the agents fell. He wasn't obsolete yet.

That would teach Sturlusson to discount his opinion.

The sounds of shouting faded behind him as he ran, but the time between jumps was growing longer. His movement forward was increasingly linear. The vest was running out of juice.

He had no way of knowing if it would recharge, and few other defenses. When it reached the point that he was only running in a straight line, he tucked the pistol and cane back into his belt and began to wrestle the vest off. It dropped to the floor behind him, sparking a twinge of guilt.

At least it was still in ENIGMA hands. Maybe one day they'd be able to finally broker a peace treaty and it could be returned to Reclamation, but that day was looking further and further away.

When the next group of guards approached, Rhett plastered himself to the wall and held his breath. This time, they ran right past him, too focused on getting to their injured brethren to notice any slight inconsistency in the shadows at their feet.

He reached the entrance of Valhalla at last. Two very young and nervous-looking people hovered by the entrance, holding rifles in a manner that made it quite clear they had no idea what they were doing with them. When they saw Rhett, one of them started so badly that the rifle slipped out of her hands, and would no doubt have hit the floor if it wasn't on a strap over her arm.

Rhett looked at the two of them with pity. "I don't want to shoot you," he said wearily. "And I very much doubt that you want to shoot me... or that you could, even if you tried. Why the hell do they have you two guarding the exit?"

The young man, still holding his gun, gulped so hard that his throat visibly bobbed. "They thought you'd be below," he said. "Raiding the vault, like Apollo did on his mission."

He let out a frustrated sigh. What a mess. "Well, I'm not. So are you going to let me out, or is this going to get ugly?"

The two of them exchanged shifty glances, clearly wondering about the consequences for letting him leave unscathed. The clock was ticking, and the longer he waited, the more likely it became that someone would catch up with him. While the two of them waffled, Rhett grabbed his cane and slammed the tip into the boy's gut hard enough to knock the wind out of him. The electrical jolt that followed only added insult to injury.

The girl squawked in alarm and tried to dodge, but Rhett prodded her before she could get away, and she went down, too. They'd be fine, but at least they wouldn't get in trouble for aiding and abetting his escape. Before either of them could rise again, Rhett hurtled over them toward the exit.

Kári's boat was still bobbing outside, and Rhett leapt into it, gritting his teeth against the pain of impact. Distant alarms began to blare in Valhalla's interior as he powered up the engine. Clearly Kári hadn't been worried about him making it this far. No one had, and why would they? They must have assumed that, if he *was* working with the Hand, his priority would be in getting to the vault's interior rather than doing everything in his power to get the hell out of Dodge.

He aimed the prow in the general direction of the mainland, hoping that the rising sun would burn away the fog enough to let him find the point-to-point teleporter pole. Porter was going to be disappointed when he found out what a mess he'd made of things...

It was only then, halfway between the coast of a foreign country and a hostile vault, that Rhett remembered handing the belt to Kári. Even if he *could* find the pole, he couldn't use it.

He was stranded.

12 FABIEN

FABIEN HAD ONLY VISITED Rome twice before. Once, when he was a schoolboy, a friend's parents had brought him along on holiday. They'd visited the usual tourist attractions, marveled at the galleries, shuffled along in the press of people wending through the Sistine Chapel, and returned home with armloads of trinkets and souvenirs: bottle openers with the Pope's face printed on the handle, postcards of the Parthenon, plastic molds of the Colosseum.

The second time he'd gone, he'd been paid quite a lot of money to do a very bad thing to a very bad man.

The address Finder had dug up for Annamaria was on the outskirts of the city, far away from the bustle of the tourist districts and even the residential neighborhoods where Fabien had found his mark on that second visit. He made his way along quiet roads between sprawling villas, the boundaries of each property denoted by spearlike groves of cypress trees.

"Why didn't you drop me closer?" he asked Finder.

"The use of relics leaves a... trace. Think of it as an energy signal. If I dropped you on the front lawn, it would likely alert her to your presence." Finder hummed. "Then again, I have no way of knowing if the Hand can track these things."

"Better to be cautious," Fabien said, although if this woman really *was* a Hand agent, she might already be on the alert.

He wondered where Rhett was; a little backup he could *trust* wouldn't hurt. Hopefully, he was off securing an alliance with Aethelstan or whatever that man's name was. When they regrouped, they could boast about their exploits.

Assuming, of course, that they both made it back in one piece.

His path ended at a sprawling estate. The building was set back from the road, behind an ornate and carefully tended garden. Paths lined with topiaries and mathematically precise hedges snaked through the greenery, partially obscuring the house beyond. The other villas along the road had been two or three stories high with off-white stucco walls, but this building was older and far less modern. It might have been lifted out of the Roman period and shuttled, intact, through time. The sloping roof was covered in lapped red tiles, and the roof of the peristyle was supported by dozens of painted columns.

The hair on the back of Fabien's neck rose. *How old is this lady, exactly?*

He checked the local time on his tablet. Four a.m. The villa was dark, but the moon was close to full, and it was a clear night. As long as he was careful, he should be able to do a good bit of snooping before sunrise.

"I'm going in," he told Finder. "I'll need you to be quiet."

"You got it, boss," Finder whispered, although there was no one outside to hear them. "I'm going on mute. If you need me, just ask, but in the meantime I'm going to focus all my attention on the vault. Be careful!"

He wasn't sure that strolling into the house, which might be a trap, counted as *being careful,* but he didn't point that out. Instead, he closed the screen on the tablet and tucked it into the safe part of his pack. Then he started pulling things out.

The black balaclava he pulled out was of the perfectly ordinary kind, but the gloves were new. They were magnetized, designed to match with the contact points on his smart-targeting rifles, of which he'd brought two. He'd dropped one too many weapons in the midst of a fight over the years.

He pulled one rifle into place, left the other strapped across his back, and flipped the rifle's setting to *stun.* Then he checked the blades on his right hip and the trio of grenades at his belt. He set the last device, a heat sensor that Finder had suggested he bring along, to highlight anything within ten meters of him. Reassured that all was in place, he pulled on his gloves and set off through the villa's gardens.

Judging by the precision of the boxwoods, whoever was responsible for Annamaria's gardens was clearly anal-retentive about their appearance. The recent rain had left the ground soft, and when Fabien stepped onto the lawn, he left a footprint in the grass. There was no way a line of footprints wending through the gardens would go unnoticed the next day. After a moment's hesitation, he stuck to the paths instead.

He passed pristine reflecting pools and several hardscaped

patios with garden furniture laid out around cast-iron fire pits. *This could be a summer home,* he thought. *If there were a bunch of people around, surely there would be at least one light on inside? A forgotten lamp left burning in an empty room, or someone who can't sleep flipping through a book?* He was going to feel pretty foolish if he broke into some poor schmuck's empty vacation rental.

Halfway to the house, his heat sensor vibrated, and Fabien froze, scanning his surroundings. When he spotted the culprit, he let out a shaky laugh. Apparently, Annamaria had *rats.* The fat rodent stared at him, its nose twitching, its eyes bright red even in the moonlight. Its body was highlighted with a pale green grid generated by the sensor, although the light didn't seem to bother the beast at all. As Fabien watched, it skittered across the path and into one of the nearby reflecting pools, where it paddled about undisturbed.

Not a rat, then. A mink. Even the local rodents were classier than he was used to.

The obvious entryway sat at the front of the building, but Fabien bypassed it. He had yet to encounter any security, but whoever owned this place would, no doubt, have alarms on the front door. Instead, he stuck to the outside wall, beyond the peristyle—just in case the residents had security cameras aimed at the walkway—and made his way around the back of the estate.

It was brazen, to be sure, but if the police showed up, he could handle them. If the *Hand* showed up...

Well, that was the whole point, wasn't it?

There was a gate on the back wall, wrought of heavy iron

and secured from the inside by two sturdy latches and a massive
rusty chain looped three times through the gates. Through the
gaps in the metal, Fabien could see the courtyard beyond. It was
even more beautiful than the gardens.

His gloves might have helped with the latches, but there
was no getting around that chain. Not without making a racket.
Instead, he turned his attention to the nearby trees. There was
an orchard at the back of the house, and a few trees that reached
over the red-tiled roof.

Fabien grinned. He'd climbed his fair share of trees over the
years. It was almost funny, really, that the owners of the villa
had taken such pains to lock the gate while leaving the courtyard open to the sky.

He shimmied up the trunk and along the sturdiest branch
before gingerly lowering himself onto the tiles. One careless
step might knock a tile free and send it tumbling to the stone
courtyard below. Rather than risk the noise, Fabien took his
time, testing each tile before he put his weight on it. His knees
protested when he made the jump from the roof to the courtyard, but it was only one story.

Besides, it was worth the momentary pain. He was *in*.

Two walls of the courtyard were exterior walls, but the
other two abutted the residential portion of the villa. Fabien
slipped silently toward the doors. One looked into a kitchen.
Servant's quarters? Anyone who could afford a fleet of
gardeners could afford housekeepers, too. He left that one alone
for the moment and approached the other one.

This time, when he peered through the glass, he caught his
breath. He was looking into a deep hall with a long table set for

sixteen. The far wall was hung with paintings. *Old* paintings, by the look of them, many of which were portraits.

At least four of them included figures that were quite clearly Annamaria Vizzini. Fabien took a few deep breaths, fending off the lightheaded sense of dread and wonder that swept over him. There was no denying that he was in the right place.

He tried the handle, but of course it was locked. That was no problem; he'd been picking locks for years, and a deadbolt wouldn't be anywhere near as loud as a heavy, rusty chain. He peeled off one of his magnetized gloves and fished his lockpick set out of his pocket.

Fifteen seconds later, the door swung open. Fabien hastily stepped through, although he took care to pull his glove back on first. Fingerprints were the least of his worries. If a relic could track him with a strand of his hair, who knew what else the Hand could do?

The left-hand hall led through to the kitchen, so after a quick sweep of the dining hall, Fabien went right. He held his rifle at the ready and tiptoed as he went. *Please let her be here.* His heartbeat roared in his ears.

The hallway was lined with doors, and he stopped at each one, listening through the wood before turning the handles to peer within. The first was a storage room. The second was an office. When the third door opened, Fabien bit back a yelp of triumph.

Inside were display cases. A private museum of relics behind glass, the much smaller cousin of an ENIGMA vault.

And there, in pride of place behind a locked case, was the

very same two-handled cup that Ronnie had found. The cup that ENIGMA's records had called the Holy Grail.

He was already stepping into the room when his heat sensor went off, but it was too late. Something large and cold and very solid slammed into his side at waist level. The pain arrived a moment later as his nerve endings caught up with him. An enormous, many-toothed jaw clamped down on his thigh and *shook*, tearing him open even before he hit the stones. His vision exploded with stars when his skull met the floor.

He rolled onto his belly in a vain attempt to crawl away. Seams gave way as the pack he'd been wearing was shredded open and cast aside. His attacker tore into him again, and he flipped onto his back, trying to bring the gun between himself and whatever was on him.

Something clamped around his neck, and Fabien froze.

A woman was screaming in Italian. Whatever had grabbed his thigh let go, but the pressure on his neck intensified as a blade dug into the tender skin above his Adam's apple.

When his vision cleared a little, he found himself staring up at Annamaria Vizzini. Her hair was wild, and there was more silver mixed in with the black than there had been in her old portrait, but it was clearly her. She was wrapped in a loose robe over floral-print pajamas; she held a polearm of some kind, only instead of ending with a blade, a spiked metal half-collar was mounted to the end. This was pressed against the floor, pinning Fabien in place. If he tried to sit up, he'd end up with a throat full of sharpened metal.

"Who the *hell* are you?" Annamaria snarled in English.

Fabien kept his lips pressed together. He wasn't going to tell her a damn thing.

Also, his thigh was on *fire*. If he opened his mouth, it was entirely possible that he'd let out a helpless whine of pain, and that wasn't going to happen.

The heat sensor was still buzzing at his hip, but the green grid it cast only highlighted Annamaria, not the thing that had attacked Fabien first. Without turning his head, he lowered his eyes to the figure at the woman's side.

It was a dog, but not. Made of metal plates and panels, it was as much a *Canis familiaris* as Finder was a member of *Homo sapiens sapiens*. Its tiny eyes burned with a hateful red light, and its back was arched. A digitized growl ripped from its throat. Its razor teeth—not merely razor-sharp, but *actual* razors, designed for maximum damage—dripped with Fabien's blood.

"Answer me!" Annamaria bellowed. When Fabien didn't comply, she twisted the end of the polearm's handle.

The world went white. Fabien's back arched off the floor as he coughed and sputtered. He was distantly aware that, in his writhing, he'd pressed his throat to the metal spikes of the collar, but he couldn't stop.

The pain subsided abruptly, and Fabien went limp.

"For the third time, I ask you, *who are you*." Annamaria lowered his face toward his, her teeth bared. They weren't as sharp as the razor-lined mouth of her mechanical guard dog, but her fury was just as dangerous. "If you don't answer me, I will let Brutus have you."

"Brutus?" he choked. Hot rivulets of blood were dripping

down his neck. "You named it *Brutus?* God, what is it with the Hand and your stupid, dramatic names?"

Annamaria paled, and she rocked back on her heels. "You know—?" she began.

He hadn't been thinking clearly, and he *certainly* hadn't expected to catch her off-guard with this knowledge. Through the floaty, dissociative haze of his pain, it clicked.

She wasn't expecting him, because the Hand hadn't warned her he was coming.

Any advantage he had wouldn't last long, and if she hit him with another jolt of whatever powered that polearm, he wouldn't have much fight left in him.

Fabien didn't let himself consider what would happen if the dog attacked again. He wasn't thinking at all. *Don't plan too much. Follow your gut.*

Both of his hands closed around the handle of the polearm. He arched his back again, careful not to impale himself any further, and kicked Annamaria in the stomach as hard as he could. The polearm slipped out of her grasp as she tumbled.

He was on his feet in an instant, dropping her weapon and lifting his own gun instead. He aimed it dead in the center of her heaving chest.

"Call your dog off, or I'll shoot," he said. She didn't need to know that the rifle was set to stun.

The mechanical hound growled again, but Annamaria hissed, "*Aspetta!*" and it fell silent, although its unblinking eyes never wavered from Fabien.

"Porter sent you," Annamaria said. There was no question in her voice. Like the dog, she kept staring at Fabien, not at his gun but at his face. Her eyes were coals, burning into him. "He armed you poorly, I saw you the moment that you left the road." Her lip curled in a sneer. "All those relics, all that power, and yet you never seem to come prepared."

"Who else is here?" Fabien snapped.

In all the years since she sat for her old portrait, her smile hadn't changed. Despite staring up the barrel of his rifle, she seemed almost amused. "Wouldn't you like to know?"

His leg was trembling, and the wound from where Apollo had once stabbed him was ached in sympathy. *You're losing blood, and fighting two to one. Get smart or get out, dipshit.*

There was no way he was leaving without her, not now that she knew she was caught. If he fled now, she'd be long gone by the time he returned. He needed an advantage.

To his left lay an open door to a room full of relics. Annamaria narrowed her eyes. He'd have to move fast, or that dog would maul him beyond repair. The longer he waited, the weaker he got.

You could just shoot her, he thought. *Stun her.* But the dog might attack again if she went down, and those teeth would tear him in half in an instant. He needed a way to fight back before he took that risk.

Three.

Two.

One...

Annamaria must have seen some warning in his expression, because she was already shouting in Italian when he leapt through the door. He slammed it closed behind him and braced his back against the wood just as the dog's weight collided with the far side.

Think, think, think. Your grenades might take her down, but you need to target the dog first. Neutralize the threat. The mechanical beast kept flinging itself against the wood, and the hinges groaned under the strain. In the meantime, the heat sensor that had been buzzing against his hip ever since Annamaria came in range fell silent.

She was getting away while Fabien bled out in her private collection. Or, worse, she was calling for backup from the rest of the Hand. How pathetic would it be if, instead of capturing her, Fabien ended up in Hand custody?

No way was that happening. Not today. If Annamaria Vizzini was going to defeat him, she would damn well have to kill him in the process.

13 DINAH

"FINDER?" Dinah asked in a low voice. "I don't mean to be rude, but how did you manage to get the calculations with the Gravitas Engine so spectacularly wrong?"

The android hummed. "I wouldn't say spectacularly wrong. If they'd been all that bad, we'd probably be blown up right now, and we wouldn't be having this conversation to begin with. But yes, I admit, that was not my finest moment. It's nothing to worry about."

It's nothing. That was what Dinah had told Lane, what Lane had told Marcus, and now it was Finder's excuse. *It's nothing* was starting to sound suspiciously like bullshit to her ears.

"True," she said, "we didn't die horribly." *Yet.* "But the fact remains that we've run into several, erm, minor issues that neither of us thought of to begin with. Doesn't that worry you?"

"Marginally." Finder waved a hand. "But I'm learning all

the time. After all, the scientific method requires trial and error. Some of the greatest minds in history have been wrong about their initial theories. Take Linnaeus. Dead wrong about evolution, but he still made incredible contributions to the field. And of course, there are thousands if not millions of individuals who've made advances in other fields whose names are buried in the annals of scientific discovery—"

Dinah was used to the android prattling on about anything and everything, but this particular monologue had an air of desperation to it. On top of that, the android's expressive eyes had taken on a decidedly shifty appearance.

"That's the problem? The scientific method? Because we're not just coworkers, Finder, we're friends, and if there's anything you want to talk about..."

"Oh, look!" Finder said, pointing a little way ahead of them. "We're here."

This was, perhaps, a clever distraction, but it also seemed to be true. A low, squat building lay before them with its bay windows dark. Metal grates barred them from the outside, protecting the glass.

It wasn't exactly a fortress, and it was much humbler than a vault. An odd place to store powerful otherworldly treasures, to be sure, but at least it didn't appear to be too heavily fortified. The pair of them approached the metal door that led into the warehouse from a side street. There were no doors along the main road—assuming they were on a main road, which seemed hard to believe given the narrow, modest nature of the thoroughfare.

Over the years, Dinah had had to do a fair bit of traveling, and she'd often found herself in cities. More than once she'd been walking down a quiet street only to realize she had entered a neighborhood or suburb that wasn't welcoming to strangers. To her immense relief, nothing had ever come of it, but there was a familiar quiet hostility in the air as she and Finder approached the door. She was certain that there were eyes on her, that their every movement was being observed.

How deep do Apollo's roots go? Dinah wondered. For all she knew, Apollo was holed up inside. Having to face off against the man again would be terrifying, but what if she was able to bring him in after Rhett and Fabien had failed to do so?

The door—which only reached the height of Dinah's shoulders—was locked, and when she bumped her shoulder against it, she elicited the dull thump of reinforced metal.

"How do we get in?" she whispered. "Should I shoot the lock, or...?"

"Allow me." Finder slipped its metal fingers through the slight gap at the top of the doorframe and yanked. The door peeled back like the lid of a sardine tin, buckling as it went and taking the interior hinges along with it. The android set the ruined door aside with incongruous delicacy. "Voilà," it said with a self-satisfied little flourish.

Dinah whistled. "Damn. Remind me never to start a fistfight with you."

"It would be most unwise, to be sure," Finder agreed.

Something moved on one of the nearby rooftops. Dinah squinted up into the darkness, but the moonlight revealed nothing, and the dimly-lit streets didn't offer enough illumination to reveal the identity of whoever, or whatever, was up there.

"Come on." Dinah dipped her head and crab-walked through the too-small door before it occurred to her that sending Finder through first might have been the wiser course of action.

The warehouse was as dark within as without. It took a moment for Dinah's eyes to adjust to the darkness, and when they did, she peered around in bewilderment.

"Oh!" Finder's eyes lit up, quite literally, sending washed-out beams of light skidding around the warehouse whenever the android turned its head. "Look, it's a trash heap." The android clapped its hands and shuffled forward.

"Yeah," Dinah agreed, minus the enthusiasm. Instead of organized shelves and distinct categories, the warehouse was filled with little mounds of what looked like nothing more than junk. Twisted metal scraps; a hill of broken glass in every color; a heap of pebbles; a mound of broken plastic; stacks of flattened fabrics; palettes groaning under the combined weight of old bricks... it was either a scrapyard or the private residence of a fanatical hoarder.

Finder squatted down next to a pile of metal refuse and picked up an unrecognizable object between its thumb and fore-finger. "You're trained in archaeology, so you must have some reverence for the educational value of rubbish, Dr. Bray. They can tell us an enormous amount about a civilization—"

"About defunct or historical civilizations, yes." Dinah waved to indicate the city outside. "But we're already in the civilization, so why are they using this place to store trash?"

"It could be a recycling center," Finder mused.

"Hm." Dinah crossed her arms. "Maybe." *Although why Apollo would be hanging around a recycling center, I can only imagine.* "And you're sure that the resonance stone is here somewhere?"

"Oh, yes." Finder straightened up, dusted off its hands, and moved between the piles of refuse toward the back of the warehouse. The play of light coming from its eyes made strange, uncanny shadows dance across the walls. More than once, Dinah thought she saw something else move in the corners, or along the seam between the wall and the floor. When she turned to look, however, there was never anything there, just the silhouette of unfamiliar trash or a reflection in the dome of her helmet.

"This is all truly fascinating," Finder said. "You know, I've been taking samples here and there, and this world's atmosphere has almost the exact same blend as that of Earth. Now, it's possible that's artificial, given that the dome over the settlement must allow them to circulate an artificially blended atmosphere, but the presence of plastics on this world suggests not only a parallel chemistry, but a parallel development in their industrial processes. What are the odds of that? For creatures with such wildly divergent biology from that of your own to evolve almost in parallel?"

"They aren't that divergent," Dinah observed. "They're mammals, aren't they? I mean, yes, their evolutionary tree is likely very different, but mammals didn't come into prominence until after the time of the dinosaurs, so it's possible that this world has some level of shared... you know..." She waved her wrist in a slow circle as she searched for a word that wouldn't come.

"Convergent evolution?" Finder suggested.

"I guess. Remember, I'm a historian, not a biologist."

"To me, as a non-biological entity, it's entirely fascinating. I couldn't have come into existence without human intervention, so I'm perhaps more aware than you are how unlikely a coincidence it is that the species would end up building a society that bears so much similarity to your own, aesthetics notwithstanding."

But it's not a coincidence, is it? Dinah thought. Azmera had told them that the destabilizer and its power cells had been brought to Earth from another world. A gift from an alien species. Had the rat-people of this planet been the ones to make the device and bring it over? Or had some tertiary species contacted them both? That might explain the parallels between worlds, but it wouldn't account for the shared chemistry of the planets, or the similar atmosphere.

Finder reached the far wall of the warehouse and pointed to the ground at its feet. "There you are!" it exclaimed. "I found it—"

A high-pitched chittering piped up from behind them, and Dinah whirled. One hand fell on the butt of her pistol. She raised her other arm as if to block a blow.

Even if a blow had been coming, however, her movement would have been useless, because the sound was coming from a very short—

Person? Dinah squinted down at the figure. It was similar, but not quite identical, to the figure she'd encountered in Finder's AI simulation, with pale pink ears, a glistening nose at the tip of a pointed snout, large red-tinted eyes, and stubby limbs that ended in claws. Its clothing was more refined than Dinah had expected, and had the quality of a uniform, although a rather rough-and-tumble one.

It chittered again, and from the far wall, Finder responded. The newcomer cocked his head and made a different set of sounds. As this exchange progressed, words began to crop up amid the squeaking as Finder started to translate the individual words of the language in real time. A rapid-fire exchange of questions followed, although it took several back-and-forths before Finder was able to adequately translate any of the words.

"*Eek eek*—doing here—*eek*—thief!" was the first partial sentence that came through.

"Not thieves," Finder insisted. At the same time that Dinah understood the words, she could hear that the sounds emitting from Finder's helmet were a mixture of English and the high-pitched squeaks. Finder was always doing the most, but translating an alien language on the fly gave Dinah a whole other level of appreciation for the system's abilities. "We're looking for something of ours."

"Yours—*eeeeeek!*—in here?" The creature's reddish eyes bulged. "You are—*eeeee?*"

Finder cocked its head. "We are what?"

The small figure pointed to the sky and repeated the sound. "Travelers. From another Earth."

"Another..." Finder straightened up. "Oh! Of course!" The android turned to Dinah. "I told you that the chemistry was similar. This warrants more study, of course, but I think... oh, yes, I think we might not be meeting aliens at all."

"He's a talking rat," Dinah muttered.

"Rat?" the rat asked.

"In point of fact," Finder corrected, "I believe our new friend is some variety of marsupial, but that's beside the point. He's not an alien. He's an alternate you. Not *you* specifically, of course, but a sort of *Didelphimorphia sapiens sapiens*, as it were."

"Didelian," the creature said, hooking what passed for a thumb at its own chest. Then it extended a curved claw toward Dinah. "Traveler. Yes?"

"I suppose, by definition," Dinah agreed.

The rat-man—or was he actually an opossum of some kind? —twitched his nose a few times. He was sniffing them, a fact that Dinah found extraordinarily discomfiting. "More Travelers. *Eeeeek* wasn't expecting you."

"You weren't?" Dinah said, confused. She almost asked if the Didelian was referring to Apollo, but she stopped herself from uttering the agent's name just before it left her lips. Associating herself with Apollo, even verbally, probably wasn't a great idea.

"Not me," the creature said. "*Eeeeek*. Callic."

Dinah turned to Finder in confusion.

"I'm having trouble finding a word that would serve as an adequate translation," Finder explained. "I think it's an honorific. Perhaps *Commander* would be a suitable option?"

"Callic is a person," Dinah said. She pointed to the Didelian. "And you answer to him?"

"Yes." The creature nodded fervently. "He is a friend of Travelers. Beloved of your kind. And you, you must have followed your brother here?"

"Um." Dinah fell back a pace. "I'm not sure what you..."

"You are Agent Ra? With the Hand of the Sun?" The creature's eyes bounced between Dinah and Finder. "You have come to speak with our Traveler. To put an end to *eeeeek*?"

Perhaps she should lie and agree with the creature's assessment? If she pretended to be on Apollo's side, it might buy them some time. Then again, being marched right up to Apollo in the midst of a crowd of enthusiastic marsupials wouldn't give her a lot of opportunities to attack. They'd likely be outnumbered. She could try taking this Didelian captive and interrogating the beast—

"No!" Finder exclaimed. "Apollo is our sworn enemy!"

Dinah squeezed her eyes shut. "Finder, shut up."

"The very idea that you would think we're with that man—" Finder huffed.

One of these days, she was going to have to sit the AI down and have a serious talk. Unfortunately, it looked like she might have to put a pin in that.

The creature's face split into a wicked grin, and it puffed up all its fur, standing even straighter to make itself as big as possible. "You're one of them? You're with the enemy? Ooh, he'll be so happy to know that I brought you to him. Might even decide he likes me more than Callic."

Dinah reached for her pistol while Finder stood tall, bracing its fists on its hips and lifting its chin. "You are outnumbered, sir!" the android announced.

"Finder—" Dinah began.

"You have no hope of taking us!" Finder went on.

"*Finder—*"

"It is my sworn duty to avenge the deaths of my designers by doing everything in my power to unset the Hand of the Sun and all expose the villainy of its—"

"*Finder!*" Dinah pointed to the entrance from which Finder had peeled the door only minutes ago.

"Not now, Dr. Bray, I'm in the midst of a heroic monologue! What could be so important that you would need to... oh." The beams of Finder's eyes swept toward the door, illuminating the swirling mass of gleaming eyes, glistening teeth, and sharpened claws. Their assailant hadn't come alone. "Oh, dear."

It was the last thing Dinah heard before the creatures swarmed.

Most of her life had been spent in cities. Dinah had never been a country girl. Her experience with marsupials was limited to videos, zoos, and common knowledge. From what she recalled, the North American opossum was a funny-looking beast whose two primary defense mechanisms consisted of hissing and playing dead until whoever was bothering them got bored and left.

Apparently, divergent evolution had blessed the apex species of this new world with a whole new set of built-in weapons—and, as if that weren't enough, the ability to fashion tools of their own.

As the nearest Didelian lunged for her, claws-first, Dinah whipped out her pistol, silently cursing Finder's love of vintage film. She was going to die on an alternate Earth looking like an absolute nerd.

Only fitting, Fabien would no doubt have said.

Dinah opened fire. It fired even more smoothly than the

former laser pistol she'd borrowed, and the grip stayed cool in her palm.

Fortunately for her, the Didelians were so closely packed that firing in the rough direction of their general mass was enough to hit one. Its wail was accompanied by the stench of burning hair.

Unfortunately, her shoddy aim meant that she didn't hit the one that was already on her. The creature was small but compact, and the impact of its collision took her out at the knees. She fell with a cry, and the Didelian was on her in an instant, hissing and spitting as it tried to claw the pistol from her hand.

What little combat training Dinah had ever received went right out the window. Instead of doing... well, whatever Rhett or Fabien would have done, which she could only imagine would have required more finesse and competence, Dinah went feral. She wrapped both arms and legs around the creature and rolled, pinning it in place under her greater bulk. The beast hissed and spat, and Dinah hissed right back, slamming the dome of her helmet into her enemy's face. When she pulled back, there was a pink smear of blood on the glass. Judging by the way the Didelian mewled and clutched at its face, she'd likely broken its nose.

"I don't want to hurt you," she protested. "Can't we just ta —oof!"

Another of the Didelians landed on her back and began to tear at the back of her suit. The clawing was bad enough, but then the one whose nose she had broken sat up and bit her on the wrist.

Dinah rolled again, successfully dislodging the creature on her back. She fired a few shots with the laser as she scooted away until she could press her back against the wall. Despite the pain in her wrist, and the slow trickle of blood oozing from her bite wound, she didn't want to shoot indiscriminately. Morals aside, killing any of them would be a terrible PR move. Apollo had evidently won them over, and harming any of them would only confirm whatever smear campaign he had launched against ENIGMA.

"Finder!" Dinah barked. "What's the plan?"

A Didelian with a large knife clenched between its needle teeth—*seems like overkill*, Dinah thought, *they already have so many pointy bits*—was climbing Finder's leg. The android peeled the creature free, leaned back, and hurled it as far away from itself as possible. Dinah didn't see where it landed.

"I'm afraid I don't have one, Doctor!" the android called back. "The door is quite a long way off, and so far there appear to be about two dozen of them trying to take us prisoner."

Assuming they don't kill us first. Dinah fired on another Didelian, this time hitting it in the shoulder. The beast retreated, covering the smoking furrow in its flesh with one paw and baring its teeth at her.

Dinah screamed bloody murder when another of the creatures popped up at her elbow. Instead of attacking her, it charged right past, barreling into its wounded counterpart. There was a brief scuffle, and the newcomer came out on top. It hissed until its opponent toppled sideways and collapsed.

The newcomer was small for its kind, judging by the build of the others. Its clothes were even shabbier than those of the others, and its small ears had bite marks in the thin flesh that suggested it had fought, and not necessarily won, more than a few skirmishes. What surprised Dinah the most was the fact that the creature was familiar. It was the same one she'd seen before, the one that had appeared in the simulation holding the resonance stone.

"You're with the other side?" the creature hissed. It squatted down next to Dinah at eye level.

"Uh." Dinah pushed herself a bit more upright. Another Didelian went sailing through the air above them. Evidently Finder was holding its own for the time being. "I'm not with Apollo, if that's what you mean."

"This way," the beast chirped. It dropped to all fours and scurried past her.

She had no proof that this particular creature was trustworthy, but it wasn't trying to bite, scratch, or stab her, so that seemed like a good sign.

"Finder!" Dinah called. "This way!" She stumbled after her savior, tripping over her own feet as she went.

"The name's Nibbles," the beast said over its shoulder. "If we get separated, head for the tunnels. Tell them you're a friend of the underground."

"Sure," Dinah said, mostly because there were so many questions swirling around in her head that she hardly knew what to ask first.

Finder followed them, flanked by a wave of furry bodies. Nibbles slipped through a narrow gap between a pile of old junk and the wall; Dinah would surely have gotten stuck in the passage if Finder hadn't run full-tilt into her and sent the pile of junk toppling in every direction. Their pursuers lost their footing as a wave of old cans and rusty hardware sluiced across the floor.

Dinah landed on her hands and knees several feet from a hole in the floor of the warehouse. Nibbles was holding the metal cover. "Through here!" he cried.

To call the opening a manhole would have implied that it was designed with the size of a man in mind. Such was not the case. Dinah eyed the hole dubiously, not sure that she would fit.

Better than getting bitten again, she thought, and crawled forward, plunging face-first into the opening.

Stale, fetid air engulfed her as she wormed her way through the hole. She slid forward a few feet, and then abruptly down, landing very nearly face-first on a hard surface. Her gun was still clenched in one fist, at the ready, but she couldn't see a thing in the darkness.

A moment later, Finder slid in behind her. Metal met metal as Nibbles yanked the hatch shut. "Keep moving!" he cried.

The passage was barely large enough to crawl through, but Dinah made her way forward on her hands and knees. Sometimes, from her left, there would be a gust of air when a draft swept through some unseen aperture in the tunnel wall. Finder's glowing eyes were enough to illuminate the sides of the tunnel, but the blackness ahead of them was impenetrably deep.

Then the tunnel changed direction, and Dinah's gloved hands slipped on the slick floor. She slid forward, grunting at the scrape of rough stone over her belly, until the narrow tunnel opened up to a vaulted corridor. Dinah came to a stop with her face hanging out over an underground river.

"Oh, God." She gagged and pulled back. At least in that larger tunnel, she could stand upright on the bank. The walkway that skirted the walls was clearly very old, built from stones that had sunk and shifted over the years.

Finder emerged behind her and pushed itself to its feet. "Oh, look at this! Would we call this a sewer, or a catacomb?"

"Don't you have rivers on your Earth?" asked Nibbles as the scruffy creature squirmed out to join them. "It's fresh water. Good for drinking."

Dinah squinted into the dark water, not sure if she could trust it. The real question, of course, was whether or not she could and should trust the creature who'd led them here.

Nibbles waved to the pair of them. "Come on. We need to get out of here." He hurried away on all fours until he reached a small boat moored nearby, whereupon he raised himself up on two legs, turned back to them, and cocked his head. "Are you coming, Travelers? We ought to take a look at that bite wound."

Dinah cradled her wrist to her chest and, with some reluctance, slipped the pistol back into its holster. "Should we go with him?" she whispered to Finder.

"He seems like our only friend here," the android replied. "What is your human intuition telling you?"

"That we're lucky he found us in time." Dinah sighed and trudged toward the boat. Nibbles had powered it on, and it proved not to be a motorboat at all, but some sort of flat-bottomed hovercraft that bobbed several inches above the surface of the water. Finder climbed aboard without reservation and immediately began asking their small savior questions that involved phrases like *surface tension* and *fuel cells*. Dinah followed rather more reluctantly. They'd come to find Apollo, and although she wasn't enthusiastic about being taken prisoner, she had at least been clear that their attackers from the warehouse knew where to find the agent of the Hand.

You're in over your head, she told herself as she climbed aboard the hoverboat. *Way out of your depth.*

Come to think of it, she couldn't remember the last time she hadn't been.

14 RHETT

THE BOAT'S engine was sputtering by the time Rhett came
into sight of land. He wasn't sure which direction he'd been
going, but this little strip of coastline was different from the one
he'd left behind that morning. He'd spent the crossing in a pain-
fueled daze, wondering how on earth he was going to get in
touch with Porter.

But what if you don't go back to Reclamation? he mused.
*What if Sturlusson spreads the word about what happened in his
vault? It will get back to Porter quickly enough, and word will
spread to whoever's on the inside. The Hand already tried to
contact me.*

*Maybe there's a way to salvage this that gets me more
information.*

The engine died in the shallows, and Rhett staggered out
through the ankle-deep water and across the beach. A group of
children playing on the beach looked up in alarm and ran for

their homes. He probably looked like an alien in his silver suit. It was possible, of course, that Sturlusson had contacts out there, but ENIGMA was a close-kept secret. To his relief, when a small group of adults left their homes and made their way to the beach to question him, they seemed puzzled by his appearance rather than hostile.

In broken Swedish, and with a plan only half-formed in his mind, Rhett asked to be taken to a phone. Instead of trying to find a way to reach Porter, he used his broken Swedish to track down another number entirely.

Rather than reach out to ENIGMA, he called Tera.

———

TERA ERONSDÓTTIR HAD BEEN an IT student before she became a journalist. They had crossed paths during Rhett's brief stint in Sweden, and then again, purely by happenstance, at a military base in Yemen years later. Now, apparently, she was living in Uppsala, just a train ride away. After a brief conversation with the man who'd invited Rhett into his home, he was given a backpack, a change of clothes, and a ticket to the train station in Uppsala for that very night.

The chunky sweater and loose trousers he'd been gifted weren't his usual style, but Rhett was more concerned with the throbbing pain in his hip. He spent most of the train ride with his eyes closed, leaning back against the seat, massaging the muscles with the hard press of his thumb. Usually the pressure was enough to help with the pain, but this time it only made his head spin. Only the fact that he didn't have any ID of his own kept Rhett from buying a whole bottle of painkillers and a jug of brännvin to wash it down.

Dusk was falling by the time he stepped onto the platform in Uppsala and was greeted with open arms and a familiar smile.

"Rhett!" Tera gripped him tight and let go of him just as quickly. "So good to see you. What happened to you? You said your ID was stolen?"

Rhett nodded as they made their way along the platform. "It's been a long day. I'm hoping you can pull some strings at the Embassy... I've got nothing with me."

"Don't worry." Tera patted his back. "I'll get you sorted out. It pays to have friends in high places."

"And you're that friend?" Rhett teased.

"Ever since that Kurt Schork Award, I am. Or close enough." Tera laughed so loudly that a few other travelers glanced sidelong at them.

Tera was a few inches shorter than Rhett, built like a bean-pole, with thin mouse-brown hair and overlarge blue eyes that seemed to take up half of her face. Given her stature and proportions, people often mistook her for a child, but Rhett knew better. He'd seen this petite woman crawl on hands and knees through war zones for the sake of a story, and stare down militants in the hopes of getting a good quote. Tera was either fearless or so adept at masking her fear that it made no differ-ence in the long run.

"We can go to the embassy in the morning," Tera said. "Get your papers sorted out. In the meantime, you can stay with me. I have plenty of space, and I live alone."

"Still single?" Rhett asked.

Tera wrinkled her nose. "No, actually." She held up her hand, indicating the plain band on her ring finger. "But he's in the Caribbean right now, photographing fish."

"A photographer?" Rhett laughed. Tera's familiar presence was already calming him down.

"A nature photographer. And no, before you ask, we didn't meet on the job. He'd be useless in a war zone, but he's good for me."

Rhett nodded his understanding. Being in the company of his sister Zoe and her family was a sort of healing balm. They would never understand what he'd been through, which was a good thing. Spending time in the company of happy people made the weight of his experience easier to bear.

They stopped at a restaurant, where Tera chatted away about her husband and her recent work while Rhett gorged himself on fresh fish and potatoes poached in mushroom butter. He hadn't realized how hungry he was until his head began to clear. Tera paid their bill without breaking the patter of her talk, then guided him home to the apartment.

The instant the door closed behind them, however, Rhett's host turned to him with a shrewd glint in her large eyes.

"Enough bullshit," she said, jabbing a finger in Rhett's face. "I know you didn't get mugged. Tell me what's going on."

"I can't." Rhett raked a hand through his hair and stumbled toward Tera's couch.

The journalist folded her arms and squinted. "A mission?"

"Yeah."

Tera puffed out her cheeks. "And you let them kick your

ass? I'm disappointed, Zappotis. You've lost your touch. Coffee?"

"It's late," Rhett protested, glancing toward the darkened window.

"It is, but you're not going to sleep anyway. I know you." Tera hovered by the front door. "What are the odds you were followed?"

"Low," Rhett said. "But not zero."

"Ha, as if they're ever zero." Tera disappeared into the kitchen and clattered around for a few minutes, giving Rhett time to gather his thoughts. He owed Tera an explanation, but more importantly, he needed help. Help from someone he could trust. Explaining his plan without revealing too much promised to be almost as difficult as speaking to the Oraculum, and he'd made a shitshow of that.

Tera returned with a tray carrying two cups of coffee, sugar, a pot of cream, and two tumblers of potent spirits. She passed over the liquor first and raised the glass in a toast. They drank together. Rhett's throat burned as he set his tumbler back on the tray, but the resulting heat in his belly was more than worth it.

"So," Tera said, "you called me rather than just approaching the embassy yourself, which means you've either stepped in shit so potent even the government can smell it, or you need intel. Which is it?"

"Mostly the latter." Rhett accepted the small cup of piping-hot brew and let it warm his fingers as he considered his next words. "I'm not working for the government now. I've gone private."

"Oof. That's no good, not if they've turned on you."

"It's not like that. I've landed myself in some hot water, but the real problem doesn't have a face."

Tera's brow wrinkled. "Explain."

Rhett closed his eyes. "This is big, Tera. I don't want to drag you into it. There are some dangerous people out there with secrets they would kill to keep. I don't know who they are, but they have long arms and deep pockets."

A smile flashed across Tera's face. "What do you mean? Like the Illuminati?"

"Something like that."

"Interesting. And if I can give you a lead, how will you know it's the right one?"

Rhett mulled that over before admitting, "I'm running on instinct mostly, I'm afraid. I've only ever met one member of this organization, and I don't even know his name."

"Can you narrow it down for me?" Tera waved her hand in a lazy circle. "A country? A territory?"

Rhett shook his head. He set his cup of coffee back on the low table, untouched. "It's likely a global network. Small, but powerful. Maybe interested in acquiring antiquities."

Tera nibbled her bottom lip as her eyes unfocused, combing the depths of her memory. Rhett waited, holding his breath in anticipation. If anyone outside of ENIGMA, but within Rhett's wider circle, were to know anything about the Hand of the Sun, it would be Tera.

"Antiquities," Tera murmured. "I wonder... have you ever heard of Gold Bar Holdings?"

Rhett shook his head. "The name doesn't tell me much."

"That's the point," Tera said, warming to her subject. "I've looked into them before, but finding any information is tricky. It's all very smoke and mirrors. On the surface, it's a conglomerate of smaller brands that they've bought up over the years. Cheap garment companies based in China, paper products in Brazil, programming startups in Indonesia. Random things, almost. But I've been watching them, because even if the companies themselves seem random, the places they're located aren't."

"What do you mean?"

A blush rose in Tera's cheeks. "This is going to sound a lot like a conspiracy theory," she warned.

Rhett snorted. "Trust me, I'm deep in the weirdness. Give me what you've got."

"There's a definite pattern. Wherever Gold Bar Holdings has a foothold, things go south shortly thereafter. Not in a big way, nothing extreme, but the usual stuff. Civil unrest. Other projects start to quietly shut down. Things go missing. People, too. That's why it came to my attention, actually. A contact of mine in Bandung told me that he was going to look into Gold Bar's dealings with a local tea plantation, and he disappeared. When I looked into it, the plantation he told me about was closed. Scrubbed from any records I could find. There was a bill of sale for the land, linked to a shell corporation affiliated with Gold Bar. Crates being shipped out with no labels. A whole hillside stripped away like a mining site. But no tea."

Rhett scratched his neck as the skin along his spine prickled. Maybe it was nothing. But...

"I've been tracking them for a couple of years, but I haven't found anything definitive," Tera went on. "People who go miss-

ing, research sites that lose funding, civil unrest and archaeo-
logical sites that close. Every time I brush up against them, I
think of the Germans stealing the head of Nefertiti, packing it
in mud brick and greasing a few palms so that the guards will
look the other way. There's a lucrative market for that sort of
thing."

"Do you have proof that they're selling things off?"

Tera lifted her hands. "Me? No. And I'm not sticking my
neck out here."

Rhett's bark of laughter echoed through the apartment. "Is
this the same Tera who I once saw walk through a live mine-
field?" he asked.

There was no mirth in the journalist's expression. "This is a
whole different world, Zappotis. None of the men we faced
down in Yemen can reach me here, and if they did try, they'd
leave a trail. A company like Gold Bar could make me disappear. And not just me, either."

A lump formed in Rhett's throat as he nodded. Tera had a
point. If Gold Bar really was run by the Hand, they could do a
lot worse than kill a person. With the right relics, they could
make whatever remained of his life a living hell.

"You're having second thoughts," Tera observed.

Rhett bit the inside of his cheek. After what he'd done to
Apollo, and that note he'd received in Reclamation, he was
already square in the Hand's sights. The danger wouldn't go
away if he buried his head in the sand. This was his best chance
to get on the Hand's good side. If he failed—

He couldn't think about that.

"I'm in deep," he murmured. "If you want to throw me out

on my ass and protect yourself, I understand. This isn't your fight."

"Maybe not." The grin that stole over Tera's innocent face transformed her into something wild and feral. "But if I do help you, do you promise to give me the inside scoop?"

"Gunning for another Schork Award, I take it?" Rhett held up a fist. "I'll pass along anything I can."

"Good enough." Tera tapped her knuckles against Rhett's, then reached for her laptop. "I'll tell you what I can. Gold Bar headquarters is in London, as you might expect. I can give you the address."

She was still talking when she opened the offline document she was working in, which included dozens of notes, as well as photographs, maps, and blurry snapshots of locations. Tera scrolled down through the document in search of something until Rhett gripped her arm.

"Wait," he said. "Go back up."

Tera scrolled up a little. "How far?"

"Back to the photo of—*stop!*" Rhett's fingers tightened on her friend's arm. "Oh my God. That's him."

"Him who?" Tera asked.

A photograph of a handsome man with thick black hair, heavy brows, and dark, piercing eyes smiled out at her. He was wearing a suit that was obviously tailor-made, a dusting of black stubble covered his strong jaw, and his posture spoke of confidence and long hours at the gym. If he'd popped up on a Google search three months ago, Rhett would have done a double-take. He was good-looking. Model handsome, posing like an up-and-coming businessman or a Gucci advertisement.

Emilio Brais Sambueza, read the caption beneath his photo.

"Who is he to Gold Bar?" Rhett asked.

"On paper? No one. His father owned a company outside Barcelona that manufactured electrical components. One of Gold Bar's subsidiaries bought it up a few years ago for a few billion Euro. Emilio went missing a couple of months later. I assumed he was dead."

"He's not dead," Rhett muttered. *Not unless his little tumble through the seam finished the job.*

He'd seen Emilio Sambueza only a few months ago. At the time, however, he'd known him as Agent Apollo.

15 FABIEN

IF ONLY THE automaton would stop bashing itself against the door for a minute, maybe Fabien could think clearly. He wasn't holding his breath; the beast's relentless hammering rattled through him with each impact. He was losing ground, too. The blood pooling down his leg and into the treads of one boot caused him to slip a little further with each blow.

The weapons he was carrying on his person wouldn't do much good against an android. Every swallow reminded him of the way Annamaria had pinned him with that polearm in the hall; *that* might have helped, but it was outside, and there were no similar weapons in the little display room where he found himself.

Cups, trinkets, whistles, jewels... none of the objects locked in with him were familiar enough to be useful. He could have asked Finder, except that his tablet was in the bag, and the bag was in the hall, and the tablet had probably been destroyed when the bag was mauled off of him.

Go with what you know, Fabien thought. He twisted around to bolt the door shut behind him.

The automaton had paused its attack for a few seconds, and Fabien used the respite to fling himself forward, putting as much distance between himself and the door as possible. He twisted as he went, landing on his butt with his back to the display case where the Holy Grail was housed. He fumbled with his rifle, setting it to the laser output.

One breath. Two. What Fabien did best was shoot to kill, and he was going to do his damnedest to take the beast out of commission.

Despite its relentless attacks before, the automaton was oddly silent. Maybe it had followed Annamaria now that she was out of range. He lay there, trying to catch his breath, wondering what his next move would be if the dog really *was* gone.

It was then that he realized that the door was smoking.

He blinked at the small gray plume issuing from the wood. It was about the height of where his head would have been if he hadn't moved.

The longer he sat there, the more smoke issued from the door, leaving a black smudge on the wood in its wake. By the time he realized what was happening, it was already too late. The dog slammed into the door one last time, with such force that the whole entrance collapsed inward. It hit the floor with a mighty smash that sent little motes of dust and plaster flying. The beast's smoldering eyes were aimed upward, sending pinpoint-accurate beams of red light in their wake. They were still aimed high, so instead of searing their way through Fabien's flesh, they struck the glass of the cabinet door above his head.

The reflection was thrown back into the dog's eyes, and the beast winced, shaking its head. Even that brief moment of contact was enough to melt a small section of glass, which dripped down toward his shoulders.

Shit. Fabien didn't have time to push away from the door before the thin trickle of molten glass seared a hole in the back of his shirt. He couldn't risk getting hit by those beams. If they could melt glass...well, he'd seen what the Hand's weapons could do to human flesh.

Instead of flinching away, he took the shot that he'd lined up while he waited.

Only he hadn't set the gun to laser fire after all. Perhaps it was because his hand was shaky with blood loss. Perhaps the magnets in his gloves had messed with the settings. For whatever reason, instead of launching return fire, the barrel issued a live round.

His aim was perfect, so it shouldn't have mattered. With a regular rifle, it *wouldn't* have mattered. But the smart-targeting rounds were designed to fire on a living target, and the automaton wasn't alive.

Fabien realized his mistake and rolled sideways just as the glass front of the cabinet exploded in a shower of tempered shards. He swore as the dog pounced, and adjusted the settings. This time, when he fired a laser round, he hit the android squarely in one eye.

It let out a surprisingly realistic yelp and fell back a pace, shaking its head as if in pain. The beast's metal casing was undamaged, but the eye he'd hit had gone dark.

"Ha!" Fabien sat up amid the rubble. "That'll teach you, *tête-de-nœud!* That'll teach you to—"

If he'd injured a living thing, it would have taken a moment to regroup. The android, however, was barely deterred by the damage. It bared its razor teeth and charged again. Fabien squawked and tried to push himself to his feet, but he slipped, and ended up with a thigh wound full of tempered glass fragments for the trouble. This time he rolled *toward* the display case, slipping between the shelves and the supports.

The cases in Reclamation were made of sturdy metal. Annamaria, however, had preferred to display her collection of relics in beautiful, antique wooden pieces that were works of art in their own right. All the animatronic dog had to do to get to him was slide between the shelves and force its way upright. The wood splintered, and the few relics that hadn't already toppled came crashing down against its back.

Fabien kicked out with his boot and slammed the dog's nose away. His timing, however, left something to be desired; the dog's teeth closed around the thick sole of his boot, and it lunged backward, dragging Fabien through the broken glass and dislodged relics. He grabbed at the broken struts of the furniture and succeeded only in overbalancing it, but it fell the wrong way. The dog growled and shook its head. The razor-filled mouth tore Fabien's sole to ribbons. He clawed at the carpeting, then the slick, cool tiles of the villa.

The dog pulled him almost to the door before it released his mangled boot. Fabien managed to roll onto his back at last and aimed his rifle directly into the beast's one good eye.

The eye lit up.

He pulled the trigger.

His shot connected before the dog could sear him alive. It must have tried to activate its eye just as he fired, because the resulting explosion sent a shower of electrical sparks bursting out of the dog's metal casing like an American fireworks show. The dog reeled and shuddered, whipping its damaged head back and forth.

In the time it took to regroup, Fabien rolled past it. Clearly, shooting it in the head—*twice*—wasn't going to be enough to bring it down. He'd need something a little more effective, and he needed to figure it out fast, before Annamaria could get away.

The polearm with its spiked electric collar lay abandoned in the hallway. Fabien scooped it up and rounded on the dog. It was whining and scratching at its face with one metal paw.

It can't see me, right? he thought. *No eyes. I have the advantage.* He plunged forward with the collar aimed right at the dog's neck.

He'd been wrong about the eyes. Maybe its hearing was on-par with that of a living dog; maybe the limitations of biology had been rectified in its design. Either way, it didn't need eyes to see him. It dodged his attack, aided by Fabien's compromised balance. Between his shredded boot and the wound in his leg, he wasn't at his fighting best.

The dog growled and backed away. He caught a flash of the company name and logo, *SyberHund*, before the panel on its back peeled away and a nine-chambered rotary cannon rose up from its back.

"Oh, come *on*," Fabien groaned.

He fell to his knees as the cannon opened fire and the stone wall above his head exploded.

The longer this goes on, the less strength you'll have. This damn thing can go forever. It'll wear you down. You need to move. Move. NOW.

A scream of wordless rage ripped out of him as he threw his weight forward in a clumsy somersault. He was carrying too many weapons for the movement to be smooth, but it got him where he needed to go: close enough to the dog to jam the prongs of the metal collar up under its jaw and force its head upward into the line of its own fire. The dog's claws raked at empty air as it was lifted upward. Fabien leveraged his own weight until the mechanical beast was pinned upright against the wall, its back paws scrabbling at the ground as it tried to get to him.

He wedged the handle of the polearm against his side and used the stones for support as he tried to figure out the mechanism in the handle. His hands were coated in a sticky mixture of his own sweat and blood. It took three tries for him to twist the handle and send a jolt of electricity through the SyberHund.

The dog's limbs stiffened at the jolt, and its writhing became even more frantic. An electrical buzz, like a fuse about to blow, filled the air around it. Popping sounds and blooms of white sparks sprang outward from its metal shell.

Eventually, the polearm shorted out, and the dog fell slack. Its metal limbs twitched a few times before falling still entirely.

Fabien let it slide sideways. Once it hit the ground, it didn't move again.

He lay on his back, panting, beneath the beams that supported the villa's ceiling, and took stock of the damage to his person. One of his gloves was missing, and his balaclava had been lost somewhere in the fight. The muscles in his back and shoulders ached, but the most upsetting damage was to his leg. Leg wounds like that could be dangerous. He'd seen people bleed out from a badly-placed wound.

But you're not dead yet, he told himself, *so you'd better get to Annamaria Vizzini before she finds a way to finish what she started.*

He rolled onto his belly with a groan and took a moment to get his feet under him. On his few visits home, his parents and grandparents had waxed endlessly poetic about the troubles with getting old. He'd rolled his eyes at their complaints, but he couldn't help thinking, *This wouldn't have slowed me down so much five years ago. I've lost more blood than this and kept moving.*

Which maybe said more about his lifestyle choices than the murmurings of his grandparents, but whatever.

He collected his rifles and recovered his damaged backpack. He pulled the tablet out and powered on the screen. "Finder, can you help me?"

The light came on, showing the various apps available for his use, including the still-active map, but the speakers stayed dead. Several large cracks spiderwebbed their way across the screen, although it was still responsive enough to tab through the apps when he tapped them.

"Finder?" he repeated.

Nothing.

With a quiet curse, he thrust the tablet back into the inner pocket of his pack. He was about to take off down the hall when the goblet lying on the floor amid the wreckage of Annamaria's collection caught his eye.

The Grail.

And sure, maybe it was just an old cup with a codename that made it sound more important than it really was. But there were dozens of portraits in the dining room of the villa that raised questions, at the very least.

Just in case, he scooped it up and dropped it into his bag before limping down the hall in the opposite direction from which he'd come. This was the direction that he'd heard Annamaria's footsteps fade when she fled.

The wounds on his neck throbbed, but Fabien pressed on. He tried the handle of every door that he passed, but the rooms on the other side were still and quiet, with no sign of the Hand agent. He looked back only once and grimaced at the trail of blood he'd left in his wake. If the police ever looked into this, his DNA would be *everywhere*.

If the Hand acted fast enough, no doubt they could use his blood for all sorts of nefarious purposes.

He was almost to the end of the hall when he passed an open door leading out to the side of the villa. A strange low thrum came from outside, like the whine of a jet engine layered over the pulse of helicopter blades. The sound was accompanied by a resonant pressure that echoed in Fabien's chest.

It was a motorbike unlike any that Fabien had seen before.

Instead of wheels beneath the frame, there was only empty air, disrupted by the subtle shimmer of heat rising off of tarmac on a summer day. In the seat was a woman dressed all in black. A helmet with a tinted visor covered her head and obscured her face, but he was sure it was her.

Annamaria drove the heel of her boot against the bar on the side of the bike, and it zipped away almost impossibly fast, and with barely a sound.

Fabien tilted sideways and caught himself on the doorframe. "*Putain de merde*," he muttered to himself. How was he ever going to catch up with her?

Then his eyes landed on the second bike she'd been forced to leave behind.

16 DINAH

"OW!" Dinah yelped.

The gray-furred female Didelian that had been rubbing ointment into her bite wound looked up at her with a frown.

"Sorry," she mumbled, knowing full well the creature couldn't understand her. She'd had to remove her helmet in order to peel off the suit, so the translation feature was unavailable for the moment. Fortunately, given that they were on another Earth, the only problem with the air was the faint but constant smell of wet fur that accompanied the Didelians everywhere. It was perfectly breathable.

Finder, on the other hand, didn't need the suit at all. The android had set its undamaged suit aside for Dinah's use once her wounds were covered and treated, and was busy chatting with the small group of locals who inhabited the little camp where Nibbles had brought them.

She had, at least, managed to work out that 'Nibbles' wasn't their guide's real name. He had been reluctant to reveal his true identity—not that it would have meant anything to Dinah, but when he'd said this, he'd gotten a sidelong look from their rescuer.

You're both Travelers, Nibbles had said, and left it at that. Apparently, Apollo had made as much of an impression on the population of this new Earth as on the old one.

Dinah sat still until her host's ministrations were complete. The salve she'd smeared on the wounds tingled slightly, and was unpleasantly sticky, but it numbed the pain of the bite. The suit had withstood the scratches on her back and protected her skin from anything but the lightest abrasions, although the silver material had been torn to ribbons in the process.

She was examining the thin, breathable bandage, more like spider silk than gauze, when Finder dropped down next to her with a bowl in one hand.

"This is really fascinating," the android exclaimed. "They offered to feed me, but you know how it is... can't eat anything. Don't have a mouth. It's a real shame, but look." It held out the bowl toward Dinah. "You can sample the local cuisine, and then you can tell me all about it!"

Dinah peered down into the bowl, and her stomach heaved. She had eaten bugs before. Her officemate had gone on a kick in which she'd insisted that crickets were the food of the future, and had bullied her into trying all sorts of cricket-based snack foods for a six-month period shortly after she was hired to the history department. At the time, she'd thought it was some sort of hazing ritual, even as she knew that insects had always been an important part of human diets over the years. Lots of Westerners turned up their noses at insects and then happily dug into lobster or crab.

So yes, Dinah was familiar with eating bugs. But there was a difference between eating a fried mealworm and... whatever was in that bowl.

"Are those—" She swallowed hard and pressed the back of her hand to her mouth. "*Ticks?*"

"I don't think so." Finder shook the bowl a few times, and the plump, purple insects within shifted, waving their tiny legs in dismay. "I've never heard of a tick that big, have you? They're like grapes! And I'm told they're very nutritious."

Dinah tried to imagine popping one of the plump bodies into her mouth. The Didelian who had applied her bandages nodded her head encouragingly and said something to her in her squeaky native tongue.

"High in protein," Finder urged.

"I... I can't." Dinah shook her head. "Not raw."

Finder translated, and the bowl was taken away. There might come a point where Dinah would be hungry enough to stomach the offering, but she wasn't that desperate yet.

"What are we waiting for?" she asked Finder. "Are we their prisoners now? What's happening?"

"Apparently, we're waiting for someone." Finder leaned back, perfectly at ease, and crossed its ankles. "Someone very important. I'm not entirely clear on the details, but I think it might be some sort of elder or spiritual leader. Someone who will decide what to do with us. Mr. Nibbles admitted that they aren't sure what to make of us here. It sounds as if they're familiar with ENIGMA, or a sort of proto-ENIGMA from a very long time ago. It's strange to imagine that there are living organic beings that serve as knowledge repositories, just like I do." The android hummed and looked up at the ceiling above them, tapping its toes in time to some internal metronome.

It was obvious why Nibbles had called this 'the underground.' They had never left the subterranean river, and the rough-and-tumble encampment wasn't far from the water. The residents lived in paneled huts that could easily be dismantled and carried away. Everything about the setup spoke of impermanence, even the portable light fixtures that illuminated their seating area. Dinah was perched on a repurposed shipping crate of some sort, into which belongings could be packed when the time came to move on and find a new home base.

"Have you made contact with the mainframe?" Dinah asked. "Is there any word on Rhett or Fabien?"

Finder turned its head sharply to avoid meeting her eyes.

The healer returned with the bowl she'd taken, and held it out to Dinah for inspection. The insects were still inside, but they'd been cut in half and fried with some sort of aromatic herb that reminded Dinah of basil but was entirely the wrong color.

"I think you'd better at least give it a try," Finder said, still looking everywhere but at Dinah. "She might be offended otherwise."

Dinah took the bowl. "Tell her I said thank you. Do you know her name?"

A brief conversation ensued before Finder said, "You can call her Karen."

Dinah's head whipped up from the bowl. "...*Karen?*"

"Apparently it has a very specific meaning in Didelian!" Finder said, lifting its hands in self-defense.

"Right, I... right." Dinah's eye was twitching, but she tried to ignore it. "Thank you, Karen. I can't wait to try these." She wasn't sure what the insects had been mixed with, but at some point she seemed to have stepped outside of her own body, and was watching her own actions from afar with a sort of remote dispassion that might earn her a trip to the ENIGMA medic if she wasn't so very far away from home. She forced a spoonful of the dish into her mouth, and surprisingly found it pleasant enough, if she didn't think too hard about its contents.

While she ate, she let her mind wander along the topic of alternate realities. She'd always thought of the butterfly effect as something that would change the world forever onto an entirely new track, but judging by what she'd seen so far, the Didelian world wasn't entirely different from her own. Some elements had diverged wildly from her Earth, while others were shockingly familiar. Perhaps it was a coincidence.

Or perhaps something made it that way. After all, if the Didelians had a word for people who were visiting from another reality, they couldn't have existed in total isolation. And someone had made the destabilizer...

"Finder—" Dinah began.

The android flinched. "If you're going to ask me about the mainframe, please don't. There's nothing I can do about it now."

Dinah lowered another spoonful of the unmentionable soup into her mouth. "What do you mean?"

Finder shuddered. "It really doesn't bear thinking about."

"What doesn't?" Dinah demanded.

Finder folded in on itself, cradling its metal head in its hands. "You were asking me earlier about all my miscalculations, and why the other unit was struggling to control the Gravitas Engine? I think... I think there may be something wrong with the software." The android sniffed. "With *my* software."

The hand holding the bowl began to shake, and the metal spoon rattled against its side. Dinah took a deep breath. "You didn't mention this before."

"I didn't want to worry you," Finder said. "But I've been thinking about it, and something was off when I linked back to the mainframe before we left. I've been running background processes ever since we arrived, and I've identified several changes to my coding."

Dinah sucked in a breath. "Errors?"

"They appear to be deliberate alterations." Finder squirmed under her scrutiny. "Do you recall mentioning that we found it just a touch too easy to retrieve the destabilizer from inventory? I don't think that was by accident."

Doing her utmost to remain calm, Dinah set her bowl aside. Panicking wouldn't help either of them, but if Finder was right, that could mean that Reclamation was in deep trouble. She, Rhett, and Fabien were on missions, and were heavily reliant on Finder's assistance. If Finder was compromised, they could all be completely stranded.

And Reclamation was left with a skeleton crew, surrounded by erratic androids, with a traitor in their midst.

She pressed her shaking fingers to her lips and breathed deep: once, twice, thrice. When she spoke again, she managed to sound convincingly like a woman who wasn't in the midst of a full-scale panic attack. "Is there a way you can check in? Or warn Porter?"

"Doing so would mean reconnecting to the mainframe," Finder said. "Right now, I'm essentially an independent process. Sharing data with the mainframe could result in my programming becoming further compromised." The android's pixelated eyes brimmed with digital tears. "It's like being sick at the same time that my parent is sick, and knowing that they're much worse off than I am. If I pop in to see how the main database is doing, I could go from having a head cold to being..." Its voice petered off before it added, "Converted. Or worse, what if I reached out and there was nothing left of the mainframe at all?"

She had no idea what to say, so Dinah settled for reaching out and patting the android's shoulder. She didn't know what words of comfort might be helpful under the circumstances, and even if she had, she was feeling a bit selfish at the moment. If something dreadful happened to Finder, or to Reclamation as a whole, she might be stuck on an alien world forever.

Or worse.

She and Finder were both wallowing in their combined misery when two Didelians approached. One was recognizable as Nibbles; the other was the oldest of its species that Dinah had yet encountered. It sat in a hoverchair that rode as smoothly over the rough ground as the hoverboat had ridden over the water. *Guess they've moved on from the wheel,* Dinah thought.

"Travelers." The aged Didelian lifted one stumpy paw in greeting as Finder translated his chittering speech. His nails were cracked and worn, and there was a rheumy mist to his eyes that suggested he was at least partly blind. "I never thought I would live to see the day..."

"One moment," Dinah said. She reached for her helmet and set it over her head; even without sealing it onto the suit, the translation function worked, and she could understand the elder's speech.

Nibbles approached Dinah's side and pointed to the bowl. "You gonna finish that?" he asked.

Dinah shook her head and watched in mute discomfort as Nibbles began spooning the stewed insects into his mouth. After a moment, she returned her attention to the elder, who was watching her just intently enough that she was sure he wasn't entirely blind.

"Sorry," Dinah said, tripping over her own tongue. "You were saying?"

"I have heard stories of your kind." He held out his paws and reached for Dinah's arm. "May I?"

Dinah held out her hand at once, and the elder took her hand, tracing those worn claws over her forearm skin. "Fascinating... Nearly hairless, but that you can be from one of our sister-Earths there can be no doubt." He released Dinah's hand and settled back in his chair. A handful of onlookers had gathered around the open portion of the camp, watching the exchange with glittering eyes and raised ears. Even the youngest of them listened to the elder with quiet reverence.

"You know, I assume," the elder went on, "that there are many Earths with many divergent paths. Some were friendly, in the old days, when Travelers came through more often. Others arrived with ill intent. Some were like us, while others..." The elder's mouth twisted into a wry smile. "Others were as different as can be imagined. But we were kin, all of us, after a fashion."

Dinah rubbed her wrist self-consciously. The elder's words were calm and kind, but she had trouble imagining that most humans would feel the same way. Hell, they could barely get along with members of their own species most of the time.

Instead of voicing these concerns aloud—no point in suggesting that the Didelians turn on her, after all—she asked, "Do you remember the last time Travelers visited?"

The elder stared at her for a long moment in utter silence, so long that Dinah began to wriggle and squirm under the old creature's intense gaze. His black lips twitched, and he let out a bark of laughter. The laughter grew into a high, keening howl, and he used his dulled claws to wipe tears from his eyes.

"Remember?" he asked. "Oh, Traveler, that was so very long ago. It has been many lifetimes since the last visit... and from what I understand, the ones who visited us then were not of your particular kind. No, I'm afraid we have not met Travelers in living memory. Some believe they never came at all. But we have proof now, don't we?" He sat forward in his hoverchair with newfound excitement. "I am very excited to meet you, yes. But I am afraid we also have a shared problem."

"Apollo?" Dinah guessed.

"Apollo?" The elder cocked his head. "The other Traveler, you mean. Yes, he is a problem. He has emboldened those who seek power through cruel and selfish means. From what I've heard, they plan to move against us, to take total control of the fractured city and then the world at large."

Dinah blinked at him. "But... why?" Perhaps that was a foolish question; men like Agent Apollo wanted power, and taking control of an alien world must be appealing in its own right, but Dinah couldn't see the point. This couldn't have been Apollo's plan all along, surely? To take control of a world full of —no offense to Nibbles and his friends—hip-high rodents, with what appeared to be a damaged atmosphere?

It was Nibbles and not the elder who answered. The younger Didelian tipped his bowl to his lips and slurped down the last of the insects before wiping his mouth on the back of his paw. "As a launchpad," he said.

Dinah looked from Nibbles to the elder in confusion.

"You've got launchpads on your Earth, yeah?" The young warrior hopped to his feet, set the empty bowl aside, and began to pace. "I've been getting reports from the inside and inter-cepting messages, listening when I can, and from what I gather, Apollo's interest in taking over our world is little more than a passing fancy. We don't have a force here that can stand up to him. Since the city fractured, we've been scrambling to survive. Didn't have a ruling faction or anything like that, just a bunch of us doing our best to preserve the world we were left. Most of us were just happy to be aboveground and have something like a future ahead of us, but Callic and his lot... well, they don't think there's much left around here to save." Nibbles waved a paw at their little encampment. "They want more, like in the old days, and look where that got us. But Apollo is promising something more."

Dinah blinked at him. "He wants them to help him invade Earth? My Earth, I mean?"

"*Our* Earth," Finder corrected.

Nibbles wrinkled his long snout. "You think he'll be satisfied with that? Have you managed to keep your Earth in perfectly good health? Respected all the biomes, have you? Taken good care of all your fellow species?"

"Er..." Dinah bit her bottom lip and glanced around at the other Didelians, who were still watching their conversations as if entranced. "Not all of them."

Her self-consciousness was swept away as the implications of Nibbles' words washed over her. The Hand of the Sun had been doing its damnedest to acquire the disruptor: not because it was trying to gain an advantage back home, but because it wanted to expand. ENIGMA's goals were modest: protect the history and cultural significance that the relics in their care represented. Maintain something like balance. Porter and his ilk saw all that power and were content to lock it away behind glass for safekeeping. Fabien, and even Dinah herself, had questioned the wisdom of such an act, but quite suddenly she was able to picture hundreds upon hundreds of mirror universes fanned out before her like a deck of cards. *Pick one...*

And hadn't she just been thinking that humanity barely had its collective shit together? What would any government on Earth do if it had access to every other alternate reality? How many wars would be waged across such a multiverse in the quest for more wealth, more power, more resources...

And even worse, what would the Hand do with all that opportunity, given the chance.

"Oh, God." Dinah leaned forward, cradling her head in her hands as the stew she'd so recently eaten threatened to make a second appearance. "That was their plan all along. And now the Hand has got a mole in Reclamation, which means that they practically own the destabilizer."

"Oh, dear." Given that it was made of metal, Finder couldn't manage to go pale as it, too, calculated the danger of their predicament. Its dismay, however, was obvious, not the least because of the way it wrung its hands. "Oh, curses. We really should report this to Porter."

An hour ago, this would have seemed perfectly feasible, but given what Dinah now knew about the mainframe, things were looking worse by the moment. "Is there a way to get a message back to ENIGMA?" she asked hopefully. "Maybe not by contacting the mainframe directly, but through some other means? Email? Text? Surely you can hack a satellite or something."

"Not from here," Finder said. "I could do that back home in a matter of moments, but I'm afraid I'm not *exactly* in range. The only way I can contact our Earth would be to go through the mainframe. Which I can, of course, but I would open myself up to possible infection."

Dinah held her hands up at once. "Don't do that." The only thing worse than being stranded on an alien Earth would be finding herself stranded alone. Or, worse still, with an android that was suddenly operating at the Hand's behest. "We'll have to find another way." After a moment's hesitation, she turned to the elder. "Is there another way?"

The elder's clouded eyes crinkled at the corners with the ghost of a smile. "Our options are limited, I'm afraid, but there is one way that I know, one thing that might be helpful to you."

His ears twitched, and he extended one trembling arm to point at the uneven stones below them. "Do you see that?"

Dinah looked down at the ground. The walkway lining the underground river looked more or less like old cobbles whose faces had succumbed to frost heave. In between the bricks grew what looked like moss, although it was more yellow than green. Little red tongues licked up from its carpeted surface as if they were tasting the air.

"Moss?" she asked, somewhat skeptically.

"Moss finds a way," the elder said.

Dinah had gotten so used to the silence of the onlookers that when they echoed, in eerie tandem, "Moss finds a way," she nearly jumped out of her skin.

"That is the name I have chosen for myself," the elder said. "Moss. It is of great significance to our people, regardless of whatever creed we ascribe to. And this is the promise that I make you, the oath of the underground—if you have a need, Traveler, we bring it to fruition, so long as our interests align."

"Oh, um." Dinah fidgeted on the spot. "Thank you, Elder Moss."

"According to the old stories," Elder Moss said grandly, spreading his hands wide and turning his face toward the sky, obscured though it was by the arc of the tunnel above them, "the Didelians of old possessed a sacred stone, one so unique in its chemical composition that it was never truly separated from itself. Its vibrations could transcend space, even theoretical space. Using this stone, Travelers could speak between the universes as easily and readily as if they stood side-by-side. No such stone belonged to us—"

"But that Apollo fellow has one," Nibbles grumbled.

"A sacred stone?" Dinah sucked in a breath. "It's true, Apollo had a resonance stone. And a lot of other stuff, too, that fell through the seam with him when he arrived."

"I know." Nibbles crossed his arms and twitched his whiskers a few times. "That's how we met the first time, if you recall. I got my paws on the stone, but after we connected, I didn't want to touch it again." He shook himself, and the fur that wasn't contained within the confines of his clothes fluffed up and stood on end. "Perhaps I should have taken it, just so that he couldn't use it again, but I was afraid." He shot a guilty glance toward the elder. "I'm not used to any of this."

"It's all right, pup." The elder's head bobbed back and forth on his shoulders. "We are all out of our depth. Besides, we weren't ready to reveal ourselves, and if we'd taken the sacred stone, we would have risked giving away our true intentions."

"Oh, dear," Finder murmured again.

Dinah pivoted toward the android. "What? Did something happen? Did you find more system errors?"

"No." The android unfastened a panel in its stomach to reveal a small cavity, inside of which rested a familiar object: the resonance stone in its mounting plate, propped in place with metal pins. "I may have, ah, lifted it during the skirmish. But if I wasn't supposed to—"

The elder sat forward. "I think you've given away your presence quite effectively," he said in the same gentle tone he'd used to assure Nibbles. "Now is the time to act. This agent of chaos is cut off from his allies at home, and we know where to find him."

"That's right, Travelers." Nibbles stood a little straighter and crossed his arms. "No time like the present. What's your plan?"

Dinah was keenly aware that everyone was looking at her, and her brain had chosen a most unfortunate time to short-circuit. What was she supposed to say? That she didn't have the faintest beginnings of a plan? That she was much more concerned with her own predicament?

Apollo was building an army. All Dinah had was an android with software trouble, a small troupe of ragged allies who only sort of trusted her, and a magic rock that would only let her contact one person on her Earth.

The person who had turned against her and her friends. The one person, in short, that she absolutely could not trust.

She remembered Lane throwing herself on the destabilizer just before the seam closed. *Shit, shit, shit.* She might be the only honest member of ENIGMA that knew what was going on, and there was no way to share what she'd learned. No way to call for backup.

She needed a damn plan.

After a few shaky moments, she reached up to wipe the sheen of sweat off of her forehead, only for her hand to meet the glass dome of her helmet. It thumped to an abrupt halt.

"Dr. Bray?" Finder hissed. "Are you all right?"

Dinah kept staring at her hand, and the dome that protected her face. The dome. Like the dome that covered the fractured city.

"I'm fine," she said. "Nibbles, you said that you can get close enough to Apollo to spy on him. Is he still in the city?"

"Last I checked. He's been using Callic's warehouse as a home base." Nibbles cocked his head. "Why?"

"If we get him and his crew out of the dome, do you think the underground can take the city back?"

Nibbles scratched his chin thoughtfully. "Maybe. At the very least, we could divide up his forces. But good luck getting him to leave. It's dangerous outside the dome. There are other... things out there."

"Yeah." Dinah said. "To lure him anywhere, we'd probably need some pretty good bait."

17 RHETT

RHETT HELD up the Canadian passport that Tera had procured for him and plastered a smile on his face. The photo was real enough, even if the rest of the information on it was fabricated. His borrowed name was Ioannis Stamatopoulos, although Rhett didn't know if there really was a Ioannis Stamatopoulos living in Toronto or not.

The dead-eyed agent behind the counter plucked the paperwork from his fingers. "Welcome to the UK," the younger woman droned. "Please state the purpose of your visit."

"Business," Rhett said. He leaned on the counter, subtly taking the weight off his throbbing leg. Between his little stunt in Valhalla and the cramped plane seat he'd just escaped, his body was furious at him. He would have liked to use his cane, but he'd tucked it into his checked bag, and he was keenly aware that there could be, and likely were, hostile eyes on him at all times. Maybe it was paranoid to think that the Hand was always watching, but he hadn't been able to shake the sense of unease that had descended on him last night as he and Tera pored over the journalist's research into Gold Bar Holdings.

And now here he was, in London, steeling himself to walk into the spider's web.

Unlike Rhett, the young woman behind the counter didn't have the faintest hint of nerves. She glanced over Rhett's passport, checked his papers, and thumped a stamp against one of the pages. "Good luck, then," she said with total indifference, and waved Rhett through.

It was still early afternoon. Even after his time with ENIGMA, Rhett was impressed by how quickly Tera had managed to pull the necessary strings to make this happen. He'd fallen asleep on his friend's sofa with the laptop's battery almost dead on his lap, and woken to a coffee, fake documents, and a plane ticket to London. He was going to owe Tera for this, big time.

Especially if I'm able to snare Agent Aten before all this is over.

With his small bag in tow, Rhett headed to the airport bathroom to make himself presentable, then headed out of Heathrow in search of a cab. As he went, he felt himself sliding into that old routine, that old rhythm. He'd had plenty of beloved associates on his old assignments, but he'd also had to dive head-first into trouble on more than one occasion. If he let himself think too much, he'd start to question the wisdom of his next move.

This is my best chance to make direct contact with the man in charge of it all, he reminded himself. *So long as ENIGMA*

THE SACRED STONE   205

believes that I'm a traitor, I've got the perfect opportunity. And sure, Porter and his little crew would know better, but Porter had always been ENIGMA's black sheep.

His little slip-up in Valhalla would no doubt set them back, but as he slipped into the back seat of a taxi, Rhett tried to picture the look on Sturlusson's face when he delivered the Hand of the Sun on a silver platter.

That would certainly change his tune.

STANDING on the walkway outside the global headquarters of Gold Bar Holdings, Ltd., Rhett had to admit that he was disappointed. The building itself was nothing remarkable. Its stone edifice boasted the usual mismatched jumble of Greco-Roman features so common in London architecture, but it was blank. Sterile.

Boring.

Not that his first impression of ENIGMA had been much better. At least the abandoned Ohio mall had been intriguing. This building had about as much personality as a bank.

He shook a few painkillers into his palm from the bottle Tera had given him and tossed them back with a swig of the overpriced coffee he'd picked up along the way. The coffee was bitter, and it mingled unpleasantly with the coating of the pills on his too-dry tongue. Thank goodness Tera had thought to acquire a suit in roughly his size. It wasn't tailored, of course, but at least he wasn't strolling into Gold Bar Holdings in his street clothes, or the chameleon suit. That was safely rolled up in his oversized handbag, just in case.

He'd debated the merits of sneaking into the headquarters, but to attempt a mission like that alone and largely unarmed would be a fool's errand. If he was going to make it seem like he was defecting to the Hand of the Sun, better that he should do so in a manner so brazen that the Hand would have no choice but to believe his intent.

Rhett tossed his coffee cup in a nearby bin and mounted the steps of the building.

The lobby was quiet, and just as plain as the entrance. The furniture was respectable and high-end, but not ostentatious. A desk sat against one of the far walls, at which sat a middle-aged woman wearing spectacles and a perfectly tailored pantsuit. She looked up from her computer screen as Rhett approached and offered the sort of close-lipped smile that managed to convey the idea of a greeting rather than any real warmth.

"Good morning," the woman said. "May I help you?"

Rhett answered with a cool smile of his own. "I'm here to see Mr. Rooke."

The woman wrinkled her nose, just for a moment. "Do you have an appointment? I don't believe he's expecting anyone."

"Not as such." Rhett kept the fake smile in place, as if this was nothing unexpected. He and Tera had found Mr. Rooke's information on the company's website, although neither of them had been able to turn up anything useful on social media. Which made sense, if Rooke was who Rhett thought he was. Operating under that assumption, he added, "Mr. Rooke contacted me with an... open-ended offer of employment."

The woman nodded blandly. She was more attentive than the customs agent, but she, too, was looking straight through

Rhett, as though he was of no greater importance than a delivery driver or a janitor. "Your name?"

Rhett hesitated. He could give the fake name on the passport he was carrying, but the Hand wouldn't know that one, so he blurted, "Rhett Zappotis."

"One moment, please." The woman reached manicured fingers toward the landline at the desk beside her and cradled the receiver against her shoulder as she dialed three numbers. There was a brief pause, through which Rhett could just make out the distant shrill of the phone ringing, and then a man's voice, unintelligible to her ears. "Good morning, sir. I have a Rhett Zappotis here to see you?" More mumbling. "He says you've corresponded...?" Her perfectly manicured eyebrows rose as she watched Rhett's face.

Rhett merely kept smiling.

After a few more seconds, the woman at the counter simply said, "Yes, sir." She set the phone down and offered Rhett a saccharine, sympathetic smile. "I'm afraid that he's not available just now."

"Perhaps I can wait?" Rhett suggested, knowing full well that he was pushing his luck.

"I'm afraid it's not a good day. Mr. Rooke is quite busy."

"Perhaps tomorrow would be better?"

The receptionist's smile had taken on a strained quality. Her keep calm and carry on attitude was clearly wearing thin. "Or perhaps you should reach out to him again via whatever channels by which you were first contacted and schedule an appointment."

To be perfectly honest, he hadn't been expecting that. Rhett had been prepared to walk into a trap, and he'd braced himself to shamelessly lie about his intentions, but he hadn't expected to walk into the Hand's grasp and then be turned away.

Maybe he was wrong about all of it. Twelve hours ago, he'd never heard of Gold Bar. And what were the odds, really, that Tera would be able to cough up the exact information he needed, information that ENIGMA had never managed to get its hands on, despite all of its resources?

The secretary's mouth pulled down into a sympathetic frown. Rhett's stunned expression must have softened her. "Would you like to leave a calling card? Or a phone number?"

"I—" Of course, he had nothing of the sort. Rhett ran his hand through his hair. Short of telling the Hand to give Porter a ring, what more could he say? "No, thank you. I'll speak to our mutual friend."

He turned away, wondering what in the hell he was going to do next. Slip on the jumpsuit and go sneaking around through Gold Bar's offices, just to be sure? Not that he was expecting to find any clues now. At least he had enough money, thanks to Tera, to cover a ticket back to California. He could regroup at Zoe's, and then...

The phone rang again, and the receptionist called out to Rhett, "Mr. Zappotis?"

Rhett stopped in his tracks and looked over his shoulder.

"Mr. Rooke's personal assistant just called. One of his calls was canceled. He has a fifteen-minute opening, if you'd like to speak with him now."

Rhett's throat closed up for a moment before he was able to choke out, "Yes, of course."

"His assistant will meet you at the elevators." The receptionist pointed the way before returning to her work.

On shaky legs, Rhett tottered over to the elevators. There were two of them, and he waited as they descended, watching the numbers shrink as they approached the first floor.

Either the receptionist was an excellent actress, or she was clueless about what was going on. That wasn't surprising. Gold Bar Holdings' stock profile suggested that they did millions of pounds of legitimate business each year, inasmuch as any of their business dealings could be called legitimate. There were no doubt hundreds of people who cashed paychecks from the company each year without knowing what they did abroad, and many more who did know but were unaware of the company's relationship to the Hand.

Assuming he was right.

The first set of elevator door opened, disgorging half a dozen individuals in business suits talking about market rights. They hustled past him without a second glance. He was still watching their departure when the second elevator opened.

The man inside was perhaps in his sixties, or a bit older. His salt-and-pepper hair erred on the side of salt, and his eyes were so shockingly blue that Rhett thought he might be wearing contacts. They were, perhaps, the most remarkable thing about him. Like the Gold Bar Holdings offices themselves, he wouldn't have looked at the man twice under other circumstances.

"Please come in, Mr. Zappotis," he said coolly. Rhett hesitated, just for a moment, and the man smiled at him almost kindly. "Come along. Mr. Rooke is very busy."

"So I've heard," Rhett said thinly. He forced his feet to carry him into the open elevator. "I'm glad he was able to make the time to speak with me."

The assistant folded his hands in front of him as the door slid shut. In the last moments before the door closed behind them, Rhett resisted the urge to bolt back through the door, away from Mr. Rooke and whatever awaited him in the private offices of the company. The doors closed, and the AC kicked on, humming above them despite the cool weather as the elevator jolted to life.

The assistant dipped his head toward him. "My apologies, Captain. I shouldn't have called you mister before. Or are you going by Stamatopoulos now? I can never keep up." The crisp pop of the consonants in his mouth, the rigidly British pronunciation of the borrowed name, made Rhett bristle. How the hell did he know about that already?

"Rhett will do," he said. "And what might I call you? Mr. Rooke, or...?"

He laughed. Only then did Rhett realize that the fluttering in his stomach wasn't just nerves; the elevator wasn't rising, but sinking beneath floor level. "I'm afraid you won't be meeting Mr. Rooke today."

Rhett licked his dry lips. "He offered me work," he said, hating the uncertainty in his tone.

"I very much doubt that, my friend," the man said. "Mr. Rooke is an admirable CEO. Runs things quite smoothly, much better than his predecessor I can assure you, but he's not in the business of hiring staff. He has other people to do that for him."

"People like you?" Rhett guessed.

The man glanced sideways at him and smiled, as if they shared a secret known only to the two of them. "I don't hire for Gold Bar Holdings," he said. "With the singular exception of Mr. Rooke himself."

So much for being an assistant, then. He'd suspected as much.

"To be quite frank," the man went on, "I'm not hiring anywhere else, either. My, ah, social circle is complete. I don't need any more friends than I already have."

Rhett's head spun. "Then why make the offer?" His voice sounded wavering and strange, slightly slurred, as if he'd been drinking.

"I'm afraid I don't know what you mean."

"Aren't you Aten?" he asked.

The whole mission was going poorly, he knew that, but he couldn't seem to pull himself together. When he turned to face the man, he staggered sideways, catching himself against the railing that circled the enclosed space.

"Of course I am," the man said, in a tone that implied he was being quite silly, "but that's beside the point, isn't it? You tried to kill one of my associates. What makes you think I would want to talk with you?"

Rhett fumbled in his pocket for the note, the one he'd found in his quarters, the one from the mole. The one that had gotten him in so much trouble with Sturlusson's people. Still clutching the rail, he held it up between them.

The older man read it, then smiled. "I see. You assumed that one of my people reached out to you? An intriguing idea, Captain, but I'm afraid you've gotten it wrong. In my circles, trust is earned over many years. We are not the same breed of the ragged little militias you're used to working with, no. We're not so easily infiltrated. I don't know who this offer is from, but it's not from me."

The pressure behind Rhett's eyes mounted, and his stomach heaved. *Say something smart*, he scolded, but when he tried to speak, he ended up heaving a thin trickle of the coffee from that morning onto the toes of his borrowed shoes.

That damned AC. It wasn't pumping cool air; it was pumping some sort of gas into the elevator, and for some reason it was only affecting him.

He lunged for the man, but instead of crashing into him, he passed through, tripping over something small at his feet and landing in a pathetic heap on the floor. Aten flickered for a moment, just long enough for Rhett to realize that what he'd stumbled over was a small black puck.

A hologram projector.

No wonder the nerve gas, or whatever was flooding the elevator, hadn't affected him.

As Rhett choked and sputtered, clawing at his collar, the image of Aten crouched down beside him. "See you soon," he told him. "I look forward to meeting you in person."

Rhett's eyes fluttered shut and failed to open again.

18 FABIEN

FABIEN HAD RIDDEN A MOPED BEFORE, and even a proper motorcycle, but nothing could have prepared him for the speed of the stolen hoverbike, or the delicate handling that made it possible to turn on a dime. The wind whipped at his face, making his eyes sting so badly that he could barely keep them open, which was a real problem given that he was sailing down unfamiliar roads in the dark at a hundred kilometers an hour. It would have been wise to slow down.

But then Annamaria would have gotten away. Instead of pumping the breaks, he leaned on the pedals. Tears streaked from his eyes as he squinted against the wind. If the Hand agent had a second helmet, he hadn't wasted time mucking about in an attempt to find it.

Annamaria's bike was ahead of him, a faint bobbing light in the distance as she whipped along side roads. Fabien had to keep his head down to avoid being blinded, using the bike's small windscreen as protection. As a result, he had to twist and contort his back until he was hunched over the steering column. The new position awakened a whole new level of pain in his wounded leg and his stinging throat. That only added to his misery.

He was keeping pace with Annamaria, but he'd never catch her at this rate. He wasn't close enough to fire off another round, either. If he was going to gain ground, he'd need to find a way to cut corners, but he didn't know the area well enough to risk losing sight of her for long.

At an intersection, she hooked a sharp left, disappearing behind a row of cypress. What little math he remembered from primary school kicked in: *the shortest distance between two points is a straight line.* Dinah would have been proud of him for remembering that.

The academic might have been *less* impressed with the choice Fabien made next, which was to swerve left as well, although he didn't wait until he was at the intersection to do so. Instead, he cut across a sprawling lawn. The hoverbike plunged through a dense row of shrubbery. The branches clawed at his arms and legs, striking the exposed meat of his thigh. He gritted his teeth against the pain and squeezed his eyes closed, just for a moment.

When he opened them again, it was to discover that he was on a collision course with a low-lying stone wall.

There was no time to hit the brakes, unless he slammed them so hard that he would likely be sent flying over the front of the bike. In the three seconds between seeing the wall and ramming into it face-first, he drove his heels against the pedals and leaned back to yank the handles.

If he was on an ordinary bicycle, he would have lifted the frame so that his whole weight was balanced on the back tire. Rather than popping a wheelie, the movement sent the back half of the hoverbike dipping toward the lawn so that it scored a deep furrow in the otherwise pristine grass. The front of the bike surged upward, so that its undercarriage was almost parallel with the face of the stone wall.

Fabien had to clamp his thighs to either side of the bike to keep from sliding off. He was certain it was going to overbalance and come crashing down on top of him. He'd end up as nothing more than a heap of meat and an inconvenient mess for the villa owner, who would be forced to report the dead stranger on his lawn to the authorities come daybreak.

The hoverbike launched upward, sailing over the wall and beyond, carrying him over the tops of the narrow cypress trees. For a few brief but thrilling seconds the whole countryside sprawled beneath him. The lights of Rome proper glowed in the distance, and all Fabien could hear was the rush of wind in his ears and his own frantic breathing. He spotted Annamaria's headlamp below him and noted her position. He was technically closer now, for what it was worth.

And then he reached the apex of his arc and began the breakneck plunge back toward land.

Stomping on the pedals did nothing; whatever unit powered the hoverbike wasn't able to arrest his fall.

Relax, he told himself, *you'll break fewer bones that way,* but that was easier said than done, all things considered. When he looked down, he saw the shimmering blue waters of an open-air swimming pool beneath him, illuminated from beneath by underwater lights. All around it was hardscaping.

Aim for the pool! he thought, but there was no way to aim, no way to alter his course.

The smart thing to do, perhaps, would have been to tip sideways over the water. There was no telling if it was deep enough to keep his bones from shattering, and couldn't hitting the surface of the water at a high enough velocity knock you unconscious or cause your organs to rupture or something? Dinah would have probably known, but she wasn't here to ask, and Fabien had only a fraction of a second in which to decide his next move.

If he hit the pool, he might live. But he'd lose Annamaria, and she'd go underground, and this would all be for nothing.

To hell with it. Fabien clung to the hoverbike like a baby chimp latching onto its mother, and closed his eyes.

He didn't see the ground rush up to meet him, but he felt the exact moment that the bike's mechanisms kicked in: not enough to arrest his fall entirely, but enough to start actively propelling him forward again. The front of the bike scraped against the pavement with an ear-splitting screech that reverberated through his whole body. It was like someone was dragging chalk the wrong way along a chalkboard while simultaneously running Fabien through a clothes dryer.

Then, almost miraculously, the bike righted itself and sped across the hardscaping and the lawn beyond. He'd only just managed to get his palms back on the handlebars when he whipped between the cypress trees out into the open road, crossing it at an angle.

The other hoverbike was only a few meters ahead of him.

Thank God for math. Fabien banked sideways and fumbled for his rifle with one hand. Fortunately, he still had one of the magnetic gloves, which allowed him to grip the rifle steadily enough to aim. Of course, he had to do it with the rifle strap still slung over his shoulder, but he could work with that.

The more pressing issue was the fact that he couldn't aim through the rifle scope without exposing his face to the wind. He tried once, but there was no way to keep his eyes open long enough to aim before they filled with tears from exposure to the slipstream. He cursed to himself and took his eyes off of Annamaria just long enough to check the settings on his rifle. He'd have preferred to stun her, but if he used the laser setting, he stood a better chance of damaging the bike and arresting her flight.

Laser it is, then. This time, he made sure that the magnetized points of his glove didn't pull the damn settings out of whack. Satisfied that they were right, he did his best to line up the shot and fired.

His first shot went wide, and several of the branches of a cypress tree lining the road smoldered with sparks. He tried again, and this time Annamaria swerved. He was ready to slam his foot onto the brakes and lunge toward her if she fell, but she only wobbled; she must have realized he was taking potshots at her, even if they hadn't hit.

Fabien's finger was on the trigger in anticipation of a third shot. Before he could take it, Annamaria threw her bike into reverse. He sped past her. The change in her velocity had been so abrupt that there was no time to recalibrate his aim.

As the person doing the chasing, he hadn't fully appreciated the advantage that being in the rear had given him. Aiming at her now would require twisting around to figure out where she was.

Fortunately, she hadn't tried to escape altogether. Fortune, of course, being relative, because she'd produced a familiar pistol from somewhere on her person. Even the brief flash of it that Fabien caught was enough to confirm that it was of the same variety as the one Apollo had carried. Fabien had seen that feisty little gun melt more than a few faces, both in the hologram imaging of Apollo's incursion on the Ohio vault, and in person within the halls of Laputa.

He had zero intention of letting Annamaria fire that gun at him, but she was right behind him, taking aim from behind the protection of her tinted helmet visor.

This left him with another snap decision to make, but this one was easier. He hit the brakes hard and skidded sideways, blocking the middle of the road.

And yes, it made him a sitting duck, but Annamaria wasn't the only one with a gun. This time, he fired-point blank.

He couldn't tell where she was hit, but she dropped like a stone. Her bike kept moving, however, and he barely had time to throw himself free before her bike collided with his in a sudden burst of sound and shrapnel and shattered glass. What was left of the two machines tumbled along the road.

Fabien knelt with one arm over his head, breathing hard.

His leg burned from hip to knee. It gave him a whole new appreciation for what Rhett dealt with every day.

If she could keep fighting, so could he. He lifted his head and scanned the street.

Without the headlamps of the hoverbikes to light the way, the only artificial light came from the villas set away from the road. The sky, once black and alive with stars, was fading to a paler gray with little streaks of pink evident on the clouds closest to the horizon.

Annamaria Vizzini had rolled onto her side and was gripping her shoulder with one hand. The visor of her helmet was cracked, and parts of it had broken away entirely. One half of her face was visible, revealing a vicious snarl.

"You'll pay for this," she hissed.

Fabien emitted a breathless laugh. "Really? That's all you've got? Do you know how many times I've heard that over the years?" He sat upright and pushed himself to his feet. There was no need to keep the rifle-strap around his shoulder anymore. Fabien shrugged it loose to increase his range of motion. He aimed the barrel in her direction.

Annamaria snorted. She lifted the remains of the damaged helmet and flung it away into the road. Her lips twisted in abject disgust. "You're not the only one who's armed, Fabien LeRoux."

"So you *do* know me." He used the pause that accompanied their banter to get his feet under him again.

Annamaria, still lying in a heap, spat into the dusty road. "A Frenchman in Porter's employ who talks too much? It doesn't take a genius to work *that* one out." She tried to lever herself up onto her elbow. When she fell back with a gasp, he caught a brief flash of the seeping, half-cauterized wound in her shoulder. A good hit. Too good, honestly. If she died from it, this endeavor would be for nothing.

His eyes flicked toward the gun as he adjusted the setting to stun. In the moment his attention faltered, she managed to aim the pistol at him.

"Stop moving," she panted. Her face was terribly pale in the dawn light. The fight hadn't left her, but her strength was flagging. "Don't you think I'll shoot?"

Fabien shrugged and adjusted his grip on the rifle. "You can try, but good luck hitting me. I can see how badly your hand is shaking from here."

Annamaria's eyes widened slightly, and she shifted the pistol so that it jutted up between her own chin. "I won't miss this, will I? I know what you want. The same thing everyone wants."

"Power?" he asked, already bored with the patter. He was light-headed from blood loss, but she was fading faster than he was. "Money?"

"*Information,*" she snarled. "If I die, you lose all I have to offer."

Fabien resisted the urge to roll his eyes. "You know what I think?"

Annamaria's chin tilted up another defiant centimeter.

"I think—" He lifted the rifle as he spoke, so fast that she didn't have time to react. With the stock braced against his shoulder at an angle, he fired. Annamaria's head tipped back and the pistol dropped from her limp fingers.

Talking. Talking was *always* how it ended. For someone as old as Annamaria appeared to be, she hadn't learned enough to wise up over the years.

He staggered over to her and knelt down beside her just as his brain registered the whine of an engine. They'd made enough racket—one of the neighbors must have called the *polizia*. There was no time to flee. He'd have to drag Annamaria out of the road and wait until law enforcement moved on.

Fabien didn't have a plan to contact the Roman vault. He'd been relying on Finder for that, but with the tablet broken, he'd need a backup plan. He slid one arm under Annamaria's shoulders and braced to hoist her upright.

The vehicle that zipped along the road wasn't a police car. He'd had enough trouble with the law to know what official vehicles looked like in *most* countries, and this one certainly wasn't the usual fare. It was much too long, and segmented like some cross between a city bus, a row of train cars, and a centipede, and appeared to rely on thrusters rather than wheels.

It pulled up to a stop beside him and the doors opened, folding upward to reveal a host of armed troops. Their uniforms were all-black, but their rifles were familiar enough—perfect twins to Fabien's own.

He fell back to one knee with a relieved sigh. "ENIGMA?" he asked. "I work with Porter. Excellent timing, I just caught up with a member of the Hand and—"

The first of the armed soldiers reached him, but instead of reaching for Annamaria, her fist struck Fabien in the teeth. New stars burst behind his eyelids, and he tasted blood.

"Don't talk to us," the woman spat. "Don't look at us. I know exactly who you are, *traitor*."

Fabien blinked up at her in mute shock. *Traitor?* He'd nearly died for ENGIMA yet again. He'd caught one of the enemies, something that the rest of the organization had deemed impossible. There must be some misunderstanding.

While two other ENIGMA agents hauled Annamaria upright and carried her to the transport vehicle, the woman loomed over Fabien. She was short, probably only shoulder-high if they'd been standing, and Fabien wasn't a tall man in his own right. She was quick, though, and strong, if that blow to his face was any indication. Only part of her face was visible, but the fury burning in her dark eyes couldn't be denied. Her Italian accent was thick enough to indicate that she must be with the regional vault. Not that he'd been expecting a warm and fuzzy welcome from the local branch, but this was more hostile than anything he'd anticipated.

Her nose wrinkled like she'd stepped in dogshit. "You are our prisoner, Fabien LeRoux, and you are lucky I don't shoot you dead on the spot. It's better than you deserve." She whirled away from him and stalked off to the transport vehicle.

"What did I do?" he asked. He got no reply other than a blow to the temple that made his vision blur. He didn't see the faces of the two guards who dragged him to his feet and secured his hands behind him. If the Hand had come for him, he'd have fought tooth and nail to escape, but these were his allies—supposedly. Fighting back would only confirm their belief that he'd done... whatever they thought he'd done.

Porter will sort this out, he thought.

At least the cup he'd reclaimed from Annamaria was still in his backpack, along with the broken tablet that might have exonerated him. He let himself be dragged along in the Italian commander's wake, wondering what in God's name he was supposed to do now. They hadn't even told him what was wrong.

He was being strapped into one of the transport's seats when it clicked. Whatever had the Italians up in arms might not be the result of his own actions.

Which raised another question.

Where the hell was Rhett?

INTERLUDE
THE RIGHT HAND OF THE SUN

Aten sat across from the ENIGMA agent, watching him sleep, although perhaps that was too kind a word for it. More accurately, he watched him groan and shift against the bonds that held him in place as he sipped from the cut-crystal glass of porter that he'd been nursing for the last hour or so.

Usually he preferred cognac, but he'd been saving this particular bottle of spirits for a special occasion. Call him sentimental, but the little joke amused him. He'd been waiting years to finish what an earlier generation of Porters had started; had waited so long, in fact, that he'd begun to wonder if he would be the one to bring the house of cards called ENIGMA crashing down. These things took time, and Aten's mind was always on the long game, on the gradual payoff, on the inevitable moment of triumph that, at times, had to be left to percolate over years or even decades.

But now, he was on the brink of accomplishing a new level

of success, one that few of his predecessors had ever dreamed. He wouldn't merely drive his bootheel into the collective throat of ENIGMA; he would be master of many worlds. Aten's rays would spill across neighboring Earths.

Imagine what we could build. Imagine the legacy I could leave. No more piddling about with currencies and politics, no more skirting international law, no more erasing our tracks. The Hand will finally claim its place in the spotlight, at the pinnacle of not only world power but of every Earth ours brushes up against, and beyond.

He closed his eyes, imagining the worlds splayed out before him like a chessboard, plotting every move. With Reclamation overtaken, he would have access to every artifact within its walls... power over the most advanced AI on this Earth... and with one swift, decisive move, he could both suppress ENIGMA and make his move against the other worlds, cementing alliances where possible and eradicating the enemy when necessary.

The comm in his pocket chimed.

He lifted the object from his pocket and held it in one lazy hand while he sipped his drink with the other. "Ray Twelve," he said mildly. "Funny you should contact me just now."

"...*Is it?*" The junior agent's voice wavered with uncertainty.

"Oh, yes. You see, I have a visitor here. I believe you're acquainted with Captain Rhett Zappotis?"

Agent Ra sucked in a breath that sounded like static through the voice scrambler. "*What's he doing there? How did he find you?*"

"Apparently he was following up on an offer of employment," he said. "I thought perhaps you might have given him a clue."

"*Never!*" There was a touch of fear in Ra's voice, but even more fanaticism. "*I would never betray the cause, not to one of them.*"

Aten smiled to himself—there was pleasure in letting his inferiors squirm. "Are you quite sure of that? Perhaps you let something slip. And the note he showed me is rather suggestive."

"*I never contacted him,*" Ra insisted. "*I am not aware of having made a mistake, but if I did, it was entirely in error.*"

"I have no use for an agent who's gotten sloppy," Aten warned.

There was a prolonged beat in which Ra said nothing. Aten sipped his drink, letting the other agent's silence play out, letting him stew. He suspected that the younger agents had designs against him. Frankly, he would be disappointed to learn that Ra wasn't ambitious enough to hatch his own schemes. Ambition was what drove the Hand, after all. An open palm was only the precursor to a fist.

"*If I have disappointed you in any way,*" Ra said at last, "*I will accept my fate.*"

Ah, false modesty. The younger man was wise to bow and scrape, so Aten relented. "I will find out what he knows soon enough, Ray Twelve. In the meantime, are you ready for my arrival?"

"*Not yet, but only because I have news. Apparently, Captain Zappotis' recent attempt to connect with one of the other vaults went poorly. Several branches of ENIGMA have decided to take action. They have requested permission to visit Reclamation for themselves and will be arriving shortly."*

Aten reeled back against his chair. "Other commanders will be there? Gathered together?"

"With their eyes on the wrong enemy," Ra confirmed.

Aten rose to his feet and began to pace the narrow strip of floor available to him. The arrangement of his imagined chessboard shifted. He'd been prepared to take the queen, so to speak, but the opponent had made a larger mistake than he could have dreamed. *Checkmate.*

"You're prepared to recall Apollo?" he asked.

"I'll inform him of our next move, and will alert you as soon as they have arrived. Be prepared to depart at a moment's notice. Our window of opportunity will be narrow."

"If I didn't know better, it would sound like you were giving orders," Aten observed. He stopped in front of the case that contained his armor. It hadn't been worn in many lifetimes, but he had always dreamed that he would be the one to wear it. Before Ra could protest his innocence, Aten added, "I will alert the others. We will be ready."

"I haven't heard from Ray Seven in some time, sir."

"Leave her to me. You have done well, Ray Twelve, very well indeed. I will remember this when the time comes."

He cut their contact and tucked the device back into his pocket, still admiring his armor. From where he stood, reflected in the glass, it seemed to him that he was wearing it already.

This is destiny. This is my divine right. He tipped the last of the porter down his throat, set the glass aside, and unlocked the case.

19 DINAH

THE FRACTURED CITY had given Dinah the creeps, but that was nothing compared to the spot aboveground where Nibbles led them. Dinah was wearing her full suit, and Finder had donned the damaged one, insisting that it would be unwise to leave any more human technology behind. Call it littering or call it contamination; Dinah could see his point, although it seemed like too little too late, given how many relics Apollo had brought with him when he fell through the seam.

Regardless, she was less worried about the butterfly effect her presence on the other Earth might lead to than she was about their current environs.

"What are those things?" she asked, pointing into the skeletal trees and stone outcroppings that surrounded them.

Nibbles glanced upward. Unlike Dinah, he hadn't donned a full suit, only a breathing apparatus designed for his narrow snout. "What, those?" he said, unperturbed. "Spiderwebs."

Dinah wrinkled her nose. "*Spiderwebs?*" she echoed. The thick, sticky ropes dangling from above were much too big to be made by any spider she'd ever seen, and that included the photos her officemate had sent her from her family home in Australia. *They'd have to be the size of cars, at least.* The farther they walked, the denser the webs became. At this rate, she'd be forced to confront one of the awful things.

She shuddered and ran her hand over the butt of her laser pistol. "I hate spiders," she whispered.

Finder gave her shoulder a reassuring pat. "I'm not confident in my translation," the android said. "It's possible that he's referring to some sort of large herbivorous arachnid, although my scans do indicate that this material has almost the exact same chemical composition as the spiderwebs I'm familiar with." It must have noticed that these words of comfort weren't having the intended effect, because it hastily added, "But don't mind me! My systems are all muddled, so maybe I'm wrong about this."

One of these days, Dinah would finally have that much-needed conversation about bedside manner.

Nibbles snorted. "Herbivorous? You wish. One of them can drain one of us dry in a single meal." He stopped short and pointed to a dull gray lump only a few yards away. "It's not pretty."

Dinah took a cautious step closer, and the lump resolved into something recognizable. It was a Didelian, or what was left of one, now little more than shriveled skin and brittle fur wrapped around a pile of loose bones.

"Seriously?" she whined.

"Don't worry," Nibbles said, "you're a lot bigger. I bet you'd make two meals." He pointed to Finder. "You're the lucky one, though, you're not edible."

"Too true," Finder chirped. "I do hope we get to see one, I'm compiling a catalog of every new species we encounter here."

Dinah shuddered. "I sure as hell hope we don't. Remind me again why we're doing this?"

"Because it's going to be three of us against your fellow Traveler and however much backup he brings." Nibbles rolled his eyes and waved a dismissive hand. "You wanted to lure him out of the safety of the city, away from all his little toys. Well, that's what we're doing. My people are going to be focused on taking the city, and we don't want to get surrounded. Spiders don't care who they eat, so if we end up outnumbered, odds are in our favor."

Dinah retreated from the desiccated little corpse. "Right. Odds." She should probably have asked more questions before agreeing to this plan, but she'd assumed that if part of the mission involved traipsing around in a giant spider's nest, Nibbles would have mentioned it. Not explicitly, of course, but just as a sort of general rule.

Never assume. She turned away and let Nibbles lead them onward, deeper into the maze of webs.

Although she hadn't properly understood the bit about the spiders, she was still pinning her hopes on the part of their plan that she'd understood: she, Finder, and Nibbles would lure Apollo out of the safety of the city, while the underground attempted to secure the city itself. Divide and conquer, as it were. If Dinah could take Apollo in the struggle, excellent. If not, then Nibbles could lead the two ENIGMA representatives underground again, and Apollo and his crew would be trapped outside the city. Then, at the very least, Dinah and Finder would be able to secure the warehouse where all the relics were kept and figure out what to do next, and how to use the relics to their advantage.

There were a few potential issues with this plan, including the very real possibility that Apollo would be more interested in killing Dinah than capturing her. Nibbles had sworn up and down that he knew the terrain outside the city better than anyone, and that he would do his best to help Dinah and Finder flee if—or rather, *when*—things went sideways.

Now that she was aware that giant spiders were an unspoken part of the plan, she was beginning to wonder what else she'd taken for granted.

As they walked, Nibbles kept looking up, not just at the webs but at the canopy above. Every so often, his eyes would narrow and his skinny tail would stiffen in surprise, but he said nothing.

Dinah was starting to wonder what she'd missed when Nibbles' ears twitched sharply. "There!" he hissed.

The sun that the other Earth orbited was rising, and the temperature had begun to climb. Dinah was sweating in her suit, but despite the heat, the light itself was watery and thin. In that dim glow, she couldn't tell what she was looking at until the creature on the cliffside above them scurried away.

"Spider?" she whispered.

"Nah," Nibbles replied, "too small. It was a Didelian, no doubt one of Callic's people."

"One of *Apollo's* people," Dinah corrected, even though she felt a bit strange calling the diminutive alien a person. She was still getting used to the fact that her current allies were as different as they were. The academic portion of her brain—in other words, the majority of her gray matter—wanted an opportunity to delve into whatever archives the Didelians kept.

Nibbles shrugged. "Same difference. Looks like they saw us, anyway. Come on."

Dinah tried to reassure herself that it was a good thing that one of Apollo's underlings had spotted her, since that was the whole point of the exercise, but she couldn't help but feel that she was trapped between a rock and a hard place. Only the rock was a murderous enemy agent, and the hard place was a den of carnivorous spiders.

Finder fussed over her as they walked. "Your heart rate appears to have spiked significantly in the last minute. Are you all right? Are you dehydrated? Do you need rest?"

"I'm fine," Dinah said, mostly in an attempt to buy a few moments to get her thoughts together, but what a thing to say. Had any words she'd spoken ever been less true?

They crested a hill, and whatever chance she might have had to clarify the state of her mental health was blasted out of her mind at the view that lay before her. The path sloped sharply down into what appeared to be a crater or a sinkhole. Stone walls rose around them, encircling the massive pit. Dangling above that were more webs, from which were suspended enormous cocoons.

Nibbles had led them right to the nest.

"Oh, God." Dinah pressed her palm to her stomach and

swayed on her feet. *Please don't let me puke in my helmet...* *please don't let me puke in my helmet...* The only good news was that, so far, none of the inhabitants of that awful place were visible. A faint mist hung over the declivity, girdling the hive with an eerie beauty.

Dinah dropped into a crouch, still clutching her stomach. She was doing her best not to panic. It wasn't going well.

Finder's hand landed on her shoulder. "Look at this!" the android chirped. "It's very Gothic. Very festive."

Dinah turned her head slowly and glared up at the android.

Finder bent lower and dropped its voice to a whisper. "I'm trying to make you feel better. Is it helping?"

Dinah opened her mouth a few times, closed it, opened it again. "Sure," she croaked.

"Good." Finder straightened up and dusted its hands off. It seemed that sarcasm wasn't part of the AI's vocabulary.

Nibbles surveyed the hive, nodded once, and turned back to face the road from which they'd come. He, too, squatted in the dirt at Dinah's side. He fidgeted with the mask covering his face and adjusted the straps that had left pink marks on the backs of his protruding pink ears.

"And now we wait," he said.

"Wait," Dinah echoed. "Here. Right next to..." She pointed into the heart of the nest. "That?"

Nibbles glanced over his shoulder and shrugged. "At least we know that Apollo and Callic won't sneak up on us from behind."

Dinah's stomach burbled, and she thought again of the stew she'd picked at earlier. If she'd known that they'd been marching into a den of giant arachnids, she might have held off eating those ticks earlier. It was all feeling a little too 'circle of life' for her.

"Shouldn't we be worried about the spiders sneaking up from behind?" she asked.

Nibbles shrugged again. "Not really." He pointed one stubby finger at the webbing that spanned the arch over their heads. "They're more likely to attack us from above."

Which was about as comforting as anything that Finder had said.

DINAH WOULD NEVER HAVE BELIEVED that she would nod off while waiting for an attack from two directions, but as she squatted between Nibbles and Finder, she found her chin tipping toward her chest against her will. Each time, she snapped awake again, but her vigilance was increasingly abysmal. She and Nibbles faced the road, while Finder watched the nest, humming to itself as it observed.

Eventually Nibbles swatted her shoulder. "Eyes up," the Didelian said.

"Sorry." Dinah blinked a few times and tried to rub her eyes, forgetting that she was wearing the helmet. The sky was the same dull color it had been for hours. "What time is it?"

Nibbles squeaked something, but what Dinah heard was a mechanical voice that intoned, "*Translation error.*"

"What does that mean?" Dinah asked.

"*Translation error.*"

Dinah groaned and turned to look back at Finder to ask

what the problem was, only to find that the android had fallen silent and was staring into the distance with a disconcerting intensity.

"Finder?" she asked. *Please don't let it be a programming error.*

To her short-lived relief, the android answered in its usual voice. "I think I saw something move. Over there." It pointed a slim metal finger up into the hanging cocoons.

Dinah lurched to her feet. Even before she was upright, her eyes skimmed between the webs in search of whatever Finder had seen. Would they look like the spiders she knew from home? Clearly this Earth had plenty of things in common with hers, but that didn't guarantee that spiders would have evolved the same way, given that marsupials had taken a very different evolutionary route. As for the fate of the local primates, she hadn't dared to ask.

Try as she might, she didn't spot any movement in the unsettling canopy.

"Is this a system error?" she asked Finder under her breath.

The android tilted its head. "I'm confident that I saw something move, although I'm not sure what. It might have been the wind."

Nibbles grunted. "No wind."

Finder peered down at him. "Are you sure?"

"By the time of the fracture, our ozone layer was shot." Nibbles picked up a stone from the ground by his feet and flicked it away down the road. "We don't get breezes anymore. The only type of wind we get now is strong enough to strip a landscape bare. It hasn't happened recently, at least not that I've heard, but that's one of the reasons we built the bubble. That, and the air quality." He snorted. "Well, and the pollutants. They're the only reason we aren't being cooked in these suits right now."

Dinah made a mental note to ask more about the fracture, but the more pressing question on her mind was the nature of the mystery movement above them. "Where did it go?"

"I'm not sure," Finder admitted. "My visual sensors only picked up a peripheral reading. Even when I play it back, the results are inconclusive, so—"

The android was cut off abruptly by a humming sound from within its chest. Both Finder and Dinah stared down in surprise.

"What was that?" Dinah demanded.

Finder placed a hand to its chest. "I believe it was an alert," it said.

"You mean, like a parts failure?"

"No." Finder opened its chest cavity to reveal the resonance stone still stored inside. It plucked the stone free even as it hummed again. "I think Apollo might be getting a message."

Dinah recoiled. "Can whoever it is hear us?"

"Not yet." Finder turned the stone over in its fingers. "Would you like me to answer?"

Dinah sputtered incoherently.

Finder's cartoon eyes flicked from the stone to her face. "I assure you, I'm perfectly capable of mimicking his verbal patterns, and the voice scrambler already makes it difficult to identify the speaker. We may learn something that will help the others."

For a fleeting moment, she imagined what it would be like to know who was speaking into the twin of this stone, to know exactly who was trying to sabotage Reclamation, and still be completely cut off from her friends and allies. If she knew who was threatening them, but couldn't warn them, wouldn't that be worse than wondering?

Finder was staring at her, and she could feel Nibbles' eyes on her back. Dinah swallowed hard. "Answer it," she rasped.

The tone of the humming shifted. *"Ray Six, this is Ray Twelve,"* a crackling voice said.

The voice didn't sound right. It reminded Dinah of old documentary TV shows, where some interview subjects were revealed only in silhouette, their speech overlaid with voice-changing technology that made it almost impossible to identify them.

"Ray Twelve, this is Ray Six," Finder said, scrambling its own voice to match that of the speaker. There was a pause before the android added, "What is your status?"

Dinah mouthed the words, *Ray six?* That was frustrating. Not that she'd expected the Hand agent to use their full government name in greeting, but at the very least, she'd hoped for a clue. They were currently engaged in the equivalent of a wiretap, and the more talking Finder did, the more likely it was that they'd give themselves away to the enemy agent.

"Good news, Ray Twelve." Even through the voice-altering tech, the voice was smug. *"Two of the agents have been brought in, one by ENIGMA, and one by the Right Hand himself."*

Dinah bit back a cry of dismay. The ENIGMA agents most likely to have been brought in were Fabien and Rhett.

"The only one left is the useless one who came after you. Have you encountered her yet?"

That brought Dinah up short. She scowled at the stone. *Useless?*

"Not yet," Finder fibbed.

"Then leave her. Let the locals handle her. Return to the crossing point, and I'll open the seam."

Dinah wasn't certain what the spy meant by a 'crossing point,' but she could guess. Each time that the disruptor had been activated, it had led into the fractured city. Judging by the way Apollo had been able to use the device back home, this probably meant that it wasn't opening a wormhole, but was instead breaking down the walls between realities, as it were. Opening a seam in New York City wouldn't be of any use to someone in Boston, because the door between worlds would probably connect one version of New York to the other. The fractured city had been built on the Didelian version of Reclamation, which implied that the geography of the two worlds was different, but not so different that the disruptor failed to recognize them.

And that meant that if the agent opened a seam in the fractured city, it wouldn't matter who had the resonance stone. Instead of Apollo calling home and plotting with his contact, all the spy would have to do would be to activate the device, and...

And Apollo could stroll into Reclamation anyway.

Dinah let out a choked sob. The agent was right. She was useless. Instead of fighting Apollo head-on, she'd come up with yet another stupid, pointless plan that wouldn't help anyone in the end.

The sound must have picked up through the stone, because the scrambled voice asked, *"What was that?"*

Finder shot Dinah a quelling glance. "I said, Good work. I'll be there as soon as I can. It might take longer than you expect. Dinah Bray isn't as useless as she looks."

Even through the haze of her dismay, Dinah had the wherewithal to make a rude gesture at the android.

"She's come up with a very clever plan to stop me," Finder went on. "So don't activate the device until I tell you so. Otherwise, she and all of her allies will come pouring through, and they'll make the next stage of the attack on Porter's new vault very difficult indeed. Let me handle this sorry excuse for an agent first. I'll tell you when I'm ready."

For an android that claimed to be malfunctioning, Dinah was impressed by Finder's ability to think on its feet. If the agent bought their story, it would give them at least a little time to come up with a new plan.

"Don't waste your time with her, Ray Six," the spy snorted. *"We don't need prisoners anymore. We've got all the leverage we need."*

"Understood," Finder said. "I'll be in touch soon."

The humming from the stone stopped, and Finder fiddled with it for a moment before tucking it back in its chest cavity. Dinah stared down into the spider's nest, not really seeing. She was glad, at least, that Apollo hadn't received the message to kill her, but it still shocked her to think that someone who knew her, who had worked with her, was capable of ordering her execution.

What did you think the Hand was planning? she asked

herself. *How many times did Apollo try to kill you? This was always the plan.*

And yet, that one brief conversation drove home the true cruelty of the Hand. Apollo had never pretended to be her friend, and yet someone in Reclamation had sold them out and was actively planning their deaths.

Someone who had Fabien and Rhett in his clutches.

"Well," Finder said at last. "I suppose we should come up with a new plan."

"I'm the worst at plans," Dinah said. To her horror, she felt the familiar tickle in her nose that told her she was about to well up. Fabien would tease her relentlessly for crying, but Fabien wasn't here, and nothing Dinah had done mattered. She'd made mistake after mistake. Working with Fabien and Rhett had given her an inflated sense of her own usefulness, but Porter had known that she wasn't as valuable as the others. It had been reflected in that first offer.

Dinah wanted nothing more in that moment than to curl up on the ground, wrap her arms around her helmet, and disappear.

"Don't worry." Finder nudged her shoulder. "There's still time. You and I are very competent individuals. We can get back to the city and find another solution. There's still time."

"But we don't even know who we just talked to." There was an embarrassing whine in Dinah's voice.

Saying so aloud stopped her short. They hadn't heard the agent's unfiltered voice, but she *did* know that the person they'd spoken to had access to the destabilizer. She'd seen Lane power the device down as they'd fallen through the seam. Lane, whose former partner had been killed by Apollo, but who'd been left alive during that first incursion on the vault. Lane, who had approached them in the vault as they prepared to go after Apollo.

That *bitch*. Fabien shouldn't have stopped at shooting her in the leg.

"We have to get back," Dinah said. She tugged on Finder's arm. "Maybe we can trick them into opening the seam for us, and then we can stop them before Apollo catches up with us."

Nibbles spoke from behind them, and Dinah jumped; she'd almost forgotten that the Didelian was there. "It's nice that you want to change the plan again and all, but we've got another problem."

He was pointing out along the road they'd taken to the hive. In the distance, a plume of dust followed the track. If Dinah didn't know better, she'd have guessed it was a small tornado making its way up the track. As it swept in toward them, the webs above them began to shift and sway.

If these space-spiders work the way ours do, all that movement will draw them right to us. Due to the single gap in the stones, whatever was coming wouldn't disturb the whole nest, just the filaments that spanned the crevice. It would likely have the same effect as a fly plowing smack into a cobweb.

"I thought you didn't have wind in your atmosphere," Dinah said.

Nibbles shook his head. "We don't. Whatever's coming must be bringing its own."

"Bringing its own wind?" Dinah repeated. Not that it would be impossible, but she wasn't sure what Nibbles meant. A car would kick up dust as it passed, not send a burst of wind ahead of its path.

"Whistles," Finder said.

Dinah frowned up at the android. "Huh?"

"Whistles," Finder said again, retreating a step. "It must be Apollo's people."

She could have kicked herself for being slow. Of course... she, Rhett, and Fabien had used whistles on their squirrel suits to call up wind when they'd left Laputa. She'd seen some of the very same whistles inside Reclamation when Apollo first destroyed it. They'd been pulled through the seam with him and heaped amid the mounds of treasures piled on the warehouse floor.

In an instant, the laser pistol was in her hand, its bulbous barrel aimed into the midst of the artificial tornado. "Stand with me," she said. "When that dust reaches us, we'll be fighting blind. If we block the passage, at least they won't be able to surround us." As for what the spiders might do, she could only guess, but she didn't have time to come up with a better plan.

And anyway, as she'd just asserted, she sucked at planning.

Nibbles reached her side just as the dust swept over them. She felt Finder's elbow bump her own, but couldn't even see as far as the arm against which the android had brushed. Fortunately, her suit filter was able to sift out most of the dust, but the sound of tiny flecks of stone striking the mask of her helmet was like rain dropping on a metal roof. Her suit was thin enough that she could feel the stones through the material. They were more irritating than painful, but if they tore through the material, her access to breathable air would be compromised.

Aiming into the obscured space before her, Dinah fired at random. Each time, she felt the laser pistol jump in her hand, but she had no way of knowing if she'd hit anything. Not even the bolt of the laser was visible.

"Aim down," Finder's voice said, easily audible over the peppering of little stones that droned in Dinah's ears. The android must have connected directly to her audio system to bypass the rush of the wind. "They're short, remember? If it will help, I can link through heat-signature readings... now."

For half a breath, her helmet clouded over as the visual augmentations kicked on. When it cleared, she could make out a dozen or more heat signatures, blurry representations of Didelians that followed after one leader at the fore of their attack. The one with the whistle, presumably.

"How do I know which one is Nibbles? Nibbles, can you hear me?" Dinah didn't get an answer, but when she turned her head, a reddish-orange blob was still standing directly beside her several feet away. If Nibbles moved, she'd hold her fire, but for the time being she could avoid friendly fire.

She'd never thought of herself, and likely never would, as combat-ready, but she could think just far enough ahead to know what to do next. The Didelian leading the charge was almost certainly the one carrying the whistle, so Dinah aimed roughly into the center of its blurry mass and fired.

The figure collapsed. Immediately the wind began to die, and the other attackers began to shriek at one another, speaking so quickly that Finder's translation program struggled to keep up.

There were perhaps a dozen more Didelian soldiers, but no

sign of Apollo. She aimed at a second one, and missed when it dropped to all fours and began to run.

Now that the dust was settling, Dinah could see a bit better, but so could their attackers. Nibbles let out a ferocious screech and dove forward, crashing into the next-closest attacker. Dinah fired on another, and managed to graze its ribcage with the blast.

She'd been prepared to face a maelstrom of teeth and claws, but not for the little beast to toss something into the air. All she saw was a flash of metal—no doubt one of the myriad tiny relics that had followed Apollo through the seam—that exploded in midair with all the volume and glitz of a firework display. She used one arm to block her eyes, and in so doing left herself open to attack. Before the lights faded, a small, dense body crashed into her knees and sent her sprawling.

Dinah was dimly aware that Finder was also engaged in some sort of tussle, and that the android wouldn't be coming to her rescue. The laser pistol slipped from her hand as she hit the ground.

Last time she'd ended up on her belly, the suit got torn. She couldn't let that happen again, out here, where the atmosphere hardly qualified as 'air' and whatever chemicals swirled about them were unbreathable. She flipped onto her back just in time to avoid being clawed.

The Didelian that had knocked her over hissed at her through its breathing apparatus and poised to spring again. Dinah didn't stop to question what she was about to do. Her arm moved of its own accord to snatch the mask from her opponent's face.

The alien howled and tried to grab it back. If its claws

hooked into her suit, she'd be finished, so rather than engage in a deadly game of keep-away, Dinah heaved the mask away.

Into the hive.

It slid downhill, far out of reach, and the Didelian staggered after it. The creature didn't get far. It couldn't catch its breath in the thin atmosphere, and its desperation made its furry body run through oxygen even faster than usual. Its panting heightened to a whine, and the marsupial stumbled, then collapsed into the dust and began to writhe.

You killed it. Dinah pushed herself into a crouch, her eyes fixed on the doomed creature. It wasn't human, but that hardly mattered. Other members of its species had met Dinah with kindness, and now she'd murdered one of them. *I'm supposed to be an intellectual pacifist, and I killed it...*

Her personal crisis cost her valuable time. The Didelian was still thrashing in the dust when Dinah groped for her gun and found it missing. Another aggressor had scooped it up in the meantime, and had it aimed right between her eyes.

"Surrender," it snarled, "or I'll break that helmet. I don't care what our orders are. You killed my sister, Traveler!"

Dinah pressed her palms to the earth. *Useless.* The spy was right about her. She'd bloodied her hands, and for what? She was still going to end up in Apollo's clutches.

Movement shimmered above them. Both Dinah and the Didelian looked up at the same time. The heat-signature function on Dinah's helmet was still on, but while the Didelians were overlaid in warm tones at its warmest points, the thing above them was mostly accented blue and green.

To call it a spider would have been to ignore just how horrifying the creature was. Its limbs were much longer proportionally than those of a spider, and the enormous churning mouthparts would have been less out of place on a machine than on a living thing.

It was hung suspended upside-down from the web above them, its myriad glossy eyes fixed on its prey.

Dinah screamed, and the Didelian screamed, too. She didn't need the translate feature to tell her what it was saying; cursing took on the same tone in most languages.

Galvanized by their cries, the spider dropped. Dinah flung herself out of the way, but the Didelian wasn't so lucky. Perhaps the spider recognized familiar prey, because it ignored her and dove for Dinah's would-be attacker. The two spindly front legs snatched the Didelian up. It screamed until it reached the spider's mouthparts.

The cries faded over a matter of seconds as the spider fed, deflating the wretched creature before Dinah's very eyes. It couldn't just be sucking its prey's blood. There must be a fair bit of soft tissue being slurped up as well.

Dinah fell back a step and looked around. She'd lost her only weapon, Nibbles was nowhere to be seen, and Finder was in the middle of more or less punting a Didelian back down the road.

And there were spiders everywhere. Their long, stick-like limbs didn't look like they were built for speed, but they moved faster than Dinah would have credited. They descended en masse upon the battling group.

"Come on!" Nibbles' voice called from somewhere. "They'll

take the easy prey, Traveler! Shoot one and the rest will back off!"

There was another blast of sound, another flash of starbursts, another distant scream. Dinah bolted forward, weaving between the stiltlike, brittle legs, dodging screaming Didelians, not fully sure where she was going, but knowing that she had to get away.

She collided at full force with Finder, who grabbed her by the arm. "Lead the way, Doctor," the android cried. "I'll cover you."

They staggered out of the rift between the stones and left the nest behind as they hurried back along the road. Nibbles was waiting for them. His mottled fur was ruffled, and there was a nasty bite on his ear, but other than that he didn't seem much worse for wear.

"It worked!" he cried.

"Did it?" Dinah panted for breath as they kept jogging. The screams faded behind them, but she wasn't taking any chances with those spiders.

"I don't see any more of Callic's folk on our heels, do you?"

Sure enough, there was no sign of the little raiding party, other than the footprints in the newly-stirred dust and the fading screams of the ones who were still alive.

"Being alive is a win," Finder said from a few paces behind Dinah. "And now we have the opportunity to—" The android's words were cut off in a garbled mess of static.

Dinah pivoted back. She expected to encounter one of the spiders, or a rear guard of Didelians, but it was much worse than that.

She'd been lamenting Apollo's absence as a missed opportunity, but here he was.

The Hand agent wore a modified version of the mask Nibbles wore, one which covered his head and sealed into his battered suit but which, unlike his old helmet, revealed his face. Beneath the shield, his eyes were bloodshot. His cheeks were so hollow that the bones of his face were visible beneath, and he seemed hunted.

Haunted.

Merciless.

In a single, smooth movement, he twisted Finder's head free of its body and tossed it aside. Dinah reached for a weapon that wasn't there even as Apollo knocked the android down and yanked open its chestplate.

"You stole from me," Apollo snarled. He bent down and plucked the resonance stone from Finder's chest. And then, right before Dinah's eyes, the agent flickered. Like static on an old TV screen.

Dinah flinched. Something was very wrong with the Hand agent, that was obvious. Something that had changed not just his mind, but his biology as well.

Apollo rose to his feet and stalked forward. When Dinah risked a sideways glance, Nibbles was gone. He must have vanished into one of his hidey-holes.

"You are a disgrace," Apollo snarled. Dinah scrambled away, but there was nowhere to run, and she'd abandoned too many friends already. She'd rather die standing her ground at Finder's side than with a bullet, or a laser, to the back. She sank into a fighting crouch and raised her fists.

It was over so quickly, she hardly understood what was happening. Apollo's fist struck her chest hard enough to knock the wind out of her. Another blow, and she was down, curled up like a useless grub as she tried fruitlessly to defend herself.

Apollo raised his boot and brought his full weight down on Dinah's helmet. The first stomp resulted in a surge of pressure that left Dinah's ears ringing. The second sent a spiderweb of cracks scrawling across the visor.

"Waste of air," Apollo hissed. He must have activated the stone, because his next words were not aimed at Dinah. "Ray Twelve, this is Ray Six. I'm ready. Activate the device at your discretion..."

His voice faded as he walked away. Dinah lay perfectly still, holding her breath as long as she could.

Do something. Be smart. Be useful. You're not dead yet. But a series of disjointed messages flashed across her broken visor, alerting her to the plummeting pressure inside her suit, and to her thinning oxygen. There was nowhere she could reach in time by walking, no one to call for help.

So no, she wasn't dead. Not yet.

And then the spiders came.

Dinah broke her promise to herself to lie still and lurched to her feet. She scrambled upright and sucked in a breath that left her lungs burning. One of the long-limbed arachnids descended on her and swept her up. She wriggled ineffectually in its grip.

It didn't bite her, though. It held her up and spun her like a shawarma, wrapping her in its web as it went.

She couldn't even muster terror. She couldn't breathe.

And the world went dark.

20 RHETT

HE WOKE with the taste of bile in his mouth and a pounding migraine. His hands were bound behind his back, and something was keeping him upright. A chair? Where the hell had a chair come from? The last thing he remembered was...

The Hand. He'd found the Hand. And Aten had taken him prisoner.

His eyes struggled to focus as his head lolled forward. His mouth was a dry sponge in his mouth, and he shifted against his bonds, his arms and shoulders screamed in agony. He was on the brink of being sick, but there was nothing in his stomach to expel. All he could do was heave weakly.

"Ah," said a cool voice, "you're awake. It took you long enough. I fear I may have overdone it with the gas."

Rhett lifted his chin and the room swam into focus, or something like it. The man sitting in the chair before him had his legs crossed. He was dressed in an exosuit similar to the suit Apollo had worn—it looked like royal armor, but the man he'd met was hardly young, and the easy way he shifted as Rhett watched made him think that the material must be some sort of ultralight composite.

His face was obscured by a strange mask, but Rhett knew it was him. He wasn't relying on process of elimination, either.

Rhett was watching the people who surrounded Aten.

There were eight more of them gathered in the room. All of them wore gold, though only some of it was armor. Others favored flowing robes, but all of them had donned masks and headdresses that obscured their identities. The styles had been borrowed from a variety of locations; like ENIGMA, the Hand drew on many backgrounds. Out of all of them, only Aten was sitting, while the others gathered around him in a loose crescent formation.

It's not an organization, he thought. *It's a damn cult.*

"We should kill him," one of them said. He was a big man, dressed like a horned god. A long loop of heavy chain was cinched to his belt, attached to a handle that suggested it could be used as a whip. "Why waste time with him? We don't need hostages."

"He could be useful," Aten countered. His face was still turned to Rhett's, although Rhett couldn't see his eyes within that stupid mask.

A surge of anger shot through him, accompanied by adrenaline that helped clear the fog that still lingered between his ears. If Aten and Gold Bar Holdings were anything to judge by, these people had so much. They had more wealth and power than anyone could justify, and they used that wealth and power to do harm instead of good. Even the room in which they stood, with its dark hardwood floors, illuminated display cabinets, plush furniture, and host of stolen treasures, was ill-gotten. How much more did they have, squirreled away in bank accounts and summer homes and private jets and foreign holdings? Why wasn't this enough? Having taken more than their share of this world, what gave them the right to reach for another one?

In Rhett's old career, he'd worked with civilian resistances to help them rise up against warlords and unjust regimes. Sure, the people who cut his checks had their own motives, but he'd believed in the work. Now that he'd seen the difference between ENIGMA and the Hand with his own eyes, he knew he'd chosen the right side.

He'd never been as loyal to ENIGMA as he was in that moment.

"We don't throw away useful things," Aten went on. He was holding something in one gold-gloved hand, turning it over and over between his fingers. A stone of some kind, set in a metal device. A relic, probably, although Rhett couldn't remember if he'd ever seen one like it before.

"Some might say that he's outlived his usefulness." The figure that had spoken this time was shorter than the rest, dressed in layer upon layer of gold silk and tulle. She didn't look like a soldier, but with all relics at her disposal, who knew what she could do?

Aten turned his head without moving the rest of his body, like an owl. "My apologies, Sunna. Are you in charge now? Should we be taking orders from you?"

"No," the woman said sullenly. "I was only making

suggestions. He's dead weight. With Ra's help, we've all but won. Reclamation is as good as ours."

"Perhaps," Aten said, "perhaps not. Belenos will see to him."

"I will?" the horned man asked. When Aten swiveled toward him, he nodded. "I will," he repeated, as if it hadn't been a question the first time.

"Only until we reach the vault," Aten clarified. "Ra will take him from there. We must make sure that we have every advantage, and that will mean using our little pawn to ensure our checkmate." He inclined his head toward Rhett.

"I'm not a pawn," Rhett spat. He'd meant to convey the full brunt of his anger, but his voice cracked, and in the end he sounded more pathetic than dangerous.

Aten laughed. "He speaks? And yes, Captain, of course you're a pawn. You're a useless little piece who can only see one move ahead, while others control the board. Porter has used you, too, although I barely consider him a player at this point. He's an amateur."

"Why is this taking so long?" a woman in a form-fitting gold suit asked. Her mask was a honeycomb of tiny gold plates that fit closely over her head, a much more modern design than Aten's would-be crusader getup.

"A few minutes' delay is nothing after so many years of patience," Aten intoned. In spite of his words, the room was filled with potent excitement. They couldn't wait to descend on Reclamation like a pack of feral dogs and tear the place apart.

I need to do something, Rhett thought, but whatever they'd used to secure him in place wasn't a rope, or zip ties, or electrical tape, or any of the many other restraints that he'd been taught to wriggle out of. They must have been using a relic to secure him.

The agents began to speak, focusing on each other rather than on him. He used that opportunity to keep squirming, and hopefully figure out a way to escape once they reached Reclamation. He had allies there, and if he could get to them in time, it might not be too late to stop whatever the Hand had in mind.

The chatter stopped abruptly when Aten raised one hand. The metal-encased stone in his hand was humming. A moment later, a scrambled voice said, *"This is Ray Twelve. It's time."*

A chorus of cheers and jeering rose from the gilded host, and the horned agent reached over to grab the back of Rhett's clothes. He plucked him up from the chair as if he weighed nothing. The restraints held even when he tossed Rhett over his shoulder.

He was wearing bracers rather like the ones Porter had let Fabien try. If Rhett could get them off of him, he'd be a hell of a lot weaker, and probably sore to boot. Using the relics always cost something; conservation of energy, et cetera et cetera. If Rhett could use that against the Hand before they got to Reclamation, it might help. In the meantime, he lay limp across the agent's shoulders. What had Aten called him? Belenos? If Rhett could lull him into thinking he wasn't a threat, he might be able to surprise him, but he would only get one chance. He would need to calculate his next move carefully.

A pawn might not be able to win a game, but every piece on the board mattered, and he had a feeling Aten wasn't all he cracked himself up to be.

Belenos turned, and Rhett's heart dropped. He'd been so

focused on the room before him that he hadn't stopped to think about what might be placed *behind* him. He should have known that the Hand would have a plan in place to head directly to the vault.

Sure enough, they had their very own traveling torii gate.

THE HAND of the Sun arrived in Reclamation not with a blast of gunfire or a battle cry the way he'd always imagined, but single-file and in an orderly line. They emerged in one of the upstairs control rooms, only a few doors down from where Porter had debriefed them mere days before. The tables and chairs had all been pushed against the walls to make room for their arrival.

"What is this?" the one called Sunna demanded. "Are we in a boardroom?"

"No." Rhett hadn't noticed the man standing in the corner, and he only caught a brief glimpse of him before Belenos turned to face him. "We're near the beating heart of Reclamation. It's the perfect place from which to launch our attack."

Rhett didn't know the man's voice. Without thrashing enough to attract Belenos' attention, he twisted his neck around to peer at the speaker. He was dressed in an ENIGMA uniform. A strange mesh webbing covered his exposed skin, except for his head. More of the mesh hung over the back of his uniform, as if he was wearing some sort of body suit, but the mask had been peeled away and left to hang against his shoulders like the hood of a sweatshirt. He was stocky and pale, with close-cropped hair so short it was difficult to determine the color.

Rhett had never seen him before in his life.

"Ra," Sunna said, her voice thick with disdain. "You kept us waiting."

The man chuckled and raised his hands in surrender. Rhett stared at him. How could this man be the spy? He didn't know him, and it wasn't as if Reclamation was a particularly big place —and he was wearing one of their damn uniforms.

"I kept you waiting for two very good reasons," he said. "Reclamation is currently playing host to three vault commanders. I wanted to make sure they'd all arrived, and that Apollo was ready for us. Besides." His smug grin widened. "I had to make sure that Finder was fully ours before I did anything that would set off alarms. Now they're here, and you're here, and Apollo is ready for us. It's finally time."

Aten strode forward and laid one paternal hand on the man's shoulder. "You've done well," he said. "If this goes our way, you'll have everything I promised you and more."

The stranger nodded. "Thank you, sir."

"I take it you have a plan?" Belenos grunted. "Let's hear it."

The stranger grinned. "Of course," he said. "I think you're going to like it."

21 FABIEN

FABIEN LAY TRUSSED up like a Christmas goose in one of Reclamation's secure cells. Annamaria Vizzini was secured in the next chamber. She hadn't stopped swearing in Italian since the Roman commander had dumped them both and departed, along with the newly-arrived Commander Sturlusson, to confront Porter.

Fabien had been behind bars before, sometimes on purpose—targets were easier marks when they were confined to prison, after all—but he'd never been held in a cell like this one. The walls were made of some thick, transparent material that he suspected was both bullet- and smashproof. There were three more cells in the larger room with them, all empty. How many people was ENIGMA planning to detain, exactly?

"Hello!" Fabien flopped around, slamming his heels against the floor to get someone's attention. The sound was disappointingly muted.

"You stupid bastard," Annamaria snarled. "You gave them the cup, and they sold you out. What did you think would happen? That they'd let you keep it for yourself?"

He ignored her. "Hello! I need to take a piss. Are you listening?"

"You ignorant pissant, they wouldn't care if you drowned in your own effluent—"

Fabien let his eyes roll back and tapped the back of his head against the floor. Nobody was answering his questions, Annamaria's raving was giving him a migraine, and there was still no sign of Rhett or Dinah. On the bright side, that meant there was no one around to mock him for getting caught, but it also meant he had no clue what was going on out there. How was he supposed to make a plan without knowing anything?

He was wondering how many times he'd have to knock his head against the floor to make himself pass out, and at the very least spare himself from having to listen to Annamaria's raving, when the door of the main room opened.

Annamaria fell silent. Fabien rolled onto his side. Lane was standing in the doorway, glaring at him.

"I should have known," Lane snapped.

With a groan, Fabien flopped onto his back again and closed his eyes. "Known what?"

"That a lowlife like you would sell us out." Lane closed the door and approached the cell.

Fabien didn't bother opening his eyes. "Are you really that stupid?"

Before Lane could respond, Annamaria threw herself against the glass. "Let me out!" she cried. "I can promise you wealth beyond your wildest dreams, life beyond that of any mortal span... but I need the cup..."

She fell silent again. When Fabien lifted his head, Lane was standing by her cell with a hand on the controls. Her lips were still moving without producing sound.

"Muted her," Lane said by way of explanation. "I don't want to hear any of her bullshit." She turned an accusing glare on Fabien. "Not that your bullshit is better. I shouldn't be surprised by *you,* but Rhett's a disappointment. Out of all of you, I thought we could trust him."

"Not a monologue." Fabien smacked his head against the floor again. "Spare me a monologue. I assume you're the spy?"

Lane paused. *"I'm* the spy? That's rich. I know you were covering for Agent Ra."

"What are you blathering about?"

"Don't deny it!"

Fabien sat up. "Listen, Lane, I don't like.you. I don't want to listen to you. You've gotten us in trouble, which is what you want. Rhett's been set up, I've been framed, good work, gold star, please fuck off."

Instead of sneering, Lane just stared at him, her brows furrowed in apparent bewilderment. Annamaria was still wailing behind the glass, throwing herself against the clear wall again and again.

"Wait," Lane said slowly. She shook her head as her eyes unfocused, looking for all the world like a woman who didn't understand what was happening, and not a woman whose evil schemes had come to fruition at last. "You think you've been set up?"

"I was arrested in the act of catching a member of the Hand!" Fabien barked. "How much more loyal could I be?"

"But the reports..." Lane trailed off. She wandered over to Fabien's cell and stared through the glass. "Rhett admitted to Sturlusson that he was planning to join the Hand."

"As a spy!" Fabien bellowed. "Because one of you Hand of the Sun bastards tried to recruit him!"

Lane's eyes widened. "They did?"

"They left him some note in his quarters..."

Lane lifted a hand to her face. "What? No, no, that was *me*. I was trying to get him to side with us."

Fabien squinted at her. "Who the hell is *us*?"

"Those loyal to ENIGMA," Lane said. "Azmera's still a bit iffy on Porter, that's why she sent Girom here to keep an eye on things. I agreed to help her figure out if Porter was leaking intel to the Hand, or if it was someone else. By the time I figured out who it was, Rhett had already left on his mission north."

Fabien's blood had been running hot for hours, but Lane's words washed over him like a bucket of ice water. "You know who it is?"

"I do." Lane sucked in a breath. "And then you helped him cover his tracks, and Dinah tried to help him retrieve Apollo from the neighboring Earth..."

"What do you *mean*, I helped him cover his tracks?" Fabien scooted closer to the wall. He combed his memory in search of whatever Lane might be referring to. Of course she could be lying, but she didn't strike Fabien as a mastermind.

"You knew he was messing with the perimeter sensors," Lane said. "And then you let him research the ReSkin. Because if one of us had looked into it, we'd have figured out what he'd done."

In her cell, Annamaria had gone still at last. She was still staring at Lane, with her lips pressed into a thin line. It occurred to Fabien that she might still be able to hear them, and he wondered what she was learning in the process.

It clicked at last. "*Marcus* is the spy?"

"Finder helped me review his search history," Lane said. "He wasn't researching the ReSkin at all, he was feeding little scraps of information into Ronnie's feed. Got us to focus on *this* bitch, and took the heat off himself." Lane hooked her thumb toward Annamaria as she spoke. "She was bait."

"Marcus." Fabien slumped back. He was an idiot.

"It's not *really* Marcus," Lane said. "I covered my tracks after Dinah left, and played dumb. In the meantime, I did a little digging. A body turned up around the time Apollo broke into the Ohio vault. It was never IDed, but I pulled some strings, and I'm sure that it's Marcus. He'd been dead for almost two months when they found him." Lane's cheeks flushed, and her eyes pooled with tears. "Those bastards killed him and used the ReSkin to infiltrate us. It's kind of brilliant, if you let yourself forget how evil it is. The suit let Ra *become* Marcus. Fingerprints, retinal scans, even blood tests... as long as he's wearing that suit, he'd be undetectable."

"Shit." Fabien pressed his forehead to the glass. "All this time, and I thought *you* were the biggest asshole in Reclamation."

Lane's eyes narrowed. "And you're really not working with him?"

"Why in God's name would I do that? Do you have any idea how many times these bastards have tried to kill me?" He tipped his chin toward his bandaged leg. The Italian contingent had seen fit to clean and bandage his wounds, even if they hadn't bothered to give him new clothes after the fact.

Lane watched him for what felt like a very long time. Her hand fell to the controls. There was a pop and a hiss, and the whole front wall of the cell swung open. "If you're lying," she growled, "I'll kill you myself."

She didn't wait for Fabien to respond before undoing his bonds. They hadn't given so much as a centimeter when Fabien was fighting them, but they sprang open with the touch of a finger.

As soon as Fabien tried to get up, every muscle in his body cramped. He flopped over with a little groan.

"Get up, Frenchie." Lane dragged him to his feet and threw one of Fabien's arms around her shoulders. "We need to tell Porter and the other commanders the truth."

She dragged Fabien toward the door. Annamaria resumed her thrashing, but unless Fabien was mistaken, her eyes were more sunken than before. She seemed a decade older.

All that stolen time must be catching up with her, Fabien thought.

They made it to the hallway. To Fabien's surprise, Ronnie was standing guard outside. Rather than turning on them, he merely cocked his head at Lane.

"He's with us," Lane said. "Long story."

Ronnie's eyebrows shot up. "Heard and understood. What do you want from me?"

"Get to Girom. Have him contact Azmera, tell him that Marcus is working alone. She already knows about the ReSkin. After that, I need you to get out of here."

Ronnie's eyes hardened, and he crossed his arms. "I'm not running away. I can help."

Lane shook her head. "That's not what I'm asking. Take your family and go to Atlantis. We need Captain Correia on our side, and he *has* to know about the ReSkin. Can you imagine how vulnerable we'll be if the asshole who killed Marcus reprograms it and pretends to be one of the commanders?"

"So send a message," Ronnie shot back.

"Can't," Lane grunted. "Finder's compromised."

That was enough to send Ronnie rocking back on his heels. Fabien, too, felt like he'd been sucker punched. All of Reclamation's systems relied on Finder's input. If the Hand controlled the mainframe...

"You need to get *your family* out of here before they shut us down," Lane said. "The second the Hand knows we're onto them, we'll be fighting for our lives. If you get out before that happens, at least someone will be able to warn the rest of ENIGMA that the threat is coming from inside." There was a shocking intensity in her eyes.

"Right." Ronnie swallowed hard and backed away. "I'll, um, I'll meet you there. In Atlantis. Right?"

Lane didn't flinch. "Right."

Fabien had disliked Lane from jump. He'd found the woman arrogant, unintelligent, and self-absorbed. In that moment, with that outright lie, he discovered an unexpected store of respect for her.

If things were as dire as Lane claimed, there was no reason to think that any of them would be getting out alive.

FABIEN WASN'T EXPECTING his captors to roll out the welcome wagon, or for the Italian commander to pour him a glass of grappa and ask if he wanted a snack. Her vitriol, however, was impressive. When he and Lane hobbled across the lowest level of the vault where the commanders and their entourage were meeting, she practically tackled them.

"What is the meaning of this?" she snarled. "Porter, if this is one of your games—"

Porter, standing a few paces away with his hands behind his back, shook his head. He eyed Fabien up and down. "I assure you, this is quite unexpected."

Sturlusson's lip curled back. "I wish I could believe you, Porter, but the record suggests that you're less than trustworthy."

Porter raised an eyebrow. "Captain De Stasio has already said as much several times. I have made every effort to convince you of my position, but I promise, I'm just as surprised as you are." He turned to Fabien and Lane. "To what do we owe the pleasure?"

"Pleasure?" The Italian commander—presumably Captain De Stasio—waved to the sullen cluster of soldiers at her back. "Enough. Take these two into custody. I have half a mind to lock up Porter, as well."

Fabien leaned against Lane; he'd started bleeding again during their walk, and a scarlet stain was soaking through the bandage. It would be just his luck if that damn dog had hit something really important and Annamaria got him in the end.

His patience was wearing thin as his head grew lighter, so he threw all of his remaining energy into his voice. "Marcus is the mole."

De Stasio was still talking, but Porter held up one hand to silence her. The muscles around his eyes tightened, and it occurred to Fabien that he'd never seen Porter truly angry before.

"Marcus?" Porter repeated. "Are you sure?"

Lane nodded. "He's got a ReSkin."

Everyone started talking at once in a smattering of jumped European languages, their voices twining together into an incomprehensible mess of sound. Fabien groaned as he adjusted his stance. "There's no time for this," he said, but only Lane was close enough to hear him.

"Since when does the Hand have a ReSkin?"

"*Vad är ett* ReSkin?"

"*Perché dovremmo fidarci di lui?*"

"*Perché dovremmo fidarci di qualcuno...*"

"I knew the leak was coming from your crew!"

Fabien gritted his teeth and rotated his head until it was close enough to Lane's ear that she could hear him over the din. "Don't know why I thought this would be useful. We can't wait around for them to get their act together."

He was about to do something he'd never planned to resort to, and ask Lane what their next move should be, when movement from above caught his eye. Something shifted on the catwalks overhead. It was the shape of a person, but when it moved again, Fabien saw that it was one of the androids that Finder had hacked.

His blood ran cold. He hadn't had time to worry about what 'Marcus' could do with the AI. The threat of a vault lockdown had been bad enough, but Finder had been the one to catalog the relics. Finder had taken over communications.

Finder had taken over *security*.

And the Hand had taken over Finder.

"Lane..." He tipped his chin upward to where the android stood.

Lane's face went pale. "Shit," she mumbled. "Do you think he knows? He wouldn't kick things off with all these other agents around, would he? It's too many people to fight at once."

"Unless he brought friends," Fabien said. "The Hand could strike a serious blow to ENIGMA."

Lane swore.

Pounding footsteps made the two of them turn back the way they'd come. Ronnie, in full security gear, jogged out of the corridor and into the open room. His face was ashen, and his hair was dampened by sweat. Cara was a few paces behind him, with a pistol at her hip and Perla clutched to her chest. The child was obviously terrified. She pressed her face into her mother's shoulder.

"Ronnie, what—" Lane began.

"It's already shut down," Ronnie said. The rest of the party fell abruptly silent, and every eye in the room turned on him. "I went to get Girom and the belts for the teleporter, but he was gone, and the exits are locked. The mainframe keeps giving me an error on my security clearances."

Another pair of footsteps sounded from the far side of the room, and they turned once again. Fabien froze at the sight of Rhett, being pushed along by Marcus.

"I caught him!" Marcus cried. "He was in the control room, trying to mess with Finder. I think he sold us out." He had a pistol pressed to the back of Rhett's neck; one twitch of his finger could sever his spine.

Rhett stumbled ahead of him, bound and gagged, but his eyes found Fabien's in the crowd. He shook his head and attempted to tilt his chin over his shoulder toward Marcus.

Commander De Stasio bared her teeth and jabbed a finger at Porter. "What the hell is going on? And who is this?"

Porter's stare could have bored a hole right through Marcus' forehead. "This," he said coldly, "is the son of a bitch who killed and is impersonating Marcus Michaels."

An expression of utter bewilderment settled on Marcus' face, and for a fraction of a second, even Fabien doubted his conclusions. Lane had been wrong about him. What if they were wrong about Marcus, too? Or maybe Lane was playing him, feeding him lies to implicate this man and allow herself to go undetected?

He might not trust Lane completely, but he trusted Rhett. If it really *was* Rhett. He ignored Marcus and met Rhett's gaze.

Fabien had seen relics in action. They could do a lot of crazy shit, and from what he'd been told about the ReSkin, it changed a person into someone else entirely. The body, their characteristics, even their DNA could change. But it couldn't change the person living *in* the body, and there wasn't a single ounce of doubt in his mind: the man before him was Rhett Zappotis, and *he* was sure.

Fabien's weapons had been taken away from him when he was imprisoned, but Lane had a pistol at her hip. Fabien's hand twitched toward the butt.

Rhett was watching him, too. He nodded imperceptibly.

"What are you talking about?" Marcus asked. "He failed the test with the Oraculum. He's a traitor. A liar." He glared at Porter. "Are you really going to believe whatever *they* told you?"

Doubt lay heavy in the room, but Porter never wavered. "You know," he said slowly, "I thought it might be one of you that failed to stop Apollo's entry to the Ohio vault, but Apollo walked right through you. That had to genuinely hurt. Did you plan that ahead of time?"

Fabien's fingertips brushed the grip of the pistol. Lane flinched in surprise and glanced down, but Marcus didn't seem to notice.

Another figure moved on the catwalks above them, but Fabien didn't look. It didn't matter. It wouldn't change his next move. It couldn't.

Marcus' eyes, however, flicked upward. He grinned. "You're an idiot, Porter," he drawled in a tone that sounded nothing like what Fabien was used to. "This was *all* planned ahead of time."

Rhett might not be able to see the man holding him, but he must have been able to feel that Marcus' attention had wandered, because that was when he moved. His head slammed back into Marcus' upturned chin and nose. An instant later, he twisted sideways to drive his elbow into his gut. Marcus fired his pistol, but Rhett had already slipped his grasp and dropped to the floor. He kicked out between Marcus' spread legs, not up—although Fabien would have been more than happy to see him suffer—but out into his kneecap. The joint bent sideways in a direction the human knee was never meant to bend.

Marcus screamed as he stumbled, but his cry was cut short when the bolt from Fabien's laser-pistol drove a smoking hole through his forehead. He hit the ground with a dull thud, and didn't move again.

Fabien grinned mirthlessly at the fallen man. It was probably wrong to take joy in another man's death, but after everything the man had done, he felt more than justified. Besides, he'd promised himself he'd shoot the mole. It was always nice to cross something off his to-do list.

One of the Italian agents started yelling, which set the rest of them off. A few of them lifted their weapons, which made Sturlusson's people go berserk. Rhett wriggled against the floor toward Fabien until one of Swedes drove his boot into his back.

Fabien limped forward.

"Check Marcus!" Lane bellowed. "Check him for the ReSkin!"

The Swedish agent looked to Sturlusson for confirmation. The commander shot Fabien a disgusted glare, but he strode over and dug his fingers into the back of Marcus' neck.

His fist came away gripping Marcus' flesh, which stretched and expanded impossibly far, tenting upward from his neck in a rubbery layer. As it stretched, it lifted Marcus' scalp along with it. At last the skin tore, and a gusset ripped along the back of the dead man's neck. There was no blood. No gore. Only a layer of metal.

Idiot, Fabien thought. Why would the man who'd killed Marcus walk into the midst of their group, when he could just reprogram an android and slap the ReSkin onto its metal body?

A shot through the forehead would have been enough to kill a man, and while the android was wrapped in the ReSkin, it had been a man. Now that Sturlusson had skinned it, however, it reverted to its former components.

And the android, unlike the man, wasn't dead.

Before the torn ReSkin was fully pulled away, the android's arm snapped upward and caught Sturlusson's wrist. Still half-wrapped in what looked like human skin, it rose to its knees and twisted. Sturlusson's arm broke under the force. The Swedish commander screamed bloody murder as the android dragged him to the ground, pressed his face to the concrete, and drove its fist through the back of his skull.

Sturlusson's last gasp was lost in the chaos that followed. Androids leapt from the catwalks above, landing with feline grace with an impact that would have shattered human bone. The Swedes and the Italians all opened fire. Lane dropped so fast that Fabien was sure she'd been hit, but she didn't cry out, and immediately began to crawl across the floor toward Rhett. Ronnie shoved his wife and child back toward the safety of the hallway. Perla's high-pitched wailing struck a register so high it made Fabien's head throb.

Fabien wriggled in Lane's wake, not bothering to return fire. The Marcus-android let go of Sturlusson's remains and immediately lunged toward De Stasio.

A better man would have tried to help, but Fabien had long since achieved a level of pettiness to which others could merely aspire. He left De Stasio to her fate and reached for Rhett.

Lane released the same sort of banded bonds that had restrained Fabien earlier. For his part, he focused on tugging the gag from Rhett's mouth. A second wad of fabric had been stuffed in his mouth, and Rhett sputtered as he pulled it free.

"The Hand is here!" he exclaimed. "I caught up with Aten, but I couldn't stop him."

Lane shuddered. "And they're in Reclamation?"

"They're searching for the destabilizer." Rhett pushed himself to his feet. "We have to get out of here, they're going to let the androids kill as many as they can. They're not interested in taking prisoners."

His explanation was cut short by a headless body slamming into the ground between them. One of the androids that had formerly been controlled by Finder, and been loyal to ENIGMA before *that*, loped forward. It let the agent's head drop from its hands, forgotten.

If Fabien ever doubted that Marcus had messed with the mainframe, this settled it. Finder preferred to project friendly, puppyish cartoon eyes on its ocular screens. It wasn't a killer. This thing, though? There was no soul in there, not even an artificially generated one.

Rhett dragged Fabien upright, and the two of them pelted toward the corridor Ronnie was guarding. Lane followed so closely on their heels that the toes of her boots nipped the back of Fabien's more than once.

As they stumbled past Ronnie, he fired at the android.

"Come on!" Lane bellowed.

Ronnie didn't budge. He was using one of the smart rifles like the ones Fabien favored, and he saw Ronnie draw a short breath and fix his eye to the scope before firing again. This time, he hit one of the android's eyes. The mechanical man flailed and jerked, its eyes guttering with sparks as it collapsed.

"We can't leave without Porter," he said.

"Ronnie—" Lane began.

"No!" he barked. "I'm not leaving anyone else behind." He yanked his utility belt free and held it out to Lane. "Take it."

"Take *what?*" Rhett snapped. "We don't have time for this."

But it clicked then. Lane's strange intensity when she'd told Ronnie to leave hadn't been simply friendly concern. Ronnie wasn't just carrying a message, either.

He was carrying the destabilizer.

A few months ago, Fabien would have taken the belt and left Ronnie to fend for himself. Any time wasted in trying to save his life would be that many fewer seconds he could spend coming up with a plan later. There was only one thing that stopped him from doing just that: Perla's cries, still echoing down the hall.

Fabien had lost his only chance at having a family that gave a rat's ass about him. Erik didn't need him. His son had a new father figure, one who could be an actual *parent* and not some sperm-donor who spent his days shooting strangers for a living.

Ronnie, on the other hand, loved his kid. Fabien had already cursed his own kid to grow up without his biological old man. He couldn't do the same to Perla.

"You have to come," Fabien insisted. He pointed out into the fray, where Porter and De Stasio were climbing the catwalk toward one of the display towers. "You know Porter, he's got a plan, and he's too lucky to die randomly, damn him. He knows what he's doing."

That last part was probably an exaggeration, but it worked. Ronnie squared his jaw and shoved the belt into Lane's hands. "Okay," he grunted. "You're carrying it, though. I'll cover us."

Lane accepted the belt, but she still seemed troubled as they retreated deeper into the corridor. "How are we supposed to get it out of here if Finder and the Hand have the exits locked down?"

Ronnie bit his lip. "I don't know."

Fabien glanced at Rhett. He was sweating profusely, and between their various injuries, they had to support each other to keep from toppling over.

"Any suggestions?" he asked.

Rhett shook his head. "I've got nothing," he said. "The Hand brought plenty of their own toys, and they can treat Reclamation like a toybox, too. They didn't let me hear anything useful, but what more do they need to do? We can't get out of here without Finder's permission, and they're not going to let us walk away. We're trapped."

The sounds of combat died away behind them. Fabien was sure it wouldn't last. The androids would finish their grisly work, and then they'd come looking for new prey. They'd clear the halls of Reclamation systematically, like pest control clearing out a nest of rats.

Unless...

Fabien stopped so abruptly, he nearly yanked Rhett off his feet. "There's another way out," he blurted.

Rhett massaged his knuckles against his bad hip and narrowed his eyes.

"There is." Fabien's brain whirled ahead, trying to come up with a plan that wouldn't get them all killed in the process. They'd have to fight, and it would be tricky, but unless the Hand knew what to look for, they'd likely focus their attention on the vault's exits. They might control Finder, but the AI had been faulty even before Fabien left on his mission, likely as a result of Marcus' fiddling. What were the odds that they'd gone through the vault's collections item by item? Low, probably, there were tens of thousands of relics in the cases...

"Ronnie, Lane." His unfocused eyes fixed on the wall, although he didn't see it. "You know the vault layout pretty well."

They nodded their agreement.

Reclamation was already lost, but if they could keep the destabilizer out of the Hand's grip, they could fight another day. It could work. It had to.

"Do you think you can get us to Cabinet 110, level 9?"

22 DINAH

"CAREFUL!" a robotic voice chirped from somewhere far away. "Don't go *stabbing* her in your attempt to get her free."

"M'not stabbing her," another voice grumbled. "You're too sensitive, she's fine. Trust me, if safety's your concern, I'm not the one you should be worried about."

Light filtered in from somewhere off to her left. Dinah blinked and tried to rub the crust from her eyes, but her hand wouldn't move. The bubble of the helmet still surrounded her despite the cracks.

Dinah stirred. The movement, although slight, woke a dull throb that coursed throughout her body with each breath. The sensation radiated outward from a spot on her back—not her spine, but a throbbing wound to one side.

"She's alive," the second voice said. "At least, I think she is."

"Nibbles?" The name turned to mush on Dinah's tongue.

"She's awake!" the first voice chirped. It had to be Finder.

No other self-respecting AI would choose that voice. "Dr. Bray, can you hear me? Your life signs have been stable, but they're finally picking up..."

Dinah twitched again as a beam of sunlight knifed across her face. The shroud that had protected her peeled away, and her next breath came a little more easily than the ones before.

"Yup," Nibbles said without cheer, "she's alive, all right. Luckier than a lizard in a snap-trap, it's a miracle they didn't drain her dry."

The two of them hovered above her. At first, they were little more than silhouettes: Finder, with his head now fully reattached to his body, and Nibbles without his gasmask, looking as grim as any marsupial Dinah had ever seen in her life.

"Where are we?" Dinah asked.

"Back in the city." Nibbles spared a sideways glance at Finder. "Guess you were right, although it sounds mad."

"I'm always right," Finder said smugly, which was a damn lie.

Dinah struggled upright. Her vision was still murky, and it was therefore a few seconds before she realized that in addition to her two allies, she was surrounded on all sides by dozens upon dozens of giant mutant spiders.

She did the only thing that made sense at the time: she screamed.

"Oh, that's quite enough of that," Finder said. "They've been a tremendous help, and we wouldn't want to offend them."

"Tremendous *help*?" Dinah wheezed. She tried to crawl away, but she was still wrapped in the sticky remains of what she now recognized as one of the spiders' cocoons. The pain in her back took on new meaning. She lifted one shaking hand to her back and found the suit torn open, her side inflamed.

"They bit me," she said.

"You're lucky they did." Finder tapped one metal finger against the broken dome of the helmet. "Between the venom sending you into shock, and the webbing insulating your helmet enough to keep the suit's systems from failing, I daresay they're the reason you're alive."

"Oh, right." Nibbles rolled his eyes and glowered at the silent circle of arachnids. "'Cuz they're so friendly."

The spiders were standing perfectly still and utterly silent. The only thing that proved to Dinah that they were alive was the constant wriggling of their mouthparts.

"Is there a reason they're not, you know. Eating us?" Dinah's voice rasped in her dry throat.

"They aren't eating *me* because I'm inedible," Finder announced, with more pride than the statement probably warranted. "And they aren't eating you because I asked them not to."

"You..." Dinah coughed a few times. Her lungs felt like limp balloons, empty and flat in her chest. She imagined the other-Earthly venom of the spiders flowing through her veins and putrefying her organs from the inside. She imagined turning into jelly. *Get it together.* "You what?"

"I asked them not to," Finder repeated. "Their language isn't particularly complex, but it took me a few tries to hack. Honestly, the fact that it's so simple is part of the problem, it's mostly just verbs and nouns, which you'd think would make things simpler, but in practice it's a nightmare, word order is sooooo much more important than in most human languages, where you can parse meaning even without proper syntax so long as you have a decent grasp of the vocabulary—"

The android seemed to be in no danger of running out of steam, so Dinah butted in. "You *spoke to them.*"

"Oh, yes." Finder nodded furiously. "Before they could do you any lasting harm." It lowered its voice and leaned forward, cupping one hand around its mouth before adding, in a stage whisper, "Nibbles doesn't trust them. I imagine he feels much as you would if I told you that I'd made an alliance with a school of Great White sharks. Do sharks travel in schools? Spiders certainly don't."

"And you brought them to the city?"

"Yes, well." Finder flapped one hand at the assembly. "I told them about our Earth. Did you know that there are over 50,000 known species of spiders in our world? Literally quadrillions of them. That's a mind-boggling number, and Dr. Chikki here wants to meet them. I'm adding the honorific, of course, it's not as if they have universities, but Chikki does seem to be an anthropologist or historian of some kind." As it spoke, it indicated one of the nearby spiders, which was watching Dinah with far too many eyes at once.

"You speak spider," she repeated. She couldn't tell if it was the oxygen deprivation and the venom making her brain move more slowly than usual, or if everything that Finder said was just so spectacularly odd that she would have been confused regardless.

"I was left alone for a very, very long time," Finder said. "I speak a lot of non-human languages. Didn't have a lot of options during my early developmental stages, did I? And despite the fantastic number of species, all spider dialects are pretty closely related. Even across Earths, it seems."

"Oh," Dinah said. Because this didn't seem quite adequate, she added, "Good. Okay. What happens now?"

"You're awake," Nibbles barked. "So it's time for me to spread the word through the underground. I'll get my people to pull back, and they" —he pointed to the spiders— "are going to help us overpower Apollo's forces."

"And we're going to make sure that only Apollo's people get eaten. Isn't that right, Chikki?" Finder twisted around to look up at the massive arachnid looming behind him.

The spider historian's mouthparts thrummed together. The sound they produced was low and surprisingly deep—it echoed in Dinah's chest like a drumbeat.

She hadn't considered what it would mean that Finder could understand the spiders. Finder was the one who had translated Didelian and allowed Dinah to speak with them too, via her translation program. She hadn't realized that Finder would be able to do the same with Chikki and the others, so when the basso voice filtered through her helmet speakers, Dinah shuddered.

"Help Traveler. Meet kin. Little brothers, sisters, distant kin. Spider world? Dream. Dreaming. *Hope*."

"No eating anyone unless they attack," Finder warned. "I'll make the introductions when we reach Earth, but only if I can be quite sure you won't eat the people we like."

"Patient," Chikki rumbled. "Long, long, long time. Waiting. Alone..." Its eyes closed for a moment before snapping open.

Finder faked a cough into its fist. "Ah, yes. As I understand it, this is the only hive of spiders to survive the environmental calamity this world experienced. They seem quite keen to meet their distant cousins, which is nice."

Nibbles grunted. "If you say so. I'm going to warn my people about all this." He got to his feet and offered a hand to Dinah. Despite the differences in their height, his support helped, and Dinah was soon upright. As she peeled the last of the spiderwebs away from her limbs, Nibbles scurried off and disappeared between the buildings on the edge of the city.

"I think he's upset that we compromised the city by bringing them here," Finder told Dinah under his breath.

"You think?" Dinah raised an eyebrow. "Because I have some thoughts about the wisdom of bringing them to Earth. Do you think they'll be content to visit Reclamation and exchange notes with whatever spiders have taken up residence there? Because I doubt it, and setting them loose on the world at large is worse than any idea I've had so far."

Finder studied her somberly. When the android spoke again, its voice lacked the usual forced cheer. "If Apollo's plan works, they'll be climbing through the seam one way or another. Don't you think it's better if the giant spiders are on our side when the time comes?"

Put that way, Dinah could only agree.

THE SPIDERS WEREN'T thorough as they swept through the city. They left the houses and hidey-holes alone, opting instead to follow Finder and Dinah's lead toward the warehouse. Most of the residents screamed and scattered as the spiders approached, but a few stood their ground.

"No killing!" Finder insisted. "Leave them wrapped up and keep moving. Nibbles and his people will sort them out later."

Not all of the spiders seemed happy with this order, but they followed Chikki's lead. Dinah stayed out of their way. There was no chance she'd be mistaken for a Didelian, but she didn't entirely trust that the spiders would keep their word, and she didn't want to get bitten again either way.

With Finder's help, she'd recovered her laser pistol, although she kept it holstered until they reached the warehouse. The first real resistance they'd encountered was in the streets outside, with dozens of Didelians in uniform surrounding the place. They screeched when they saw the spiders, and immediately opened fire.

From what Dinah had seen, Didelians didn't favor guns. This unit was no exception. Most of them carried mechanized slingshots, which they loaded from pouches at their belts, or from whatever else they could find nearby.

Rocks and discarded scraps of metal were painful enough, as Dinah soon discovered. She yelped when a twisted bit of metal debris slashed across one arm, shearing another tear in her suit and pulling a thin line of blood to the surface in its wake. A few seconds later, another pebble hit her in the chest with all the force of a paintball. She fired a shot in the general direction of the nearest assailant and tried to catch her breath.

The pebbles, however, were the least of her problems. Far worse, and more dangerous, were the pellets that they carried with them. The pellets spun and expanded mid-flight, with little discs of razor-sharp metal that bloomed outward like Saturn's rings. The spiders' armored bodies mitigated the damage, but when one of them was struck in the eyes, the ball ripped through the soft tissue and spun deeper into the tender flesh, breaking apart as it went. The spider swayed and toppled, Goliath brought low by a single well-aimed projective.

Puffed up with his success, the Didelian aimed again. Dinah tried to shoot the weapon out of the creature's paw, but her aim had never been that good, and she ended up shooting into the creature's ribs. The Didelian howled and stumbled. Before he could fire again, a shadow passed above him as one of the long-limbed spiders walked directly over him and scooped the injured soldier up. The Didelian's cries soon faded as the spider silk bound him up.

Finder had ignored the combat altogether and headed right for the warehouse door. Stones and pellets alike pinged off of the android's back as it shoved its way through the entrance, barely marring its metal skin. Dinah moved to follow, then thought better of it. She imagined one of those pellets hitting her in the neck or some other squishy pressure point. No, thank you—she'd rather live.

Instead, she turned her attention to Chikki. The immense spider was in the midst of wrapping up one of the soldiers, so intent on her work that she failed to realize that another of its kind was taking aim at her eyes. Dinah aimed at the Didelian's back and fired.

For all Finder's talk about not killing, there were already half a dozen fallen spiders, and a few Didelians who had either fallen in combat, or whose blood stained the snowy-white surface of their cocoons. There was no way that Dinah was going to be able to walk away from this without getting her hands dirty.

Still, when the furry body fell, Dinah fought the urge to gag. *Don't puke in your helmet,* she thought, *you'll only regret it,* but her stomach still lurched.

Chikki dropped the newly-enshrouded body of her victim in the street and turned her many eyes on Dinah. "Help. Save. Protect... friend Traveler."

Whether she was acknowledging that Dinah had helped her, or was promising to do the same in the future, Dinah couldn't say. Maybe both. Regardless, she took her address as an invitation. Dinah pointed to the roof of the warehouse, then at herself. "Up," she said. "Help?"

Chikki shuddered. "Traveler up," she agreed.

Dinah had hoped that she might be able to climb onto Chikki's back, but Chikki didn't give her the chance. Her body swept low to catch Dinah by the back of her suit, then gripped her around the middle. While Dinah dangled in her grip, Chikki charged the warehouse wall. Another Didelian tried to fire on her, but Chikki batted him away using one leg. The force of the blow sent the creature flying.

Dinah shuddered.

More Didelians had appeared at the windows of the building. Unlike their counterparts outside, they weren't waging a war with rocks and refuse, but with the artifacts stored inside. Their scruffy demeanor suggested that they were on the side of the underground, which was only confirmed when they began launching a series of chaotic and poorly-orchestrated attacks against the soldiers outside.

The soldiers in the street scattered, and the spiders pursued them as Chikki climbed the wall. She didn't seem to mind the fact that doing so required that she walk sideways, but Dinah was keenly aware that her back kept pressing against Chikki's armored belly.

It's a wonder my brain doesn't just go into shock, Dinah mused. *Someday I'm going to have to process exactly how traumatic this experience has been, and then I'm going to need a truly shocking amount of therapy.*

They crested the roof of the building. Chikki set her down at last, and Dinah's wobbly legs barely managed to hold her upright as she stumbled away.

"Thanks," she said.

"Traveler," Chikki rumbled.

"Yeah," Dinah agreed, "that's me. I appreciate the help."

"Traveler," the spider repeated. She lifted one long leg and pointed out into the city.

The warehouse wasn't much taller than the buildings around it, but the height afforded Dinah a striking view of the city. The dome above them gleamed in the afternoon light as the sun dipped toward the horizon. Spiders and Didelians still littered the streets, and the black scars of the scorched chasms in the land formed strange patterns in the cityscape, a reminder of how different this Earth was from Dinah's own.

Chikki's leg pointed several blocks away to where a tall and flickering figure awaited.

Apollo. Dinah wrapped her arms around her middle and

tried to ignore the pulsing pain that still surged through her veins with every heartbeat. The underground might have taken the warehouse, but none of that would matter if Apollo and his ally in Reclamation opened the seam.

"Take me there," Dinah said. "Now. Please."

Chikki was silent. When Dinah turned, she was gone, and she was alone on the roof.

What happens if I can get to Apollo before Ra opens the seam? Dinah wondered. No answer sprang to mind, or at least nothing clear and cohesive. Still, she couldn't very well do nothing.

She would have to fight, as she had fought ever since she'd joined ENIGMA: with everything she had, not knowing if she would win or lose, but with the certainty that she was doing everything in her power to do the right thing.

First things first. She needed to get into the warehouse and figure out what she had at her disposal.

23 RHETT

"YOU'RE LEANING TOO HEAVILY on me," Fabien complained.

"Am not," Rhett retorted. "I'm practically carrying you, even though I'm the one with a busted hip."

Fabien made an indignant noise and indicated his bandaged leg.

"Oh, sure." Rhett rolled his eyes at him. "Go on, cry about it. I've been dealing with pain for years. You've been injured for, what? Six hours? Gimme a break."

He knew he was babbling, but he was only doing it so that they wouldn't both lose their minds. This was all too familiar: the dash through Reclamation, the knowledge that the Hand was on their heels, the certainty that the other side had the advantage. He was irrationally furious with Commander Sturlusson for splitting him off from ENIGMA and then having the audacity to die before he could acknowledge that he hadn't been a spy.

Or maybe it was just easier to be angry at Sturlusson than at himself. Did he really think that, just because he'd been able to best Apollo, he'd be able to take down the Hand by himself? Instead, he'd stumbled right into a trap, and then been used as a cheap distraction while the last pieces of their plan fell into place.

"We should stop for weapons," he blurted.

From ahead of them, Lane snorted. "You want to pop by the armory? As if they'd leave it unguarded? That'll be the first place they'd expect us to go."

"Doesn't have to be the armory," Fabien panted. Despite their banter, Rhett was genuinely worried about him. He was pushing too hard, if the soaked-through bandage was any indication. He'd seen just how far Fabien was willing to go last time; he'd almost killed himself rather than let Apollo get away without a fight. "We've got all kinds of weapons in the vault itself."

"And Finder will light up like a motion-sensing Christmas tree if we try to touch anything," Lane retorted.

Fabien opened his mouth to argue, but Ronnie cut him off. "If you two want to snipe at each other, pick another time. There's no point in trying to be sneaky, Lane. We're outnumbered, outgunned, and at an obvious disadvantage. This isn't a marathon, and we're not playing the long game. It's a goddamn sprint, and my daughter's life is on the line."

Perla whimpered and pressed her face into Cara's shoulder.

"I hate the idea of just leaving Reclamation to the Hand," Lane admitted.

Given what Tera had told Rhett about Gold Bar Holdings, and what he'd seen of the Hand with his own eyes, he was unsettled to think what they could do with this many objects. With this much more power. How many civilians would pay the price if Reclamation fell?

"Do I get a say in this? As a mother?" Cara asked. She was a soft-spoken woman with a thick accent; Rhett was positive that English wasn't her first, or even second, language. He'd never talked to her much in the dining hall—casual conversations with civilians didn't come easily to him, given how soft they tended to be, and intruding on their family conversations would have felt like butting into Ronnie's personal space. Now, though, Cara didn't strike him as soft at all. She looked like a woman who would defend her daughter with her life.

"Yeah." Fabien shifted uncomfortably and didn't meet Cara's eye. Rhett knew exactly enough about Fabien's personal life to understand why Cara's presence made him uncomfortable. "Yeah, you get a say."

"I want to get out as fast as possible," she said. "We need to warn the rest of ENIGMA. You're the only thing standing between the Hand and the rest of the world, and it's not just our lives at stake. I knew that when I came here. The Hand may gain the relics, but they won't defeat the hearts of the people. ENIGMA needs you more than they need the artifacts."

"And if we get out of here," Fabien added, "then the destabilizer will be safe. That's what they want most, isn't it? To tear a hole between realities? If that's their primary goal, then that's the thing we need to stop. So let's stop fiddling around and get out of here."

Lane rubbed her temples. "Okay, okay, I'm not *arguing* that. But if we're going to go out in the open, we have to be prepared to fight. But in order to do *that*, we'll have to give away our location..."

"So we split up," Rhett said.

They all turned to look at him. Under their scrutiny, he was suddenly aware of how battered and unwashed and hunched he was. He straightened up and tried to sound like a captain and an agent, not some sad sack who kept screwing things up.

"If we take anything from the armory or the cases," he went on, "Finder will alert the Hand. They'll turn their attention to whoever's grabbing a weapon. That'll give the rest of you time to get to the relic Fabien's talking about."

"I don't like the way you're saying this," Fabien complained. "When you say 'the rest of you,' I know you're planning to be the bait."

Rhett nodded to his bleeding leg. "If you come with me, you'll only slow me down. No, don't argue, you know I'm right. Cara and Perla are civilians, so we need to get them out."

"So take Lane," Fabien growled. "Don't throw yourself into the line of fire alone."

"You'll have the destabilizer," Rhett reminded him. "Without Lane, you'll only be defending it with one-and-a-half people who know what they're doing in a combat scenario. No offense, Cara."

"None taken."

Fabien sputtered. "Does that make me the half?"

"You can't walk on your own, LeRoux." Rhett rolled his eyes at him. "So it'll have to be me. Besides, you're the one who knows the way out."

Fabien glared at him. "And what about you?"

Rhett forced a smile, even though it didn't feel right on his face. "I'll catch up," he said. "You're not as fast as you think you are, even when you're not bleeding out."

Fabien huffed, but he didn't argue again. It didn't mean he agreed with Rhett's plan, just that he didn't have a better one.

Rhett shrugged him off and let Lane step in to help support him. "Level 9," he said. "I'll find you. Once I trip Finder's alarms, give me a five-minute head start, and then run like hell."

"Hell's a bad word," Perla mumbled. One of her dark eyes fixed on Rhett. It was only a few years since Anna was that age, and the memory of his niece only made him want to fight harder for the future.

If he had to die to keep them safe, so be it. He'd always known the score.

"Sorry, Perla," Rhett said. "I'll try not to use bad words in the future." He backed up a pace.

"Here." Fabien held out the gun he'd taken from Lane. "At least take this."

Rhett shook his head. "Keep it," he said. "You'll need it more than me."

MURDEROUS ANDROIDS WERE RUNNING AMOK on the lowest level of the vault, and Fabien's crew would be exposed on the catwalks once they made their move. Their best bet would be for Rhett to trip an alarm as far from their destination as possible.

Besides, the Hand would be watching the exits. If they thought Rhett was trying to get out, they'd likely converge on him, giving Fabien and the others plenty of time to get away.

He jogged through the halls of Reclamation, pushing the pain of each impact to the back of his mind. He could worry about the pain later. For the moment, he needed to keep moving.

There was symmetry in sacrifice. Seeing Lisa Kelly walk free had eased the guilt that clung to him for years, but this sacrifice set him free at last. Whether he lived or died didn't matter, so long as his crew made it out alive.

As he wound his way through the corridors, he heard the voices of the Hand echoing from otherwise deserted quarters. He recognized the sharp, high voice of the woman codenamed Sunna, and another woman he didn't know. At another intersection, he caught snippets of a conversation between the man who'd pretended to be Marcus—he never *had* gotten his name—and the bastard he only knew as Aten.

"...just waiting for a reading. Apollo is poised to strike, and I promise you, the destabilizer is here."

"Where, exactly?" Aten asked.

"Lane had it. She was down there with the rest of them, but apparently she slipped away."

Rhett didn't wait around for Aten's reply. If he was lucky, Aten would take his anger out on the younger agent and reduce their band by one, but he wasn't counting on it. They were too close to victory for the anger to boil over.

If we get away with the relic, it'll be a different story.

The armory wasn't far, and he managed to slip through the hallways without anyone noticing him. With the fake Marcus roaming the corridors, he wondered who, if anyone, was watching the security feeds. Perhaps the mainframe's AI was doing it alone.

If so, it must know where he was. That was Finder's whole purpose, after all.

The door of the armory stood open when he arrived. The Hand must have come through already, or else the android that had been on duty had left in such a rush that it didn't close the door behind it. The room within was only halfway lit; one bank of lights was off. Rhett checked the cross-corridor to make sure no Hand patrols were on their way past before slipping into the room.

The next thing he knew, someone had grabbed his lapels and thrust him back against the wall. He hit the plaster so hard that his breath rushed from his lungs. His attacker's elbow pressed into his throat, and their knee drove into his groin. He grunted in pain, then froze at the cool pressure of a pistol barrel driven into the soft skin beneath his jaw.

"One move, and you're dead," a woman's voice snarled. The thick Italian accent blurred the words such that it took him a moment to parse them.

Another figure moved in the half-light. At first, he was only aware of the smart rifle aimed between his eyes. The rifle wobbled before drooping downward.

"Rhett." Porter's grim expression cracked into a smile. "You're alive. How fortuitous."

"You're alive," Rhett retorted. "I didn't know you were a marksman."

"I am a man of many surprises. Commander De Stasio, would you be kind enough to release my subordinate?"

The Italian commander grumbled to herself and shoved Rhett again before retreating. "What are you doing here?"

Rhett's eyes darted to Porter, who nodded in response. "I believe we can trust De Stasio, inasmuch as we can trust anyone. It is possible, I suppose, that she's also a spy, or an imposter using a ReSkin, but they are quite rare and the one we know about was quite thoroughly destroyed."

Rhett wasn't entirely convinced, but he nodded anyway. He made a private promise not to reveal Fabien's plan until he was more convinced of De Stasio's allegiance before turning his attention to the shelves. His pelvic bone ached from the Italian commander's blow, but that was just another entry on the long list of pains that currently plagued him.

"You might want to get out of here." Rhett loped over to the racks laden with rifles. Although he generally preferred subtlety, sometimes it was better to get straight to the point.

He wouldn't mind planting a live round in Aten, for example.

De Stasio scoffed. "You think we want to stay? They have all the doors guarded! Where would we go?"

"Doesn't matter to me where you go," Rhett said, "so long as it's not here. If the Hand hasn't already clocked us, I'm about to trip one of the alarms." He reached for a bulletproof vest, but just as his fingers brushed the material, he held back. It was lightweight, but not weightless, and he'd likely be fighting at close range. A vest wouldn't stop a sword or a bomb or a punch from an impossibly strong fist. His hand danced a few slots over and found another of the hopper vests Finder had offered him before they left for Valhalla.

"Interesting," Porter mused. "I take it you have a plan?"

He yanked the vest on over the clothing Tera had given him. "*Plan* might be generous, but yeah."

"And you're the bait?"

"So it seems."

"Ah." Porter adjusted his grip on the rifle. His eyes never left Rhett, and even when he turned away, Rhett could feel the weight of his gaze on his shoulders. "In that case, I think I ought to stay with you."

De Stasio made an incredulous noise. "You don't even know what his plan is!"

Porter didn't hesitate. "If you want to strike out on your own, that's up to you."

"Well," a fourth voice growled, "isn't this heartwarming."

Even before he turned, Rhett knew it would be Belenos. Rhett had never seen his face beneath that stupid, ostentatious horned helmet, but his voice was recognizable enough. He'd traveled enough over the years that he could identify his accent as South African even when it was muffled by that outrageous mask.

He whirled to face him. Porter stood perfectly still, his expression nonplussed as he took in the full span of the helmet.

Rhett immediately raised the gun to his shoulder, but he wasn't as fast as Belenos. Perhaps the bracers he wore granted him speed as well as strength, or maybe he was already poised to strike. Whatever the reason, he was able to snatch the long coil of heavy chain from his belt and whip it toward Porter in one smooth motion.

Porter should have been snapped in half, or at the very least thrown into the wall with enough force to crush the plaster. Before either of those things could happen, he raised one hand to his chest and tugged on a leather cord. Rhett caught a flash of white against his dark suit.

The chain in Belenos' grip snapped in half. Part of it whipped back toward the agent of the Hand, while the other half went flying uselessly across the room, where it clattered into a shelving unit. Containers tumbled loose, including a small box of bright red orbs the exact size and color of fresh cherries.

Time bombs. Without stopping to think, Rhett ground his heel into the whole pile of them. There must have been at least a dozen of them.

Time stopped.

The damaged shelving unit froze mid-topple; Belenos was suspended partway through stumbling back from having his balance thrown off; De Stasio crouched with her arms over her head as she ducked away from the broken shelves; and Porter stared directly at Rhett, with the leather cord looped around his thumb and the strange pendant flashing in the light.

Moving through frozen time was like swimming through cold molasses, but Rhett had the advantage of the hopper vest. He powered it on and began to blink around the room in slow motion, lingering in one place for a second that seemed to last for ten times as long as it should. At last, his random trajectory brought him close enough to Belenos that he could power off the vest and extend his arm to pry the bracers from his massive wrists. Bracers in hand, he backed away.

He'd barely made it two tedious steps when time snapped back into its normal flow. The broken chain struck Belenos' chest. When he'd swung it, he'd still been wearing the bracers, and the full force of his superhuman strength had gone into the movement. Without them, he was just a man—albeit a very big man—and the backlash carried him off of his feet and out into the hall.

Rhett dropped the bracers to the floor and charged after him. The agent lay sprawled in the hallway. His helmet had been flung free, revealing the face beneath.

He was just a man. A man with thinning hair and ruddy cheeks and unkind eyes. His mouth opened and closed like a fish drawn out of the water. The impact of the chain had broken at least one of his ribs. Belenos was no god after all, whatever he claimed.

Rhett lifted his smart-targeting rifle to his shoulder and fired three shots at point blank range. One would have been enough to kill Belenos, but he needed the release.

He stood there, panting, as Belenos' body went limp. *Zoe would be disgusted if she could see me now*, he thought. *She'd hate how satisfied I am to be the cause of another man's death.*

Still, the bastard had deserved it.

Porter and De Stasio emerged from the armory. The Italian commander was in the process of pulling on the bracers Rhett had ripped from Belenos' arms.

He tipped his chin toward Porter's charm. "Interesting device you've got there."

Porter lifted the talisman into his palm. "A good luck charm of sorts. Although that makes it sound more magical than practical. It... alters the odds in my favor, let's say. It doesn't make the impossible occur, but it does make the unlikely more probable." He tucked it back into his jacket, which was somehow still unwrinkled. "You didn't think I'd go around completely unarmed, did you?"

A smile tugged at Rhett's lips. At his feet, a trickle of blood ran from beneath Belenos' back toward his boot. "I should have known better."

"What's the next phase of your plan, Captain?"

Rhett stepped away from the bloody trail and strode off down the corridor. "I don't know about you, but I'm going to cause some trouble."

BELENOS' death may not have set off any vault-wide alarms, but all that changed when Rhett reached the first case on the top floor. It had only been a couple of months since the first time he'd set foot in Reclamation, but the vault had been rebuilt in the interim, and it had gradually shifted in his mind from a beautiful and impossibly strange structure to something a bit like home.

Watching De Stasio use the bracers to smash through one of the display doors bothered him, even though it was part of the plan. The glass was still falling when the lights overhead flashed red, the stories-tall cabinet lit up from within, and a siren began to wail.

"Unauthorized actions on case 1214," a robotic voice droned. The mainframe didn't sound like Finder anymore. Rhett knew that the Hand's tampering had undermined Finder's autonomy, but the confirmation still hurt more than he'd expected. Losing Finder was a bit like losing a friend.

"Should we wait here?" De Stasio asked. She looked ready to fight, and Rhett had to give credit where it was due: the woman was clearly loyal to ENIGMA, and wanted to lay into the Hand of the Sun agents as badly as Rhett did.

He shook his head anyway. "We should keep moving. Keep them guessing. Make the Hand spread themselves thin so that we only have to fight them as individuals—or pairs, if we can help it."

"I wouldn't like to encounter a whole group of androids either, if we can help it," Porter added.

Memory of Commander Sturlusson's bones shattering galvanized Rhett into motion again. De Stasio drove her fists through glass as they went, while Rhett took laser-fire potshots into the distance, lighting up dozens of damaged cases all over the vault.

Not so long ago, he'd have given everything to keep this place intact. But Cara was right: if he had to choose between these antiquities and the future of ENIGMA, he'd let the world burn.

They were halfway across the walkway they'd chosen when another golden figure blocked their way. It was the woman in the armored morphsuit with the honeycomb face-mask. Rhett opened fire, but the woman sprang forward, leaping higher than any human could without augmentation.

"For God's sake," Rhett grumbled under his breath. They never could make it easy, could they?

He activated his hopper vest, assuming that it would only move him forward and back along the walkway where he stood. He assumed wrong. When he reappeared, he was several feet to the right, suspended over the abyss. His stomach lurched as he dropped a few feet and skipped abruptly sideways. That wouldn't do. Rhett had no intention of falling to his death mid-combat. He lowered the vest and dropped heavily to his feet on the nearest walkway.

The pain of the impact was too great to ignore. It raced through his nerve endings up his leg and ribcage, clawing as it went. His vision went dark for a few seconds as the pain consumed everything and blanked out the world.

Shit. He wasn't going to be good to anyone at this rate.

The Hand agent was still above him, plummeting toward Porter and De Stasio. The Italian commander raised her fists.

There was no way Rhett could make it back up to their level in time, but he might be able to aim through the metal grid of the catwalk. It was a long shot, and he wouldn't normally have risked it, but Porter was wearing that lucky charm... he flipped the rifle to smart-targeting live rounds, just in case.

De Stasio struck the Hand agent with such force that the gold-clad woman fell backward. At the same time, Rhett fired upward. The bullet clipped the metal as it was propelled upward through the agent's back, and she didn't move again.

Two Hand agents down, six to go. He could already hear a

few of them bellowing to each other as they pounded across the catwalks in search of the source of the chaos.

Surely five minutes must have elapsed since the alarms went off, which meant that Fabien and the others must be making their move at last.

If only he could send them Porter's lucky charm and ensure their success.

24 FABIEN

RONNIE TOOK THE LEAD. Fabien and Cara followed behind him, while Lane followed in the rear.

"Do you need a hand?" Cara asked.

It must have been obvious that Fabien was struggling to keep up, but he still shot the woman a disgusted glance. "You're carrying your daughter," he said. "She needs you more than I do."

The simple fact of the matter was that nothing would make Fabien hate himself more than accepting help. He'd wanted this. He'd been *bored* without a fight. He couldn't make someone else drag him along. His pride couldn't take it.

Oblivious to the war within him, Cara worked her bottom lip between her teeth. She kept watching Fabien, and occasionally reached out one arm to steady him when he stumbled.

Going up the steps was the worst. Actually, wriggling through the tight gap of the device he'd used to depart for Rome was going to be the worst. He didn't let himself think about that too hard. The device would be a problem for future-Fabien, for three-minutes-from-now-Fabien, and that was impossibly far away. Stairs became the struggle that consumed his whole world.

He tried to climb fast, and only succeeded in overbalancing. There was no telling how far he'd have fallen if Lane hadn't caught him.

"Careful," Lane warned.

Fabien could have shrieked with rage. That damned dog. That damned agent. Everything had collided in a mad rush and stripped away his ability to fight back.

"You should go on without me," he told Lane. His voice could barely be heard over the shriek of the alarms that Rhett had set off several stories above.

"You're the one who knows how to use the relic that'll get us out of here," Lane insisted. "Stop whining and get a move on."

Fabien made to protest. If he hadn't slowed to a stop to argue with Lane, he wouldn't have seen the android moving silent as a cat behind them.

But he had, and he did, and he was still helpless to stop what happened next.

The android yanked Lane backward down the steps into its arms. "Device detected," it shrilled. "Destabilizer location confirmed." It wrapped its arm around Lane's neck and tightened. Lane's face turned red as she struggled and thrashed against the relentless grip.

"No!" From several steps above, Ronnie opened fire.

It was a clean shot that caught the android right in the eye.

The metal man stiffened, tipped, and crashed backward over the railing. Rather than releasing Lane, its grip locked, taking the agent with it.

The agent, and the destabilizer she carried.

Fabien howled with rage and threw himself forward. The steps were a hell of a lot easier going down than coming up, and he practically flew as he stumbled downward. He couldn't be sure if Lane was still screaming, or if the sound was coming from Ronnie and Cara and likely Perla. *She shouldn't have had to see this... we should have been able to protect her...* but that was a silly thing to think, wasn't it, knowing that any moment might be the last? Not just for Perla, but for all of them.

Three steps down, Fabien tripped, and he only picked up speed as he fell, slamming from one cold metal step to the next. By the time he came to a stop, his head was spinning and every inch of him ached.

"Lane?" he wheezed. He lifted her head.

The android must have rolled when it fell, because it lay on top of Lane. Any hope Fabien might have had regarding the woman's survival was instantly crushed by the tilt of her shoulders, facing away from where Fabien lay, and her face, which was turned so that its glassy eyes were clearly visible.

Fabien crawled forward on all fours. The alarms were still blaring, but something was wrong with his head. The floor beneath him appeared to tip from one side to the next like the deck of a ship at sea, and the rush of his own heartbeat in his ears overwhelmed everything else.

He couldn't let reality sink in. Fortunately, Fabien LeRoux had years of experience when it came to pushing things away.

Shove the emotions deep enough, and they might *never* resurface. He had to concentrate as he clambered over to Lane's corpse and ripped the utility belt free. Inside, the power cells pulsed and glowed, their green light filtering between the warp and weft of the canvas.

Take the destabilizer and go, he thought. Lane's mouth was open, and a few bubbles of blood-flecked spit trailed from between her ashen lips. *Don't look at her. Don't think her name. You need to get out of here.*

He pushed himself upright and limped away to the steps. If only Ronnie had followed, Fabien could press the belt into his hands. Tell him to get the hell out of Reclamation. Do what he had planned to do at the beginning.

Leave the useless meat behind and finish the mission.

Rhett could meet him at the case. He'd be smart enough to figure out how to use it. Speaking as the useless meat, Fabien wouldn't mind being abandoned. Getting killed would probably hurt less than walking up those damned stairs a second time.

He was so intent on staying on each shuffling step that he failed to register the man standing at the base of the stairs until it was too late.

The stranger didn't even have the decency to shoot him. He threw a punch with his bare-knuckled fist that caught Fabien square in the teeth.

There was blood on his tongue. Cold concrete at his back. He hadn't even realized he was falling until the stranger drove his boot into Fabien's chest and held him down while he yanked the utility belt away.

"I told you we'd do it, sir," he said. "The mainframe can

pinpoint every item in the catalog. I knew they wouldn't get far."

"Excellent work." The gilded figure to Fabien's left moved with all the cool solemnity of an elder deity. He held out one hand, and the stranger passed his prize over. The canvas belt looked so mundane in contrast to his backlit presence that Fabien couldn't help but laugh. It was like watching an angel stoop to retrieve a stone.

You must have hit your head pretty hard when you fell. The voice in his head sounded like him, but it seemed to come from *outside* himself. Like Jiminy Cricket was whispering in his ear. *Are you really going to let this guy step on your chest?*

He lay there like a lump of clay and let that response speak for itself.

The man in the golden armor unzipped the belt and let the power cells tumble into his palm. He retrieved the spherical core as well before tossing the belt away. It landed next to Lane's face, so that her wide eyes seemed fixed upon it.

Aren't you forgetting something? the Jiminy Cricket voice asked.

Given how poorly his brain was working, Fabien was probably forgetting a lot of things.

A few other members of the Hand wandered into Fabien's field of vision, along with a handful of slate-eyed androids. They watched in quiet reverence as their leader assembled the softly humming pieces of the destabilizer.

If that's Aten, the voice said, *then the schmuck with his boot on your chest is probably the spy. Look at his uniform. He's dressed like an ENIGMA agent, but you've never seen him before in your life. He was the one wearing the ReSkin. He's the reason the Hand was able to infiltrate Reclamation. How do I feel about that?*

Because I'd be angry.

The man stepped away, drawn to the destabilizer like a moth to flame. He didn't seem to care that Fabien was still alive. To be fair, he didn't pose much of a threat. He didn't even have a weapon—

Oh. *That* was what he'd forgotten. Lane had been carrying the pistol when she fell, and Fabien hadn't taken it. Which meant that the pistol was still over there somewhere.

Sure enough, when he rolled his head toward Lane's body, he saw the butt of the pistol poking out from under the dead woman's thigh. He shimmied a little, testing to see if the members of the Hand would notice him. None of them cared. The destabilizer spun like a top in their leader's open palms, and they clustered around it in awe, forming a circle and gradually closing the gaps between them.

He braced for the rush of wind that began when the first green sparks leapt from the assembled relic. The members of the Hand cried out in wonder and awe.

Like kids on Christmas. Like cultists celebrating when their god speaks back. Ignore them. You have one mission.

The suction from the seam grew stronger, but Fabien didn't look this time. He spread himself out against the concrete as Lane's body and the fallen android inched across the floor, pulled by the otherworldly wind.

His fingertips brushed the pistol grip. The wailing sirens mixed with the rush of the wind and delighted exclamations from the Hand. Pressure built in his ears. His palm found the grip.

And then he was yanked back again. A boot struck his bruised ribs, and he rolled over to find Annamaria Vizzini crouched above him. The Hand must have freed her from her cell, and she had saved all of her anger for him.

"*Che te pozzino ammazza!* You ruined everything for me. Where is my cup?"

Fabien's only response was to spit in her face.

She howled and ripped at his bandages, raking her nails through the open wound. "Where is it?" Her wild black hair was falling out, her skin had shrunk to her bones, and there was a milky cast to her eyes, as if cataracts were growing by the second to cover her pupils.

She was so intent on hurting him that she didn't see him lift one trembling hand to press Lane's pistol against her temple. At the last second, she flinched, but he'd already pulled the trigger.

Annamaria collapsed on top of him. Her fingers were still pressed into the meat and muscle of his thigh. She shuddered a few times before she went completely limp.

Fabien gritted his teeth as he shoved her body away. He had some vague notion that he had to kill as many of the Hand as possible. *How* he would do that, he couldn't be sure, but he was damn well going to try.

The green light that wreathed the seam between worlds had expanded almost to the edges of the massive room. A maelstrom of light and sound whirled around the destabilizer with the relic at its center, which glowed a poisonous green. The remains of the fallen androids, Lane, Annamaria, and the dead representatives of the Italian and Swedish vaults were drawn into the artificial storm. Fabien was dragged along the floor with them. He tried to catch onto something solid as he passed, but he was much too slow.

In the center of it all, half a dozen members of the Hand of the Sun had formed a circle. Their costumes had always looked foolish to Fabien, no matter what meaning Dinah saw in them. Together, they looked like a bad Renaissance faire. They'd joined arms and closed ranks, turning their faces upward as if in prayer, marveling at the watery light of the world beyond.

It's a cult. What did I tell you?

The cityscape that Fabien had seen when Apollo fell through the seam shimmered before them, as though it was one massive canvas that rippled in the wind. The city on the other side didn't quite look real.

The wind died abruptly, and the sound popped in Fabien's ears like a punctured soap bubble. The world on the far side of the seam merged with the one Fabien had always known, and in the joining, everything he'd known was undone. The whole far wall of Reclamation was gone, open to an unfamiliar sky. Fabien could *smell* it—the familiar sour scent of a lived-in city. It would have been possible for someone to follow the streets from the other world and walk right into the vault.

Which was exactly what the man waiting on the other side did. He looked battered and gaunt, but there was no mistaking him. Agent Apollo had survived his exile in the other world.

"Apollo," the leader of the gold-clad cult intoned. "You are among us once again."

What should have been the culmination of their perfect little ritual was thrown into utter chaos by a wave of...

Merde, what are *they? Spider crabs? They look like something out of an old Godzilla film.*

The spiky-bodied, long-limbed creatures swept through the opening in a wave, sending the members of the Hand scattering like ninepins. Fabien chuckled weakly to himself and tried to sit up. He didn't get far—Annamaria had made a horrifying mess of his leg—but seeing an alien population go all *War of the Worlds* on the Hand was almost satisfying enough to make up for his inevitable demise. The humans scattered for cover, while the surviving androids took up battle positions.

The thing about a proper war was that, most of the time, there were two sides. Once in a while, some unlucky fool stumbled out onto the battlefield and got caught in the crossfire. This was the position in which Fabien found himself: a nearly defenseless corpse caught between the clash of two armies, neither of which was invested in his continued survival.

He had almost resigned himself to his death when a strong pair of hands closed over his shoulders and dragged him upright. Fabien blinked at the clean-cut man, with his long and unruffled black hair, who hauled him upright.

"Porter?" he asked, although it barely came out as a word.

"On your feet," Porter said. "Rhett wanted to come, but I insisted that he go without us. Ronnie found the Picture Window... very clever thinking, by the way, I didn't realize its function before. There are so many wonderful artifacts here, aren't there? It's a shame."

Fabien let himself be lifted to his feet. He was keenly aware of what a mess he'd become.

"Gonna get blood on your suit," he grunted.

"Under the circumstances, I shall forgive you. Come on." Porter hauled him toward the steps.

"Won't make it," Fabien insisted.

In the midst of chaos and bloodshed and rampaging spider aliens, Porter smiled. *He must be mad.* "You never know," he said. "We might get lucky."

Yes. Definitely mad.

Porter half dragged, half-carried Fabien to the bottom step. "The destabilizer..." Fabien protested.

"Has done what it was meant to do," Porter said grimly. "The worlds have been torn at the seams, and I'm afraid there's nothing either of us can do about it now. We'll have to retreat. Live to fight another day. It's all we can do, really."

Even *that* seemed too much to ask, for as they approached the bottom step, a long-limbed figure bore down on them. The spider's shadow passed above them, followed closely by an android. Fabien made a halfhearted attempt to lift the pistol.

"Oh, Mr. LeRoux! Mr. Porter! You're alive!" The android drew them both into a crushing hug. Fabien went limp with relief when he registered its cartoon eyes. Somehow, this particular android wasn't under the thrall of the Hand.

Another silver-clad figure jogged up behind them, looking for all the world like a space invader from a black-and-white 1960s flick.

I'm dying, Fabien thought, *and my brain is just throwing random imagery at the wall to see what sticks. This is all the result of a lack of oxygen.* That certainly explained why the space invader was being followed by an oversized humanoid rat.

The space invader shook its head. "What happened? We tried to attack Apollo, but the seam opened up just before we could reach him."

"That's perfectly understandable, Dinah," Porter said. "I don't suppose you have a safe haven available in this other world?"

Fabien did a double-take. Of course it was Dinah. Apparently she'd been busy on her mission, whatever that might have been.

"I'm not sure how safe the underground would be for us," Dinah said.

The rat-man at her side squeaked a few times, and Dinah nodded.

"I agree... with how limited the resources are in the city, I'm not sure if we'd be able to make a stand against the Hand."

"It's just as well," Porter said wearily. "Seams will be popping up all over the world by now, I expect. Now that the Hand has managed to pull one loose thread from the warp and weft of realities, it may all begin to unravel."

The massive spider, which still loomed over them, made a deep and terrible noise. Finder made a reply in kind before telling the rest of them, "If we have another route of escape, that might be for the best."

"This way," Porter told them.

Fabien was scooped off his feet by the android and carried up the steps. Dinah and her little rat-friend came last, while the spider loomed over them all, clambering up the steps with such speed that it would probably give him nightmares later.

He wavered in and out of consciousness until they found Rhett and the Italian commander waiting for them on the catwalks. Instead of having to climb through the tiny window on his own, his friend fed him through feet-first. More hands grasped him on the other side before he could hit the ground: Ronnie and Captain Correia and Dr. Moniz settled him onto a stretcher.

Fabien wanted to tell them not to take him away. He didn't deserve to be treated, or for his pain to be taken away. He'd been so sure of himself when all this started, and he'd been reduced to a blubbering baby. He was *crying*. When was the last time he'd cried? Anger always came easier than grief.

Once again, he'd let the people he cared about down, and there was no consolation prize to be had; no other, better hero to rush in and make everything all right. He'd been the last member of ENIGMA to hold the destabilizer, and they'd taken it from him.

Reclamation had fallen, and he was the one to blame.

25 DINAH

SHE HADN'T SEEN Fabien since he was carried away on a stretcher, with Dr. Moniz fussing over him. Rhett had crawled through the Picture Window ahead of her, and they'd lingered on the deck as Finder, Nibbles, and eventually Chikki came through. Watching the giant spider contort her limbs to fit through the small gap had been unsettling, to say the least.

At his own insistence, Porter had come through last. He'd been the one to reach up and close the window from the inside, cutting them off from direct access to Reclamation once and for all.

Rhett had asked a few hurried questions, but it was obvious he was hurting. Finder had insisted on escorting him belowdecks. Correia and Porter had left to debrief.

Dinah was left alone with Nibbles and Chikki, who had made themselves comfortable on the open upper deck of Atlantis. Nibbles curled up on one of the fallow raised beds, cleared a little nest for himself, and dropped into an immediate and noisy slumber. Chikki had apparently discovered a small enclave of garden spiders and settled in for a long chat. Dinah listened in for a while, but she wanted to feel the wind on her face and skin. She peeled off the damaged suit, set her broken helmet aside, and went to stand against the railing of the floating vault.

It was a quiet night, with the sea still as glass in every direction. The moon was a bright orb above them, reflecting silver on the quiet expanse of blue-black ocean. She took a few deep breaths and reveled in the scent of the salt air.

After spending time beneath the dome of the fractured city, and two months mostly belowground, just being out in the open was a novelty. The soft susurrations of a breeze through the crops behind her made the tension in her muscles ease.

"May I join you?"

Dinah jumped when Porter joined her at the railing. "Sure," she mumbled, but she couldn't help but stare. She was used to Porter's smooth, clean-cut presence, so seeing him dressed informally—in a black t-shirt and loose sweatpants—made her do a double-take. A pendant hung around his neck and sat squarely in the middle of his chest. It appeared to be an intricate machine made of metal, glass, and wood, all molded in miniature.

"I'm supposed to see the quartermaster for a uniform," Porter explained, "but it's the dead of night, and everyone's asleep, and it can wait." He leaned forward to rest his elbows on the rail and raked his hands over his face. "What a miserable day."

Dinah nodded her agreement and went back to staring at the water. She wanted to say something, but how was she supposed to apologize for having failed as drastically as she had on the other Earth?

In the end, Porter spoke first. "I always told myself that I would atone for my grandfather's mistakes. They were exactly that, but you'd think he'd signed ENIGMA over to the Hand, the way everyone talks. I thought if I could bring the organization back together, I'd be absolved...and so would he." Porter snorted and fiddled with his pendant. "So much for that. I recovered the lost vault, only to lose it again. Protected the destabilizer, only to lose it again. I wonder what my grandmother would say, but honestly, I don't want to know."

Dinah drummed her fingers against the railing. "Sorry."

"Don't apologize," Porter said at once, "it's not your fault."

"Isn't it?" Dinah hunched her shoulders and bent over the water. "I tried to best Apollo and lost. *Again*. I couldn't stop him from opening the seam again. I couldn't stop Lane from activating it again..."

"Lane?" Porter blinked at her. "Why would Lane want to activate it?"

"Because Lane's the mole!"

A slow, crooked smile crept onto Porter's face. "No, she wasn't. Marcus was the traitor. Well, not *Marcus*... I'll have to look into the matter more thoroughly." The smile vanished again. "Another good man dead on my watch."

Dinah groaned and pressed her palms against her eyes. "Dammit. I didn't even figure out who the spy was? Then what was the point of anything I did?"

"Dinah." Porter's hand dropped onto her shoulder. "Don't be ridiculous. You made contact with another world. You managed to initiate negotiations with two species from an alternate reality. You've laid the groundwork for ongoing negotiations."

Dinah shook her head. "Finder did that."

"With your help. Do you really think that your accomplishments don't matter because you didn't complete them alone?"

"We didn't stop the Hand!" Dinah burst out. She dropped her hands and slapped them against the railing, making the metal sing. "They still took Reclamation. Apollo is still alive!"

"And?" Porter lifted one eyebrow. "ENIGMA has been operating for centuries, and we've never succeeded in stopping the Hand before. Why would you expect yourself to destroy them in a single mission?"

"If you didn't want us to stop the Hand, then why did you hire us?" Dinah bellowed. She was being too loud. Someone was going to hear them and come up to find out what was going on.

Porter whistled. He let his hand slide free of Dinah's shoulder and turned back to the sea. "Ah. I'm afraid that my communication skills are... not everything I believe them to be."

Misery settled in Dinah's bones. "I'm sorry," she mumbled again.

Porter shook his head and sighed. He cupped his face in his hands and closed his eyes. "I have an immense number of resources at my disposal," he said. "Relics and artifacts... objects that can increase strength and manufacture luck and alter the flow of time itself. I have a fair bit of money, too, though not as much as you might think. There is one thing I do not have in abundance, however, and that is trust." He let his hands droop, but kept facing forward, speaking to the dark horizon as much as to Dinah. "I have a handful of people I trust defending the Ohio vault. Many of them are dead. When Apollo first breached the vault, I knew that ENIGMA needed help."

Dinah licked her lips. She couldn't begin to guess Porter's age, but since the very first day that she'd set foot in the abandoned mall, she'd been under the impression that Porter was older. He carried himself like a professor emeritus, but in profile, in the dark, he seemed terribly young.

"In answer to your question, I hired Fabien because I trusted him to be efficient and discreet. I hired Rhett because his loyalty and drive are obvious. Two would have been enough, I thought, but then I stumbled across one of your papers, and I thought, that's the kind of person we need. Someone who cares about the artifacts, who believes in making sure that objects are respected, not treated as prizes or trophies."

Dinah sniffed and wiped her nose on her sleeve. "You read my paper on canopic jars, I assume?"

"That was the first one, yes." Porter slid a sidelong glance her way. "I know you were speculating as to why I offered you so much less than your counterparts. On one count, I stand by the decision, because they were not only much better prepared for the mission than you were, but because I needed to offer a notable chunk of change in order to get their attention."

"Whereas academics will work for peanuts," Dinah deadpanned.

Porter scoffed. "Two million dollars is hardly peanuts."

"Fair enough."

"But I also thought that if you turned me down, the mission would carry on just fine with only two," Porter added. "And on that count, I was wrong. You have proven yourself at every turn, and in spite of your many accomplishments, you're still quick to apologize for not giving more. Rhett and Fabien are the same. They both came astonishingly close to capturing members of the Hand, something we've been unable to do for generations. ENIGMA is fragmented, short-staffed, and always on the defensive. If I'd been able to allocate all of my resources to any of your recent endeavors, I have no doubt that it would have succeeded. Even on your own, you all did remarkably well. I stand by my decision to contact all three of you, and my only regret is that I didn't see your true value sooner. I will not make the same mistake again, and I promise that I *will* find a way to make it up to you."

Another silence fell between them, but this was a companionable quiet, one that allowed both individuals to catch their breaths and swallow their disappointment.

"What happens now?" Dinah asked at last.

Porter nodded out to the eastern horizon, where the sun would rise several hours hence. "We see what tomorrow brings. Contact Azmera and Tenzin, see what the damage is. We talk to your new friends and see what they can tell us, find out if De Stasio will vouch for us in the presence of the other vault commanders, track how many seams have opened all across the world, and then... we try again."

Dinah cupped her chin in her palm. "I met someone in the world we visited. Elder Moss. He seemed to know a lot about

Travelers. Maybe if we can find a way to get in touch with him, we can compare the notes we have on the destabilizer to the lore he knows—assuming we can even find him again. Everything Azmera said about the destabilizer made it sound as though misusing it would be the end of the world."

Porter lifted the pendant from his chest again. "Funny thing about the world ending, Dr. Bray. Some people seem to think there's an end date for us as a species, and yet for centuries we've been wrong about when that time will come. Perhaps our ancestors' reluctance to use the destabilizer was misguided. Or perhaps we haven't reached the end of the planet, but of an age. We don't know what will come next."

Dinah snorted. "When do we ever?"

"A valid point. And on that somewhat pessimistic note, I bid you good evening. I'm going to need some sleep before we convene tomorrow." He patted Dinah's back before turning and padding away across the deck toward the elevator that would take him down into the sub-aquatic bowels of the floating vault.

Dinah lingered a while longer. Porter's words rattled around in her mind. Of course she shouldn't expect herself to save the world, or even ENIGMA, by herself in a matter of days. That wasn't how things worked. Real progress, tangible and note-worthy progress, would take time.

And it wouldn't be accomplished alone.

She pushed away from the railing and went to check on Nibbles, who was still sleeping soundly, and Chikki, who was still speaking to her kin. Content that they would be all right for the night, she made her way across the now-quiet deck to the lift.

Rhett was probably down in the med bay, beating himself up for not being invincible. If she didn't say something to him, he would be up all night.

Porter was right. They had work to do tomorrow, and they were going to need all the rest they could get.

EPILOGUE

Another Earth

———

Q'ANAA MADE her way through the stubby grasses outside her family's shelter. She clutched a staff in her tertiary fist, letting her weight lean against the gnarled and pockmarked wood. Her primary arms were occupied with carrying the new basket her grandmother had requested. It was still early to harvest most of the crops grown in the communal garden, in the strip of fertile soil at the edge of the long-wrecked pavement, an ancient relic of the ruined city.

As it often did, her gaze wandered over the ruins, only half-aware of what she was seeing. Her primary eyes had grown inured to what remained of the rubble, which was now little more than a concrete wasteland. Twisted metal rods speared upright from the earth, pointing to the sky. Long ago, it would have been an ugly sight, but mosses and epiphytes had begun to reclaim a world that had teetered on the brink of becoming uninhabitable, and a few species of grass had formed a layer of dense turf over stretches of sidewalk. Even a few trees had sought to take root in the ruin of the old world. The eldest of them were spindly and barren, but their roots ran deep, and they had gradually cracked open the concrete beneath them, making room for the next generation.

It was these younger saplings, with their thick trunks and vibrant leaves, that gave her hope for the future. Their world would never be the same as it had been before the Great Ruination, but it would heal in time. Many species had adapted to survive, including Q'anaa's own. Those who had been unable to accept the change had died, but some had hung on, setting down deep roots like those elder trees, giving the younger generation a chance to thrive.

Q'anaa moved slowly, but with purpose. The twist in her spine required that her movements be deliberate, lest she burden herself with undue pain. Between her contorted spine and her near-deafness, she would have found it difficult to navigate the old world, according to her grandmother, but Q'anaa didn't find it difficult at all. She required accommodations, just as Q'aynor required accommodations for his night terrors, or Q'ellin required accommodations for her damaged lungs.

No wonder the old world didn't last, she thought. *It had no patience for people, and yet the environment became inhospitable to any other species. Besides, who needs to hear when one can See?*

She couldn't quite imagine what it would have been like, to see the skyline in those old days. Just imagining it made her shiver with claustrophobia.

She mounted a raised strip of road and then descended again, breathing a small sigh of relief as she descended into the food forest on the other side. The plants on this side of the border grew wild and huge: drooping gourd vines, pods bursting with legumes, upright brassicas in all their brilliant hues, towering nightshade shrubs, and a fantastic array of fruit-bearing trees. All around her, apiformes and other pollinators went about their work in droves, burrowing deep into the blossoms with unrivaled enthusiasm.

Q'anaa had left her grandmother tending mushrooms on the shaded edge of the orchard, so she retraced her steps, but there was no sign of the other woman. It should have been easy to spot her among the trunks of the trees.

She increased her pace, despite the resulting twinge in her back. If her grandmother was injured, she would need to run back to the settlement; a few more hasty paces wouldn't hurt much.

When she saw her Nana crouched next to one of the fecund logs rotting at the base of a haili tree, Q'anaa dropped the basket she was carrying. The staff slipped from her tertiary hand as she plunged to the ground at her grandmother's side.

"Nana!" she cried through a haze of tears. Her speech wasn't always clear, but Nana would understand her. Nana always understood. Q'anaa's primary arms propped her up, while her third hand cradled her grandmother's weathered face.

Every line, every wrinkle that creased the old woman's sun-bleached cheeks was the mark of a survivor. She had witnessed the end of the world—and she had come out the other side. Q'anaa couldn't imagine life without her: not only because of the hole Nana's death would leave in her own three-chambered heart, but also because her loss would mean the end of an age. Soon enough, the ways of the old world would be nothing more than oral history, a memory of a memory.

Then Nana turned to meet her gaze, and Q'anaa saw that she'd been wrong. Her grandmother wasn't ill. Her primary eyes were shuttered and dim, but her third eye, which was usually shut tight, had opened wide. The pupil had expanded so that it was huge and dark, its edges uneven as it bled into the surrounding gray iris, a monochrome at odds with all the brilliant color around them.

Nana's primary hands were braced against the earth, but unlike Q'anaa's, they were driven deep into the loose soil and loam beneath them. Her third hand groped blindly for her granddaughter's, and Q'anaa took it, twining their fingers together.

Nana's voice was too soft for her to make out, but she saw the movement of her lips and the sudden contraction of the old woman's pupil, and she understood the request.

Look with me.

Without letting go of her grandmother, Q'anaa did as she was asked, working the fingers of her primary hands into the soil. She took a deep breath—*in, out*—and let her eyes close.

It wasn't always easy to See. Opening her third eye required that she relax, and it was difficult to do so with her heart beating triple-time and her spine protesting at the uncomfortable angle.

While Q'anaa tried to catch her breath, she began to tap, sending out the first set of spidery roots from her fingers, barely more than thin threads, planting herself in the ground, a more temporary version of the myriad rooted life forms around them. As soon as the narrow roots tapped into the soil, her muscles relaxed slightly, and her breathing came more easily.

When she first learned to put out her roots, Q'anaa had been shocked to discover that she could hear, although it didn't seem to be in the same way that those with fully functioning eardrums could. Tapping was the great equalizer. It allowed her people to share a common experience despite their forms, their faiths, their inclinations, or their appetites. It allowed them to reach into something fundamental and set aside their worldly cares without giving up what made them individuals. The very act of tapping connected them to the land, to the things they couldn't live without. Things that the old world had been so eager to throw away with all three hands.

The slender filaments reached out into the soil, coiling through dirt and between stones, evading the little items that had been buried out of sight long before the old world ended. The roots began to draw up water and minerals, a capillary feeding. She heard, or perhaps *felt,* the growth of plants around her. Their climb toward the sun. Their contentment. Their harmony.

Q'anaa's head rolled back, her mouth dropped open, and her tertiary eye opened at last.

She could still feel the world around her, her Earth, but the one she Saw through her third eye was a different one. The same place, but not the same. Instead, tapping the ground of a food forest, she was looking at another version of reality, one in which the city still stood.

No, she realized, not their city, not the one whose bones she loped through every day. This was a subtly different iteration of it, built for people who were not of her kind. The inhabitants of that city spun around her, through her, and Q'anaa shuddered at their terror but basked in their presence. She had never seen so many living people in one place, and even if they weren't exactly like her kin, they were as much part of their world as she was part of hers.

Nana's grip on her third hand tightened. *Do you See them?* she asked, in the language particular to the Sight.

Q'anaa had Seen before, but never like this. Usually, opening her third eye allowed her to See other places on her homeworld. Through her sight, she had visited parts of her planet that she had never traveled to, and likely never would. According to Nana, this was part of an old mutation: their people had planted chips in their heads, then nanobots. Instead of dying with their hosts, the nanobots had colonized the species as benevolent symbiotic parasites. Inorganic, to be sure—not that it mattered. Q'anaa couldn't imagine life without them, any more than she could imagine a life without tapping.

But this... this was unlike anything she'd experienced. She had reached into her Earth and Seen another.

Nothing about the world or its people made sense, except their panic. It was evident in their half-familiar faces, in their hunted posture, in their haste. Their mouths were moving, but Q'anaa couldn't hear them, although whether that was the result of her own deafness or some feature of this new Sight was hard to say. Pressure throbbed in her ears, a dull roar in tandem with the ache of her own heart.

Q'anaa's eye slammed shut as she bent forward, heaving against the soil. As soon as her eye closed, her other senses returned. She withdrew her roots, ending the tap, and wrapped her primary arms around herself in a comforting embrace.

Her third hand was still clenched in Nana's. After a moment, the older woman took her by the wrist and moved her hand against Q'anaa's palm, spelling out the words.

You Saw it, too, didn't you?

Q'anaa nodded in the affirmative and forced her primary eyes open. Nana withdrew her hand, signing in the air between them instead. *This is important, Q'anaa. I'm sorry you are afraid, but now is the time to be brave. It has been a long time since I Saw another world.*

Q'anaa's mouth dropped open in shock. *This isn't the first time?*

No, love. I Saw one before, a long time ago. And I am afraid that it is not good news. Nana pushed herself to her feet and wiped the soil from her knees, still signing with her third hand. The basket Q'anaa had been sent to fetch lay beside her, forgotten. *I am afraid of what it means.*

Q'anaa's knees were still too shaky to support her. *Do you know what it means, Nana?*

Her grandmother spoke some word aloud, but the shape of her lips wasn't one that Q'anaa recognized. *Yes. I think I do. Come, child. I have something to show you.*

It was almost absurd for someone of Q'anaa's age to be called a child, but the term made her feel safe. The shock of the experience was already fading, and Nana *knew* what to do—or had an idea, at any rate. Q'anaa rose to her feet at last, accepting the staff that her Nana retrieved for her.

Leave the basket, Nana signed. *I will send someone else to harvest. We will need to be fed in order to prepare for what is coming.*

Q'anaa meant to ask what she meant, but before her hands could form the words, her third eye flickered open all on its own, overlaying the vision of that other Earth atop this one. This, too, was new. She'd never had all three eyes open at once, never even opened the third without tapping.

Yet there it was, not quite as sharp as the world that her physical body inhabited: another world, another people. A different one this time.

She understood it then, although she could not say *how* she knew. She had tapped into another reality because the distance between them was closing. Compressing by the instant, folding inward until they overlapped.

What will happen? Q'anaa asked.

Nana turned away from her, gazing out across the skeleton of the city, a fading echo of the hazy mirror image revealed by Q'anaa's third eye.

Another ending, Nana signed. *But if we do what is necessary, it may be followed by a new beginning. After all, it wouldn't be the first time.*

———

FIND OUT

WHAT HAPPENS
NEXT!

Click here to read
THE SECRET CITIES
(ENIGMA Book 3)

GET FREE BOOKS!

Building a relationship with readers is my favorite thing about writing.

My regular newsletter, *The Reader Crew,* is the best way to stay up-to-date on new releases, special offers, and all kinds of cool stuff about science fiction past and present.

Just for joining the fun, I'll send you 3 free books.

Join The Reader Crew (it's free) today!

—Joshua James

ALSO BY JOSHUA JAMES

Saturn's Legacy Series (4 books)

Invasion: The Complete Series (Books 1-3)

Last Stand: Gunn & Salvo (Books 1-8)

Lucky's Marines: The Complete Series (Books 1-9)

With Scott Bartlett:

Relentless: The Complete Fleet Ops Trilogy

With Daniel Young:

Outcast Starship (Books 1-9)

Oblivion (Books 1-9)

Stars Dark (Books 1-8)

———

Click here to read
THE SECRET CITIES
(ENIGMA Book 3)

Made in United States
Cleveland, OH
28 February 2025

14765206R00187